Running with Wolves

By

Summer Lane

Praise for Summer Lane's Work

Fresno Bee, Central California Life Magazine, Traffic Magazine, Lifestyle Magazine, Reedley Exponent, The Daily Bookworm, 92.6 The Blitz

"Summer Lane is giving the word 'prolific' a run for its money."

"[Summer Lane] has solidified her position as a promising young adult author."

"At a glance, you'd never guess the demure smile, soft voice and kind eyes that belong to Summer Lane, would be the genius behind a series of military apocalypse novels."

"Summer Lane's parents wanted to give her a name that would 'look good on paper.' They didn't realize just how much paper her name would adorn."

"Summer's ability to craft a compelling story that immerses her readers into the storyline seems effortless."

"The many story ideas in Summer Lane's mind keep clamoring for her attention."

"[The Collapse Series] is a frentically paced adventure story with no shortage of military action and underdog survival twists."

"The [Reedley] resident is a prolific writer."

"Reedley's Summer Lane has found success with her Collapse Series."

"Summer Lane has many talents. She is a successful publisher, blogger, writing teacher, journalist and international bestselling author."

"Prolific young writer keeps the hits coming."

"Lane, 23, has built a solid following for her different series that often explore survival and adventure after an apocalypse has struck."

Critical Acclaim

For sheer narrative tricks and turns alone, which authors many years her senior can only dream of accomplishing at the most basic level, let alone so effortlessly by integrating themselves invisibly into the main body and structure of the detail of the story itself, Lane is surely worth picking up and reading, whoever you may be.

- Daniel M. Harrison, #1 Bestselling Author of Butterflies and Senior Editor of Marx Rand.Com

Absolutely Heart stopping! If you enjoy dystopia even a little bit, you will enjoy this series.

- Leti Del Mar, Author of Land of the Unaltered

What is extraordinary is that Summer has made it so that you've come to care about these secondary characters almost as much as the main ones.

- Ruth Silver, Bestselling Author of Dead Girl Walking

The author has a real knack for writing dialogue as well as action scenes, and I'd say her newest book is her most polished yet.

- Ellisa Barr, Bestselling Author of Outage

State of Emergency is an engaging read that is compelling and believable.

- Roy Huff, Author of Bestselling Everville Series

Intense, fast-paced, never a dull moment. You feel as if you're with Cassidy every step of the way, cheering her on.

- Ellen Mansoor Collier, Author of The Jazz Age Mystery Series

[Summer Lane] is quite a talented writer with an amazing gift for narration.

- Janice White, Editor and Co-Author of Clarity: A Text on Writing

Cassidy Hart is a smart, snarky, scared and sassy protagonist.

- Brian Palmer, Co-Author of XII: Genesis

Summer Lane knows how to keep you on the edge of your seat!

- Bonnie Rae, Author of The Nether Trilogy

Like the first book in this series (State of Emergency) this sequel [State of Chaos] captured my attention and held it all the way through to the end.

- Andrew D. Carlson, Author of Sue's Fingerprint

Summer does a great job of developing her new set of characters. You may love them, you may hate them, but they leap off of the paper and are real once you read about them.

- G. Allen Mercer, Author of Worst Case Scenario

Summer Lane is an author I expect great things from.

- Jordan Page, Author of Wormwood

A compelling survival story (The Zero Trilogy)...Elle is a believable protagonist who quickly engages the reader and carries them along on her journey through a dark and dangerous landscape.

- Roberta Trahan, Author of Aftershock and The Dream Stewards Series

People disappear in this country like a pebble in the water, and with equal suddenness.

Jeremiah Lynch, Three Years in the Klondike

This is a work of historical fiction. The setting and culture of the times are based in fact.

As such, some artistic liberties have been taken in regards to certain settlements, mines, and cabin locations.

Places

Dyea
Small boomtown during the Gold Rush of the 1890s.

Skagway
Entry point to the White Pass that brought travelers to the Klondike and Yukon River.

Sitka
Capital of the Department of Alaska from 1884-1902. Also a major port.

Chilkoot Pass
Thirty-three-mile mountain pass that led to the Yukon Gold Fields. Also known as the Golden Staircase.

Yukon River
Major Alaskan/Canadian river that ultimately empties into the Bering Sea. 1,980 miles in length.

Klondike
Region of territory east of the Alaskan border where much of the nineteenth-century Alaskan Gold Rush was concentrated. Klondike was a corruption of the Han word, Trondek, which translates to "hammerstone water."

Fortymile
A small town located on a tributary of the Yukon River. Famed for their self-contained small government and justice system.

Anchorage
City in the Alaskan territory. Was virtually unsettled during the Gold Rush, sparsely populated.

Terms or People

Inuit
The native people of the Canadian Arctic. Popularly known now as "Eskimos."

Chilkoot
The native people who guarded and utilized what would later be called the Chilkoot Pass, for trading. A tribe of the Tlingit.

Malamute
A breed of working dog used for pulling heavy sleds and loads. Bred in a variety of colors. Most commonly used as a mushing animal.

Sourdough
Local mining slang for someone who had survived a winter or more in the barren, freezing wilderness. Also a nickname for someone who was considered an "old-timer."

Cheechakos
Word used to refer to someone who was new to the gold-mining territory. Literally translated, it means "tenderfoot."

Mukluks
Type of boot originating from the Inuit, made with seal-skin to keep the feet warm in subzero temperatures.

Hootchinoo (Forty Rod Whiskey)
A beverage purchased in the Alaskan Klondike, made from molasses, sugar, dried fruit, and fermented sourdough, flavored and distilled in an empty oil can. Served hot.

Double-Tents
Two layers of tenting insulated with woodchips to provide thermal protection against the freezing temperatures.

Levi Trousers

Levi Strauss invented a new type of pants in 1848 that were made of denim material. They were called "Blue Jeans." Miners commonly wore these, contrary to the popular thought that all prospectors and miners wore breeches with suspenders. Levis were durable and did not tear as easily as regular trousers or breeches.

Prologue

Jenna Renee

North of Dyea, near the Chilkat River

Alaska – 1898

The dogs run. I hang tight to the rail of the sled. The slender runners slice through the packed snow beneath my feet. My mukluk boots are planted on the footboards. Freezing, knife-sharp air burrows into the tiny cracks and crevices in my multiple layers of clothes. It is early March. The dogs pull the sled with ecstatic determination, plowing up the hill, trees and bushes flitting by in flashes of black shadow.

The Alaskan winter is full of fury and unbridled storms. The sky is darkened with clouds, even in this twilight world. I lick my dry, cracked lips and yell through the double layer of scarf wrapped around my face, protecting my exposed skin.

"Whoa!"

They do not want to stop. They want to run, always. That is their nature.

"Whoa! Easy!"

The dogs at last come to a reluctant halt.

I take a step off the sled and my mukluks sink into the packed snow, the result of months of rhythmic blizzards. Two large boulders are positioned along the trail here, nestled into the forest. I unclasp the tug line from the sled and my lead dog follows me to the sheltered spot. I feed them frozen fish. They devour the rations, and then they burrow into the snow, making a nest. The warmth of their digestion will keep them cozy as they rest. I see their white, gray and black tufts of fur sink into their spots, eyes closed, white clouds puffing around their noses. I sit with my back against the rock, two dogs curled beside me, radiating body heat. The lead dog—I call him Lincoln—burrows into the snow, laying his head across my lap. He is the wisest of all the dogs. His heart is the heart of a wolf, and he carries the instincts of ancients within him.

I pull a rough, thick buffalo robe over my shoulders and lean my head against the rock.

I close my eyes, and I sleep with my dogs.

***

We leave in the morning, before the storm hits. I can feel the oncoming flurry of snow in the air. I am so used to the cold that I am almost one with it. Numb with the acceptance of the bitter wind and icy granules making my limbs stiff.

I pull the scarf from my face for just a moment, letting the cold air pinch and redden my cheeks. I hold an iron pot over my camping stove, a new, shiny gadget called the Primus, burning hot from pressurized kerosene. I picked it up straight out of Dyea this week. I heat a can of beans mixed with bacon. Lincoln sits and watches, ears erect, eyes alert.

"I'm sorry," I say. "But this is mine. You've already had your fish."

He doesn't move.

When my breakfast is hot, I eat the rations as fast as I dare, warming a kettle of tea. I drink the tea and eat all the food, feeling the warmth spread through the insides of my body. I clean the campsite and tuck away my supplies into the sled; my only form of transportation, light yet durable. Built from thin boards of birch and oak, curled at the front to ensure that it glides on the snow. My supplies are packed into a coffin-like crate fixed onto the sled itself. Behind the supplies, a thin platform is built over the ground, where I can stand and ride when I am tired of running—and there is always running. Long, hellish, freezing weather causes bodies to shut down and blood to freeze solid. Running keeps the blood warm and the brain alive. Running is partly how we survive out here, in the unforgiving icy expanse of Alaska.

The dogs are anxious, yowling and jerking at their neck lines, dying to run. The still prologue to the oncoming storm is almost more than they can bear.

I wrap my face again and secure the tug line and the gang line on the lineup. I count the dogs: ten. Ten living, breathing, hot and powerful muscle-movers, capable of running up to eighty miles a day without any rest. Lincoln shakes his head back and forth; even he is anxious to leave. I wonder what they smell—what they sense—and decide to keep moving.

If there's one thing I know about the dogs, it's that they always know better than I.

Always.

"Mush!" I yell, cracking the whip in the air.

The sled flies. The dogs charge forward, throwing their strength into it. I am barely over a hundred pounds, and with the supplies, the sled perhaps weighs no more than two hundred. Such a light load dispersed between ten dogs makes for happy runners, and a swift journey.

I grip the handlebar as we move through the forest. Below, I see a flat expanse of ice within the trees—a tiny frozen lake. Dangerous to cross, I've been told. Nobody is sure how thick the ice is. Last year, someone took their dog team across its surface and the musher and his dogs disappeared. The mushers here fear it, so despite the oncoming storm, I avoid it. Better to brave a bit of snow than to risk plunging into arctic waters and perishing immediately. The water is too cold to survive.

Besides, the dogs know better. They do not trust the lake. They avoid it without me having to tell them to.

We move along, into the darkness. Morning here does not mean that we get to see the sun. We are submerged into a sort of permanent twilight, the edges of the horizons glowing with grayish illumination, while the sky above our heads is rippled with crystal stars. I stifle a yawn, my muscles tired and my feet throbbing with cold, even ensconced in the protection of the mukluks.

We're nearly home, *I think.*

Going into Dyea with the dogs means taking a four-day journey across the snow, alone. It means loading up the sled with supplies to help sustain us through the winter, and it means taking the risk of leaving the one thing in this wilderness that stands between us and death: warmth.

I do it often, and although I fear the cold, the dogs do not. Their courage gives me strength, and I hold on to that every time we go out into the snow, into the tundra.

And then I hear it: the howl of a timber wolf.

I look right, seeing a flash of gray movement in the trees. Panic tears through me: we are being hunted. My dogs will not survive against a pack of wild wolves. Neither will I.

I crack the whip again, screaming at the dogs to run for all they're worth.

My screaming is needless: they know. Of course they do. They fear the wolves as much as they feel a kinship with them. The wolves in this wild country are strong and dangerous. The land and everything in it belongs to them. We are merely human trespassers, nothing more than prey. I have heard stories of mushers who were found picked clean, stripped to the bone along with their entire sled dog team, staining the snow red with blood. The only clue to their demise?

The countless paw prints circling their bodies...the pack, converging before the kill.

"Mush, mush!" I yell.

The team senses my panic, and it drives them harder. They are frantic; they can smell the bloodlust of the pack circling us. I can hear the howl from the lone wolf in the distance. A ploy, meant to distract us. Wolves are clever and cunning creatures, and we are meant to think that he is alone.

He is not.

I can sense the presence of the wolves in the trees around us. There must be at least eight. A large pack for this area, and I realize that we will not make it back to the cabin before they attack. A Smith and Wesson hammerless pistol is stuffed into my belt, but in this darkness, with the forest closing in around us and the flash of the wolves' teeth snapping at our heels...I will never be able to kill them all. My dogs will be ripped to shreds. Lincoln will put up a fight, but the rest...

I see our land. The fence erected around the small claim, the cabin set against the hill, the tiny windows glowing from within, smoke streaming from the chimney. So close, yet so far! I cling to the handle like a woman drowning, afraid of falling from the sled and being left behind: an easy meal for a hunting pack.

We are almost to the boundary of the property. The gate is open—waiting for us. Even if we get inside—what then? I can't close the gate fast enough to keep the wolves out. Besides, the fence is only a few feet tall. The wolves can jump over it.

Why are there wolves so close to home?

The wolves were said to be cleared from this area—moved east, from what I heard.

The sled sails over the boundary line of our land, the fence behind us. The dogs run frantically toward the shed beside the cabin, and they claw at the wooden doors. They jerk and buck, and I am tossed off the sled, landing on my shoulder. I reach for my pistol—futile, I know. But I have to do something.

Breathing hard, I lift the Smith and Wesson into my clumsy, cold, and shaking hands. I stagger to my feet, waiting for the wolves to emerge from the shadows.

I see him...and then I see the rest of them.

Their alpha—he stands at the fence, massive and rippling with muscles beneath the white-gray fur. He stares at me, the first breeze of the storm carrying the scent of my fear to him. Around him, the rest of his pack emerges. There are ten. My estimation was wrong. They prowl forward, peering at us from the slats between the fence, eerily silent.

The alpha never moves his ice-blue eyes from mine. I feel as if I'm staring into the face of an old friend—or the face of God himself. There is wisdom in his eyes, and I am rendered frozen by it.

The cabin door slams open, and I hear yelling. Footsteps. The piercing crack of a shotgun.

The pack returns to the woods, vanishing into the darkness. The alpha watches me for a moment longer, hesitating. Why?

And then he rejoins his pack, and he is gone, and I am left shaking beside my terrified dog team, a pistol in my gloved hands, with the knowledge that we have been spared a painful death.

"Heavens, child, what on earth...?"

Marilyn, her long white hair tucked beneath a fur cap. A heavy black jacket buttoned sideways on her shoulders, covering her thick wool skirt, wrinkled fingers clinging to a smoking shotgun.

"Wolves," I gasp.

"I saw."

Her voice, raspy and brittle.

"They let us go," I say. "They spared us!"

Marilyn frowns.

"Unlikely," she mutters. "Get inside. Take the other shotgun. Lock the fence tight. Help me get the dogs stabled. If we've got wolves roamin', we have to protect the team."

The team—our most valuable asset. Without the dogs, we'll starve.

Without the dogs, we are nothing.

I know this, and so I stumble forward, flushed with adrenaline and fear and confusion. The eyes of the alpha still flash in my mind, and I imagine for a moment that he spoke to me.

Ridiculous, Jenna! I tell myself. Impossible. Wolves kill. They are monsters.

Wolves are not something to be trifled with in this country. I tell myself this over and over again as I stagger up the porch steps, pushing inside the cabin. The roaring wood stove in the middle of the room is warm—deliciously warm. I rip off my hat, long black hair falling in tangled waves to my hips. I grab our second shotgun—a Winchester pump-action, one of Marilyn's favorites—from beneath my cot and slide two shells into the chamber.

I run outside again, headed toward the fence line. While our fence really can't keep wolves—or anything else—out of our land...it at least slows them down. I find my way through the twilight darkness, hauling the gate shut, quaking. I imagine the wolves crouched in the bushes, pouncing on me, eating me alive...

I lock the gate, unafraid. I have dealt with worse.

I run across the snowy yard, into the shed. Marilyn has already moved the team inside. I close the shed door behind us, bolting it. I breathe a sigh of relief.

At least the dogs are safe.

"Far from safe," Marilyn says, as if reading my thoughts. "Once a pack of wolves get it into their head to hunt somethin', they'll always come back. They've got the bloodlust."

"They already left," I reply.

"They'll be back."

"But—"

"They'll be back."

I help Marilyn slip the harnesses off the backs of the dogs, leading them into their pens. I throw armfuls of fresh straw to the floor. They burrow into it, hunkering down for the coming storm.

Outside, the wolves howl.

I freeze, a bit unnerved, and Marilyn's watery gray eyes meet mine in the flickering lamplight.

"They always come back," she whispers. "Always."

One

I came to Alaska to survive. There's not much to tell, really. I was born in San Francisco, christened Jenna Renee, raised by a good family until the age of thirteen, and then suffered the same fate of many young, poor children in the city: I was orphaned. My parents and my younger brother perished in a ferry accident, leaving me alone and penniless in the world. It was only the generosity and kindness of my uncle Nathaniel Renee—an optimistic gold prospector—and his wife, Marilyn, that saved me from the poorhouse...or quite worse, homelessness. Living in the slums in San Francisco as a child surely would have brought either my death or corruption. Both were grim prospects.

Nathaniel and Marilyn sent for me after my parents' death. They took me into their home. Whisked me away from the warm, balmy temperatures of San Francisco and showed me what life was like in the barren wilderness of the arctic winter. It was as if I had been taken to another universe, an entirely new world. Where California was filled with color and warmth, Alaska seemed to be nothing but miles of white snow and inspirational but terrifying danger.

My aunt and uncle were kind folk—rough, perhaps, but kind. No one forced them to take me in or to care for me. After my family was killed, I spent my days staring at the wall of a friend's home, waiting for the boat that would take me away from the endless pain. When I stepped onto the boat for the first time, the San Francisco Bay to my back and the Pacific on the horizon, I felt free.

Free of the pain, free of the loss.

Alaska was the cure to my disease of despair.

The cold awoke me, the woods aroused me, and the forest nurtured my healing. I always believed the land in Alaska could speak to me, as if it was a dazzling magic show and I was its sole audience. The wild places excited me from the moment I saw the green, mountainous shores from the deck of the steamer.

Mother would be excited for me, I thought.

My mother had been a beautiful and spiritual woman, a Cherokee native from the East; a gorgeous, raven-haired waitress in a saloon in Texas. She posed as a French immigrant, the widow of a fur-trapper who had long since gone missing in Yukon Territory. Her lie was elaborate and believable. As a Cherokee, my mother had experienced cruel torture and abuse at the hands of the white settlers flooding through the West. She was cunning and clever. To survive, she became someone else entirely, separating herself from her beloved ancestral roots, desperate to make a living and find a husband outside of her dwindling tribe. She learned to speak French and called herself Louise. Her dark hair and bright eyes made the deception easier to believe, as did her fluent grasp of the French language. Had it not been for that ruse, she never would have been allowed to work, much less spend time in saloons frequented by white men.

Yet it was there, in that dark, smoky saloon, that she met my father, a rowdy and fun-loving fur trader—a true Frenchman named Jacques Renee. They fell in love—or so Marilyn has always told me—and married shortly after. My father did not even realize he had married a Cherokee until years later, much to my mother's amusement. But his love for her never faltered. The French were, after all, much more tolerant of our folk than the English or Americans. The French frequently worked together with natives to grow and expand their fur-trading businesses. They often learned to speak the language of the natives as well, integrating into their culture...rather than taking it away, as the English or Spanish had.

Mother and Father's adventures somehow brought them to California. They were a happy pair, full of love and curiosity and wanderlust. The Golden State, as some called it, sang to them, promising exciting city life and legendary crystal-blue oceans. San Francisco was an alluring place. My father worked on the docks, loading and unloading goods and supplies from near and far. My mother sought to further educate herself with dreams of being a schoolteacher. When I was born, my earliest memories of my parents were of their warmth and their smiles. I can still recall Mother's singsong laughter, whispering to me in French as a babe, singing French lullabies and reading poetry. I was as dark-skinned as she was—with the exception of my flashing blue eyes, bequeathed from my father's lineage—and Mother realized the danger. A Cherokee would not be welcome in the city...especially a *female* Cherokee.

"White people don't see us as good enough," Mother would whisper, staring out the window. *"We are French, completely, child. I want you to understand that you are Cherokee, too, but to the white man...we are wholly French. Do you understand?"*

"Yes, Mama."

I learned both English and French from the start, and could speak both fluently by the age of six. Some were suspicious...after all, we were very dark. But my Father—the boisterous, overbearing Frenchman—seemed to ease everyone's suspicions that we were not so-called *savages*. If not for Father, in fact, I don't believe we would have had much of a life at all.

Life was, I suppose, *good*.

But that was before the *accident*...

As a child, hurting from the loss of my family, I dreamed of my mother every night. We looked alike: same dark skin, same black hair, same strong, stoic spirit.

"You look like a fairy child," Marilyn told me when she saw me *for the first time. "Your eyes...it's like looking at your father and your mother both at the same time."*

Nathaniel and Marilyn put me to work. If they suspected that I was a half-breed, as some white men called children like me, they said nothing. They protected me. Nathaniel oversaw a small gold mine outside of Dyea, Alaska, not far from the primary gold fields of the Klondike. All year, the men dug. All year, the men mined. All year, the men hoped and prayed and begged God to let them find gold.

So far, they hadn't been so lucky, although Nathaniel had managed to accumulate some wealth in the time he spent in Alaska. While he managed the mines, Marilyn and I worked the land. We had a garden during the warm months of spring and summer. Alaskan winters were long and dark, so our supplies from the summer sustained us through the cold, snowy months.

Most important of all: we raised the dogs.

When the snow crusted the earth and the cold became unbearable, there was only one way to survive in the northern country...sled dogs. We owned a team of dogs, and Nathaniel taught me to handle them when I was a child.

The dogs saved me. I fed them, cleaned them, worked them, drove them and traveled with them. They were my friends, my companions and my protectors. I trusted them, they trusted me, and together, we made a strong team.

Nathaniel gave me the team; they were my sole wards, my family. I became so skilled at running the dogs that Nathaniel eventually trusted me to make supply runs into Dyea without him. It was dangerous, but I could handle myself. I could run the dogs better than most men. I never went anywhere without my Smith and Wesson hammerless or my Winchester shotgun.

The years passed. I grew up in the cold—the sharp, vengeful, powerful grasp of the arctic tundra. I learned the ways of the North, I learned to survive the cold, I learned to love the dogs, and I learned to love my adoptive parents.

All seemed well. I felt that I was finally healed, that I could move on from the pain of the past and embrace Alaska and my new life completely.

I was very wrong.

***

The wolves howl all day. I sit near the door in the cabin, the Winchester pump-action lying across my lap, leaving a crease on my blue jeans.

"Men's clothes," Marilyn had muttered when I brought home three pairs from Dyea last year. "Not fit for a girl like you to wear. I understand if you gotta wear trousers to run the dogs, but for the love of God, Jenna: why the denim pants? They're too tight for a proper lady."

"Oh, Marilyn, honestly!" I'd returned, expressionless, sighing. "Simply everybody is wearing blue jeans now. They call them Levis, on account of the fact that they were invented by a man named Levi Strauss. Imagine having a pair of pants named after you!"

"He must have a dull sense a' fashion," Marilyn commented.

Marilyn hovers now around the wood stove, nervously stoking the fire. She chews on her fingernails, jumping every time the wind blows. The storm is getting worse. Snow begins falling in sheets. The windows in our cabin are made of deerskin pulled taut, chinked with moss and strips of cloth around the edges in an attempt to keep out the cold.

In the end, it is the storm that drives the wolves away from the cabin...for now, at least.

"He looked right at me," I say, running my finger across the barrel of the gun. "The wolf...the leader of the pack. Marilyn, he looked right into my eyes and he walked away. It was somethin'."

Marilyn rolls her eyes.

"That's Louise in ya," she mutters. "Hogwash."

"Just because you don't—"

"Jenna. Stop."

Marilyn sinks into her rocking chair near the fire, huddled under a thick blanket.

"Marilyn, are you feeling unwell?" I ask, studying her face.

Marilyn's skin is icy pale, her eyes watery.

"The cold is gettin' to me this year," she replies. "When I was younger, I could take it as well as the men could, but now? I reckon I'm too old."

"You're not." I stand and walk to the back of the cabin. It's a simple structure—bare walls, a table, a small kitchen, and two cots positioned near the stove for warm sleeping. "Here."

I drape another blanket over Marilyn's shoulders.

"Thank you."

She coughs.

"Your cough is back," I say. "That's not good."

Not again. Pneumonia nearly killed you last year.

"It came back while you were gone," she replies.

"I brought back so many supplies from Dyea, Marilyn. We have everything we need until winter is over, now." I kneel next to her, placing my hand on her knee. "I made it back just in time."

"I know."

I walk to the kitchen and find the tin teapot. I scoop snow out of a bucket near the door and place it into the pot, before hanging it in its place above the flames.

"Jenna," Marilyn says.

"I'm making tea."

"Jenna, *listen*."

"All right," I say, sitting across from her in an empty chair. "I'm listening."

"I'm dying, Jenna," Marilyn says. "This farm is gonna be yours soon—*just* yours. And I want you to leave. I want you to get out of this godforsaken wilderness and go back to the city. Find a husband, start a family. You've got to, child. There's nothin' else for you here, now that Nathaniel's gone."

I stare at her.

Nathaniel is gone, yes. But why must I leave?

"No!" I exclaim. "I love it here!"

"You won't love it when you're all alone."

"I will. This is my home."

"If the wolves don't get ya, robbers will. You should know that firsthand, Jenna."

"We haven't had problems since Nathaniel was killed."

"You never know. They could come back anytime. It unsettles me."

I close my eyes, the flash of last year's nightmare dancing in my head:

Me, hiding in the woods, watching through the trees. Marilyn, kneeling on the dirt, a shotgun barrel pressed against her neck, wringing her hands and sobbing. Nathaniel, being dragged across the ground, behind the shed. His wrinkled face smeared with blood. Me again, kneeling in the woods with Lincoln, my arms wrapped around his neck, staring in horror. And there, walking slowly behind the shed, smoking a cigar, was a man I would never rightly forget: massive, a seemingly monstrous hulk of a person, skin darkened by the sun, a long coat of elk fur dangling to his boots.

Conroy Parker, I'd heard him say to Marilyn, after she'd told me to run. I reckon you've heard of me, ma'am? If not, you're sure as hell's bells about to find out who I am and what I do.

He'd laughed.

It was all a jumbled blur, now...

Conroy moving his hand in some kind of signal. The booming crack of a shotgun against the still of the land. Marilyn, screaming. Conroy saying something I couldn't make out. Me, frozen with shock and terror.

Nathaniel...dead?

Conroy Parker, that hulking beast, patting Marilyn's cheek and throwing his cigar at her feet.

"Sorry for the inconvenience, Mrs. Renee," he'd growled. "But fair's fair."

And then they'd rode out. They didn't kill Marilyn, they didn't burn the barn. They didn't even leave Nathaniel's body behind...

"It was bad luck," I say, chewing on my lower lip. "Those highway robbers just didn't get what they wanted: gold. Killing Nathaniel was a cruel method to make us pay. Nothin' more."

"Jenna, they would have killed you or *worse* had they known you were there!" Marilyn whimpers. "Good God, girl. I don't want that fate for ya. Promise me you'll leave when I die. Promise!" She is flushed, desperate.

I lean back.

"Very well," I say.

She nods.

"Good. We won't speak of it again. I'll not see you meet an end like my Nathaniel's."

"I won't," I reply.

She sighs. "Jenna, Jenna. Always calm and quiet. Your face is always so solemn, child."

I say nothing.

I return to my spot at the door, thinking of the time I have spent here with Marilyn. I was thirteen years old when I first came to the North, first came to Alaska, first came to the untamed wilderness. Thirteen, scared, orphaned and unwanted.

"I suppose we can take care of you," Uncle Nathanial had said, winking when he met the boat at Sitka, before taking me to Dyea. "Honestly, Marilyn always wanted a daughter."

"I'm not your daughter," I replied, stone-faced. "I'm nobody's daughter anymore."

"You can be ours, now."

Nathaniel was kind to me. He was my father's elder brother, someone my mother frequently poked fun at around the dinner table.

"Oh, Nathaniel," she'd say. "Seeking a fortune in the Klondike like every other stupid man in California. He'll be ruined because of it. Gold is nothing more than a yellow rock."

"A yellow rock that makes a fellow mighty rich," Father would boom, laughing.

After the accident with the ferry, Nathaniel sent for me. He wrote me a letter, promising that I could come and live with him and Marilyn. She'd always wanted a child, he wrote. He was my only living family—my only remaining bloodline. I'd never met him before. He'd always been a distant relative...someone my father occasionally received mail from, saving each letter in a drawer in his dresser.

It will be very different, Jenna, Nathaniel had written. *But it will be a grand adventure. You'll see. I promise that everything will be wonderful.*

Marilyn coughs, breaking the silence, breaking into my thoughts.

"Tea?" I ask, rising to grab the boiling pot.

Outside, the dogs whine over the wind. They sense the wolves—they sense the wild. It calls to them, like it calls to me, and I wonder sometimes if we are the only ones who hear it.

Two

$\mathcal{I}$ force myself to take another step. The snow is biting, the wind is strong. I squeeze my eyes shut and shoulder my weight against the force of the wind, feeling my hands close around the latch on the shed. Inside, the dogs are frantic and loud. They have sensed my approach, and they know it is feeding time.

I stumble inside, gripping the lantern in my right hand.

The dogs bark, whine, and growl. They jump onto the fences of their stables, tails wagging, some howling like the wolves that nearly killed us yesterday.

"Oh, stow it," I mutter. "I'm hurrying, I'm hurrying."

My hands shake as I haul their food out of the barrels in the shed. Jenna's cough is worse—her breathing is rattling, coarse. She's feverish. She lies on her cot and stares at the ceiling, talking endlessly about Nathaniel and how I must leave this farm before it's too late.

"Come on!" I encourage, tossing the rations into the stables. The dogs growl and dig into the pounded beef tongue, famished. I scoop piles of snow into their dens—in this weather, water will freeze over, and so the dogs eat snow to remain hydrated.

I stare at the dogs, my mind reeling with the reality that Marilyn is dying. I know this. After Nathaniel was murdered last year, she grew sick. Almost died. The cough never really went away. At this rate, her lungs will fill with fluid and she will die before the week is over.

The storm is bad—too bad to leave and find a doctor. Besides, what if she died while I was gone? That would be horrible.

I huddle on the ground, pulling my knees against my chest.

Alone.

If Marilyn dies, I *will* be alone. Saved once from the cruel hand that life dealt me in taking my family from me, I was given a second chance for nearly five years. But last year, after Nathaniel was killed…and now Marilyn…

Alone.

The word echoes in my head like an omen, a curse. Poison.

What will I do? Work the farm for the rest of my life?

Not a terrible judgment, Jenna. You love it here, do you not?

I squeeze my eyes shut.

"Why did they kill him?" I asked Marilyn.

I refused to cry, as I always did. I would not bow to weakness.

Not anymore.

Another loved one, dead. It was my curse. Death followed me everywhere.

Marilyn sat on the dirt, staring at the forest.

"I don't know," she murmured. "They just did."

She was ashen gray, trembling with cold. I looked at the red marks on my wrists—where Marilyn had grabbed me and screamed at me to run, to hide.

"Who was that man?" I'd asked. "Why was he here? What did he want?"

"Conroy Parker," she'd replied, simply. "It doesn't matter what he wanted. He took everything."

I shudder.

Lincoln barks, and I turn to see what the commotion is about. He rolls back on his haunches, sitting still, looking at me as if to say, *Is everything all right?*

I smile a little.

"Yes," I reply. "It's all right."

It's not all right. It's not.

Nothing has been all right for a very long time.

***

The docks are busy. It is a warm, cloudless day. San Francisco is bustling with activity. I love the smell of the city on days like this: the scent of progress and life and business. The wind tosses my hair into wild circles as I peer across the bay, searching for my family's ferry.

I see it in the distance, a small smudge.

"Someday," Father told me yesterday, "there will be a bridge that will make traveling across the bay easier for those of us who don't have boats. Mark my words."

"That would have to be a huge bridge!" I exclaimed, awed. "Papa, is it possible?"

"I don't see why not. The future is a bright place, Jenna. Believe in it."

I watch the ferry approach. Father, Mother, and Daniel are onboard. I have come to the docks to greet them, eager for them to return home. I'm hungry and Mother has promised to make a good dinner. After all, it's my birthday today. I am thirteen years old.

I am wearing a blue button-top tucked into a long skirt over petticoats, my black boots riddled with holes. I have hope that someday I will have enough money to buy new clothes and new shoes, but Mother doesn't seem to be as optimistic as I am.

And that's when it happens.

The ferry catches fire. It bursts into flame, as if something has exploded from within.

I watch it for a moment, frozen with utter shock, and then I am screaming. Frantic. People are crowding to the edge of the water, watching the accident with horrified fascination. The ferry is crackling with flames, belching black, acrid smoke into the clean bay air, staining the blue sky. I stand with my hand over my mouth, shuddering, tasting snot and tears on my tongue, watching as the ferry slants sideways. A few people cling to the bow, screaming for help. They are tiny, like ants—so far away.

Bubbles froth around the small vessel, and then it sinks below the surface of the bay. Down, down, down it goes. A slow death, a slow burn. People swim away from the boat, toward shore, but the water is cold. I count heads: twelve. That's it? The ferry was full of people when it left—at least fifty!

I just stand there, staring. Rooted to the dock.

My family is alive, I tell myself. They are among those twelve swimming toward shore. They are fine. Mother and Father and baby Daniel will be all right. This is nothing more than a nightmare and I will wake up soon. It will all be over in a moment.

It is a lie and I know it.

***

I snap awake, the nightmare flashing through my mind, the memory of my family's death like a fresh wound. I feel my forehead: slicked with sweat. I take a deep breath and rise from my cot. I press my lips together, hiding my emotion.

I am not weak, I tell myself, as if the reminder will make me braver.

I go to Marilyn, watching her sleep. She grows worse as the hours roll by. I sit beside her as her chest rises and falls, her breathing labored and her forehead covered in sweat. I press a cool cloth to her skin, despite the freezing temperature. She is burning up.

It's the pneumonia, I think, sadly. *There is nothing I can do.*

I do not have the medicine to help her.

The storm has passed. The hill and the land and the trees are covered in a stainless blanket of white snow. The air is still but unforgivingly frigid. The dogs are at peace, the wolves are gone, and Marilyn is still dying. I pick up a book of French poetry, reading each line over and over again, an attempt at distracting myself from my current sad situation.

The storm is over, I reason. *Go into Dyea, at least. It's not that far. Just a few days. Get a doctor, at least bring back medicine. Maybe all she needs is something simple!*

Perhaps, but Marilyn is fading fast. If I leave, she will be dead by the time I get back. There is nothing I can do except wait. I can make her comfortable, and I can keep her warm. I can keep the wolves from the door.

And that is all.

I close my eyes. As I hold Marilyn's hand I think of how, despite our differences and arguments, she has loved me as well as my own mother did. I could never ask for more.

My mother, Louise Renee.

I remember Mother in bits and pieces. Like a distant photograph, black and white and dusty. The older I get, the farther away she seems to become.

"Jenna," Marilyn says, fighting the rattle in her chest.

I take her hand.

"Lock the door and get the gun," she tells me, suddenly. "Somebody's here."

"Who would be here *now*?" I murmur.

She's delusional. It's nearly midnight.

I crack the door open enough to see outside, into the darkness. Sure enough, there are two dog sled teams on the edge of the fence. Our dogs begin to howl and growl from the barn. I close the door, alarmed.

Marilyn was right.

"Men," I whisper. My heart is beating wildly. "At least four. Two dog teams."

"Jenna," Marilyn rasps. "Get the *gun*."

I duck beneath the cot and grab the Winchester, dropping a handful of shells into my Levis.

"Go to the shed," Marilyn commands. "Stay with the dogs. Do *not* show yourself."

"I'm not leaving you!" I reply, angry. "I won't."

"You will." Marilyn coughs. "Quickly, child."

"You're sick and—"

"I'm *dyin'*, Jenna! You're not. Do as I say and get in the *damned shed*! Be smart, for once!"

Her words sting, but I know she means well. We have discussed this before; ever since Nathaniel's death, we agreed that the next time we had unwelcome visitors at the cabin, I would hide in the shed and Marilyn would stay inside. It was better that way, she had told me.

It was an agreement I begrudgingly accepted, if only because it gave Marilyn peace of mind.

Footsteps. I hear the barking of the foreign dogs, the low voices of men. A chill slithers down my spine. I stare long and hard at Marilyn. I pull my buffalo robe over my shoulders and slip my gloves over my fingers. I cradle the shotgun in my arms. I lean over and kiss Marilyn on the forehead.

"I'll watch," I whisper. "If something goes wrong—"

"If something goes wrong, child," Marilyn rasps, "you'd damn well better *stay* hidden."

We stare at each other. I turn away. Her eyes are hard, unrelenting.

"A good man always builds in a back door," he'd laughed. "Just in case he needs to make a hasty exit."

I step outside, breathless. I close the door and circle around the back of the cabin. I see the shadowy shapes of men moving toward the front door. My fingers grasp the shotgun. I pull my neckerchief around my face and slip around the side of the cabin. I can't see anything, but I can hear. I press my ear against the ice-crusted wood. Too cold. I pull away and listen, hunkered down, shivering in the cold.

Bang!

I hear the door slamming open. I hear footsteps echoing against the floorboards. Laughter. Someone whistles.

"Marilyn Renee," a man says, gruffly. "You look pretty damn awful, if I do say so myself."

My chest tightens. I know that voice.

Conroy Parker.

More laughter. The other men—three of them. I hear Marilyn coughing. I bite my lip.

"Conroy," Marilyn says, her tone venomous. "Get off my land, you murdering—"

"Now, now," Conroy interrupts.

I can picture him raising his hands, puffing on his cigar, feigning gentlemanly behavior.

"I was in the area," he goes on. "Just checking up on Nathaniel's old mines, you know. And I thought, lo and behold, good old Nathaniel always told me that he never had any children. He was lying though, wasn't he, Mrs. Renee? You have a child. Jacques' daughter, from what I've been told up in Dyea. Folks there says she comes in quite a bit with a dog sled team. Is that true? You let your daughter run dogs around the countryside without so much as an escort?" Conroy chuckles. "She must be a tough bird."

"My daughter no longer lives with me," Marilyn rasps. "I sent her home, to California."

"Is that so?"

"It is."

"Now, ain't that amusin', boys?"

Again, laughter.

"That's real funny, boss," somebody says.

"I see no humor in it," Marilyn snaps. She dissolves into a coughing fit.

I hold the shotgun upright, the barrel pointing toward the skies. If I could get just one shot at Conroy Parker...I could kill him, and I could avenge Nathaniel's death, and I could put a permanent end to the threat he's presenting to Marilyn right now.

What does he want? Why would he return?

"I think," Conroy says, "that you're a liar, Marilyn. I think your daughter still lives here with you. You wanna know why?"

Marilyn doesn't respond.

Footsteps boom across the floor.

"Because there's two cots," Conroy says, "and two sets of clothes, and hey, what have we got here? I believe those are Levi trousers. All the rage these days, so I hear."

Dammit, I shouldn't have left my things strewn about.

"Get out of my home, Conroy," Marilyn says.

Her voice is weak, but her tone is commanding.

"That's a mighty tall order, ma'am," Conroy responds. "I'll tell ya what: you tell me where your daughter is, and I'll let you off the hook. You can live out the rest your days in peace—and from the looks a' you, you ain't got more than a few days."

"My daughter is in California," Marilyn insists.

Don't lie again. You'll only make him angry.

"That's a damned funny story," Conroy growls. "Because the way I heard it, she was in Dyea just a few days ago, headed home with a sled full of supplies. There are no secrets in a small town, Marilyn. Not a one."

Silence.

I hear the armrests of the rocking chair creak. Conroy is probably leaning over Marilyn, leering close to her face.

"Tell me where she is, Marilyn," he says, and this time, there is no amusement in his voice, "or I will kill you and I will burn your cabin to the ground. Swear ta' God I will."

"Go to hell," Marilyn spits.

I imagine she must have spit in Conroy's face, because the next few moments are a blur of Conroy's explosive anger, the sound of a hand smacking against a cheek. Marilyn's startled gasp. The piercing *bang* of a gunshot. Conroy yelling, "Tear the cabin apart! Take the gold, take the money. FIND ME THAT GIRL!"

My heart beats against my ribs. I am frozen—with disbelief.

Did he shoot Marilyn? Is she dead? Surely that was just a warning shot!

Yet Marilyn is no longer speaking or coughing.

Hot tears spill onto my face. They freeze in streaks on my cheeks. I stand up, backing away from the cabin. The front door opens with a crash, and I slink into the shadows, into the trees. Conroy's silhouette is visible, along with two other men. Someone is still inside, tearing things off the walls, overturning the cots, cursing and swearing up a storm. Outside the fence, I see more men, maybe five more. There are nearly ten men, then.

Conroy and his boys plod through the snow. The dogs growl and bark from within their pens.

The men push inside the shed. The dogs erupt in a series of agitated barking. Strangers are not welcome in their home, and they do not like being disturbed. I hear Conroy yelling at the men to search every corner of the building.

"Find that girl!" he shouts. "Find her and bring her to *me!*"

I shoulder the shotgun and slip farther into the trees. I have just a handful of bullets. It's dark, and there are ten men—maybe more. If I tried to kill Conroy now, I'd likely die, too. I must be wiser than that, for Marilyn's sake.

I have to get to Marilyn. Surely Conroy didn't kill her. Wounded her, perhaps, but nothing else...

I know in my heart I am lying to myself.

The Parker gang trudges around the property, searching through bushes and trees and even climbing into the loft of the shed to see if I am hiding there. At last, Conroy booms, "She's not here, boys! She's probably in the woods somewhere. Marilyn was lying— that girl was here no more than an hour ago."

"What do we do if we find her, boss?" one of the men asks. "Kill her?"

"I need her alive," Conroy replies, grabbing the collar of his shirt. "Am I clear?"

The man nods.

He shoves him away, stalking toward the cabin.

"What about the cabin, boss?" another man growls. "We just gonna leave it like that? What if somebody comes across it and—"

"Burn it," Conroy says, gruffly. "Burn it all."

"What about the dogs? We could sell—"

"I said, BURN IT."

"Yeah, boss. All right."

I watch as the men tear apart the property. A piece of my heart breaks every time I hear belongings crashing against the wall inside the cabin. I wince, and then I look away. I cannot watch the destruction of the cabin. I ache to pull the trigger of the shotgun, but I have to get Marilyn out. If I draw attention to myself, I'll never have that chance.

"Let's get the hell out of here!" Conroy bellows.

He pulls his wrap around his face and climbs back on his sled. The men leave the shed and the cabin behind. One man lingers behind a little too long. He runs from the cabin and struggles to catch up with the team that is leaving the property behind.

Conroy doesn't look back—not once.

They are simply gone. In a moment, in a flash.

I run out of the woods as soon as they are out of sight. I hurry up the steps, tearing my scarf off.

"Marilyn!" I cry.

I stop dead in my tracks, inhaling. The cabin is destroyed. Furniture is smashed, dishes are shattered. The floorboards under my cot have been pulled up. Our money and gold—worth one thousand American dollars, the only thing Nathaniel left behind when he was murdered—is gone. The furnace is tipped sideways. Hot coals spill into the room. The table and chairs are burning. Smoke fills the room. I cough. My eyes sting.

Marilyn.

She is sitting upright in her rocking chair, her blankets still piled around her. A swollen blood spot has blossomed in the center of her forehead. Rivulets of blood stream down her face. Her gray eyes stare blankly at the ceiling.

For a moment, I cannot move. I cannot breathe. I feel as if I am falling into an endless black hole, being swallowed alive by the utter cruelty of life.

I hear the dogs. They are barking from the shed: it's a frantic bark, panicked.

They're alive. Marilyn is not.

This realization is profound, because it determines what I do next. I look away from Marilyn's lifeless form and pull the hammerless Smith and Wesson from a space I had long ago cut into my mattress to make hiding the weapon easier. I put the gun in my pocket and run from the burning cabin. The flames are consuming the walls. The ceiling is frozen solid. As the ice melts, it drips onto the floor and refreezes as cold air blows in through the front door.

I run outside, lightheaded with the shock of everything that has transpired in the last few moments. The shed is burning, too. The dogs are still barking. They're trapped. I hurry to the door, throwing open the bar and pushing inside. The loft is on fire.

Bastards!

Lincoln is up on his hind legs, paws on the door of his pen.

Jenna, hurry! he seems to scream. *Open the door, we're going to die!*

I move as quickly as I can. I unlock the pen doors and the dogs rush outside, into the snow. They do not leave me, though. They wouldn't dream of it. They are as attached to me as I am to them.

A burning piece of wood falls in front of me, narrowly missing my head. I grab the front of my sled and pull it from the shed, outside. I return for the harnesses and lines. The smoke grows thicker. I can taste it on my tongue. It burns inside my chest, filling my lungs and tearing at my eyes. Still, I fight through the smoke and pull barrels and sacks of dried meat from the inside of the building.

Everything we have for the winter is inside—I can't let it burn.

When the smoke consumes the shed and the flames grow too hot, I pause for a moment, exhausted. The dogs run in circles, mesmerized by the fire. The shed is little more than a massive bonfire. The smoke rises into the sky, and the land is ablaze with eerie, flickering light.

I return to the cabin. The building is writhing with flames. The heat burns my face, leaving my cheeks red and raw. Marilyn's body sits peacefully in the midst of it all. I stand in the doorway, staring at her as the flames slowly eat the wood of the chair and set fire to her clothes. She burns slowly. It's better this way. It's a sad and terrible fact of living in this country: You cannot bury your dead in the winter. I could not possibly bury Marilyn's body when there is so much snow on the ground. Despite that, even if I could manage to shovel through the snow, the dirt would be frozen. I could not perform a proper burial until spring.

So I watch her body burn, and as I do, Lincoln throws his head back and releases a mournful howl.

The rest of my family is gone. I am, at last, alone.

Three

The blazing warmth of the cabin fire keeps me alive through the night. In the early hours of the morning, the sun rises, bringing a slightly brighter light, different from the twilight glow that pervades the country for most of the day. The sky is almost clear. Clouds hover on the edges of the mountains. It must be nearly fifty below zero. Every breath hurts. My skin is numb. My feet are nearly paralyzed with cold.

The dogs nest in the snow, sheltered from the wind. I sit beside Lincoln, unmoving, watching as the last embers of the fire die. The cabin is nothing more than a hulking mass of black, skeletal lumber. The smell of smoke permeates everything.

Conroy Parker.

He did this to me. He took my life away from me. He murdered Nathaniel, first, last year, and now he has murdered Marilyn. The circle of destruction is complete. Now, everyone I have ever loved is dead. I am truly, utterly alone.

Lincoln looks up at me. The wind ruffles his ears.

Not utterly alone, he seems to say. *You have me. You have all of us.*

I look away.

If I had any chance of survival in this country, it vanished with the money and gold Conroy's boys took from the cabin. Now, I have nothing. Truly nothing.

I am homeless, penniless and without friends or family.

What is left for me?

I must go into town, I realize, vaguely. *I have to tell the constabulary what happened.*

"WHAT WILL HE DO?" I scream, suddenly on my feet, glaring at the wreckage of my beloved cabin and shed.

When Nathaniel was murdered by Conroy Parker and his gang of thugs, Marilyn and I begged for protection and justice from the Canadian constabulary in Dyea. But in Alaska, in the wilderness...there is little justice. No law. No protection. Every man protects himself, and nobody in Dyea was concerned about the safety of two women living alone. The appointed sheriff, Dan Frisco, brushed us off, saying that he would only help us if we could provide proof of the crime committed.

"You ain't got a body, ladies," he told us. *"So you ain't got a crime. I'm sorry."*

As far as everyone was concerned, Nathaniel's death had been an accident and Conroy was a figment of our imagination—the imagination of two emotional, harebrained women.

"Conroy Parker came to your farm and killed Nathaniel?" Frisco guffawed. *"Ain't possible. He's a big outlaw outside a'*

*Anchorage, but not in these parts. No need to tell wild tales, Mrs.
Renee. Tell me, how did your husband* really *die?"*

We were frustrated and humiliated, and we returned to the
cabin, angry at Dan and embarrassed that he had ridiculed us all
over town, claiming that we were little more than helpless women
with nothing better to do than spin yarns—an elaborate story, he
said, to cover the fact that Nathaniel Renee had run off with another
woman and abandoned us.

Marilyn never went into Dyea again. I went alone. For the
most part, I spent as little time in town as possible. A woman
traveling alone was dangerous enough, but some people—especially
Dan—had become suspicious of me. He had accused me of being
Eskimo, once. Marilyn had almost died of terror: imagine what my
life would be like if a rumor like that got out! Marilyn understood
how destructive it would be...and although she never asked me
outright if Mother was Indian, I believe she always knew.

If it was discovered *now* that I was Cherokee and not fully
French, my situation would only grow worse. I would be no better
than a head of cattle in the eyes of the white men coming to mine for
gold. Mine was a secret that *had* to be kept at all costs.

So I usually only traveled to Dyea when I had to, and when I
did, my visits were short.

I have no choice. I have to go back into town.

I slowly gather the supplies I salvaged from the shed. I ready
the dogs to run. They take their rightful places in front of the sled,
tossing their heads, yipping excitedly, waiting for me to get on with
it.

They know we're about to go out. They know we're about to run.

I haul their food onto the sled and I secure the tug line, the lead lines, the whip. Lincoln sits upright, his nose quivering. He is calm, yet bursting with the anticipation of the run.

Take us out, Jenna, he says with his eyes. *Let's run. Let's see the world today!*

"Have patience," I reply.

My words are flat. My face is tight. I feel like a stone—incapable of smiling ever again. Every time I remember Marilyn or Nathaniel, I feel a piercing pain in my chest, as if someone is stabbing my heart with a knife. The pain of their loss is twofold. It takes me back to the loss of my birth parents and my baby brother. I feel all of it again, and it is enough to weaken my knees and send me crashing into the snow, like a rag doll. It is enough to drown me in waves of nausea and deprive me of sleeping peacefully ever again.

I cannot bear it, and so I move. I move with deliberation, fixing my attention on the sled and the preparation for our run into Dyea.

Of the ten dogs on my team, Lincoln and I have the closest bond. He knows me better than I know myself, and his loyalty and leadership have saved my life out in the snow many times. The rest of the nine dogs are beautiful, powerful creatures; malamutes, some bred with Saint Bernards or Siberian Huskies. I have four females and six males. The females are sweet yet fierce: Patsy, Dasha, Kip, and Ella. I've raised them from pups, the only surviving babies from a litter of six. The males are domineering and strong. Lincoln is, of course, the smartest and most even-tempered of the team. Besides him, there are Moscow, Gnat, Jax, Duke, Spot, and Buck.

They all have their strengths and weaknesses, but together we make a strong team.

I hook the dogs up to the gang line, slipping their chest straps and harnesses over their thick coats of fur. They toss their heads and prance in the lineup, pawing the ground, barking at the sky.

Always, the excitement of the run infects me, breathes life into my body.

Not today. Today, I can think only of what I have lost, and what I must do to survive.

I leave what I cannot carry in the snow—it's not as if I have anywhere to store it—and grip the handle of the sled, checking the supplies one last time on the basket. I shout, "Mush!" The dogs charge forward, slicing through the snow like a line of furry, muscular bullets. I hang on, the cutting air nipping at my cheeks, the Alaskan sky opening above our heads.

It will take us four days to reach Dyea, possibly three if we make good time. By the time we do, Conroy Parker will be far away from here...but I have to tell *someone.*

The wind whistles past my fur cap and scarf and buffalo robe, my Levi trousers streaked with ash and soot beneath it all. Our journey is silent. The only sounds are the dogs' soft crunch through the snow, the quiet *whoosh* of the runners cutting a line in the icy slush.

As we move farther and farther away from the place that I have come to know and love as my home, I promise myself that I will find justice for my murdered family, and that I will take back what Conroy stole from us.

I don't know how...but I will.

Somehow.

I have to try.

***

Conroy Parker, they say, was an honest man at one time. A fur-trapper turned outlaw, driven to madness when his pretty young wife was killed in a fight with a local Inuit tribe. Something about Conroy owing them money. There was surely a great deal of whiskey involved. At any rate, Conroy's wife was killed, and from then on, he became something of an infamous scoundrel. Known mainly for stealing gold or robbing outposts, he was never known as a murderer...until he killed Nathaniel, I had doubted the very existence of Conroy Parker, seeing as how many of the stories about him were ridiculously embellished.

I no longer doubt them. In fact, I find myself rolling them over in my head as we travel, puzzling out the question that has been eating away at me since Conroy first stumbled upon our cabin last year: why kill Nathaniel? Why bother with us at all? Certainly an outlaw like Conroy had more important things to do...more important banks to rob.

The cold is biting, vengeful. I alternate between running alongside the sled to stay warm and resting by standing on the platform. If I don't run in this weather, I will surely freeze to death. It is simply too cold.

We find our way to the frozen Chilkat River. The Renee cabin is only one mile from its banks, a flowing beauty during the spring and summer month—a white, solid mass of ice during the winter. I follow the river south for a while, before crossing east toward Dyea. The journey is uneventful. The world is still; nature and all of its living things are in hibernation. It is only myself and the dogs, moving across the breadth of the land, specks in the infinite universe, the snow packed and perfect for running a sled.

No storms, no snowfall. Just cold and dark and twilight. The dogs nestle into the snow at night, digesting their fish, while I huddle inside my small canvas double-tent, warmed with a small metal stove, the smoke emptying through a hole in the ceiling, sealed around the edges. I sleep under a pile of blankets made of elk fur. Lincoln burrows beside me—the only dog who prefers to sleep next to me. In the morning, we are on our way, and I try my best to avoid thinking of Marilyn's lifeless face, her slack jaw, the blood streaming into her eyes and over her cheeks.

Think of the dogs, Jenna. That is all, nothing else.

If followed south, the Chilkat River will run all the way into the ocean. A series of massive inlets snake through the interior of this part of Alaska, making it ideal for docking steamships bringing optimistic adventurers to our country, searching for their fortunes.

Most leave this place poorer than when they arrived, half-frozen, starved, and sick. Some even leave dead. Alaska is unforgiving, and many people do not understand the harsh realities of everyday life here until it is too late.

Their lust for gold and wealth carries them here. It is also what kills them.

I cut through the forests during the day. Our only enemy now is the wolf and the occasional traveler. I trust no one out here—there are too many men like Conroy Parker in the world, and I rely on my dogs to keep me safe as we move. We stop for nothing. I keep my Smith and Wesson tucked into the belt of my Levis and a knife hidden in my mukluks. The Winchester is folded in the blankets of the sled, easy to reach if I need to use it.

The closer we get to Dyea, the more anxious I become.

Will anyone help me? I have no money. Not a cent. Just the sled, the supplies...

And I have the dogs. They're worth a lot of money.

Never!

I will never sell the dogs—they are my family. Besides, without a sled dog team, I can't transport myself anywhere during the winter. It's simply not possible. They are far too valuable to me, in more ways than one.

If worse comes to worse, I suppose I can get a job in town.

No, you know the truth about the women who work in town.

Women in this country have few choices to support themselves. The first choice, of course, is to find a man and marry him. A man will always take care of you; protect you, feed you, clothe you. The second choice is to work for yourself, and the only jobs available for a woman are saloon positions: dancing, singing, serving liquor or selling your body in the whorehouses.

To be a woman in this world is most unfortunate.

To be a woman and a Cherokee is much worse.

"Dieu merci, ma mère m'a appris à parler français," I whisper.

Thank God my mother taught me to speak French...

I drive the dogs as fast as they can go. They strain against the cold, pulling the sled as easily as pulling a feather behind them. On the fourth day, hours outside of Dyea, I see signs of civilization again. Sled marks in the snow, paw prints left by other dog teams. I smell the scent of steamer smoke, carried up the river on the breeze. The excitement of coming into town never ceases to arouse the dogs. They can sense the presence of other dogs, of people, of food.

When we come over the crest of the hill, I see the city. It lies below us, a hustling speck against the wild of Alaska. I smell the smoke of the fires burning, the cloying scent of mud mixed with snow, of horse manure from the stables, of sap leaking from barrels brought in from steamers during the warmer months.

Just outside of the city, rows and rows of double-tents are erected. Piles of supplies are stacked around the tents. Campfires burn. Men dressed in thick fur coats and tall hats gather around the fires, talking, drinking, laughing. Despite the frigid temperatures, their spirits are high. They're here to seek their fortune. They haven't yet been disappointed.

We sail past the encampment, and the town lies before us. It is little more than a ramshackle collection of buildings erected to accommodate the masses moving through Dyea, once a speck of nothing; now a bustling boomtown, a gateway to the Chilkoot Pass, known around here as the *Golden Staircase*, the trail straight into the heart of gold country.

The main street runs down the center of the city, blanketed with snow. There is a saloon, a dancing hall, hotels, baths, and a general store. Two men—fur-trappers, from the looks of it—are dragging a sled laden with supplies through the snow. Dog teams are tied to the fronts of buildings, the animals barking and howling at everything that moves. Windows gleam with lamplight. Winter twilight is dark and seemingly endless. Many people keep their homes as bright as they can afford, hoping to emulate the effect of real sunlight.

I bring my team to halt in front of *Healy and Wilson's General Merchants, Carriers and Packers.* It is here that I come for supplies during the winter, a rather dreary, clapboard structure, easily the most popular place in town. Healy and Wilson's has practically everything.

"Whoa!" I command. "Whoa, whoa! Easy!"

The dogs stop, Lincoln faithful to my command. The others are grateful to rest. I tie the sled and the gang line to the posts in front of the store, my boots crunching in the ice. Men are gathered in front of the store. They stare at my team, then look back to me.

I am used to the stares.

I'm sure I'm the only woman in these parts who drives her own team. It is heavily frowned upon. I know this, and I am running a risk by being here again so soon. I keep my head down and duck into the store. I pull my hat off, breathing in the scent of fresh straw, licorice, feed, and cotton material imported all the way from the States. Rows of fresh muslin and cloth line the wall: beautiful patterns in beautiful colors.

"Jenna?"

The store owner, Timothy Healy, is standing behind the counter. He wears a heavy coat, his glasses perched on the end of his nose, holding a bottle of whiskey in his hands.

"Hello, Mr. Healy," I say. "How are you today?"

He stares at me.

"Jenna," he replies. He is one of the few people in Dyea who have shown kindness to me—who doesn't judge me simply because of my sex. "Weren't you just here? Is everything okay up at the cabin? How's Marilyn doing?"

He knows that I do not come into town often.

"She's dead," I answer, calmly, hiding the emotion in my voice. "Conroy Parker shot her. Four days ago."

Timothy drops the whiskey bottle. It hits the counter, but it doesn't break.

"Good God!" he exclaims. "Jenna, are you *sure*?"

"Am I *sure*?" I glare at him. "Of course I'm *sure*! He *burned the cabin down*!"

Timothy shudders, picking up the bottle.

"Jenna," he goes on, lowering his voice, leaning forward, pale as a sheet of fresh paper. "If this is true, then you'd best go talk to Dan Frisco."

"I plan on it." I tilt my head. "That's why I came. I wondered if you knew where I could find him."

"The saloon, of course." He shrugs. "As always."

I frown. I was afraid of that.

"Jenna."

"Mr. Healy?"

"I'm sorry about Mrs. Renee. If there's anything I can do..."

"You can watch my dogs while I go find Dan." I nod toward Lincoln.

"Sure thing, Jenna."

"Thank you."

I leave the store and kneel beside Lincoln outside.

"I'll be right back," I tell him. "Mr. Healy's gonna keep an eye on you."

I kiss his nose.

I will be waiting, he says.

I make my way down the street, toward the saloon. The heavy door doesn't keep the sound of piano music and singing women from leaking outside. I take a deep breath and throw the door open. Inside, it is a mass of men in overalls and boots, gathered at overcrowded tables, clutching bottles and glasses of hard liquor. It's somewhat warm inside. Two massive wood stoves burn inside the building, and quite honestly, the alcohol is doing its fair share of keeping the customers from freezing to death.

Two women onstage are singing their hearts out, dressed in too-tight corsets, the material flashing in bursts of outrageous color: burnt oranges and dark maroon. Their faces are powdered white, their lips stained red. The saloon is smoky. It reeks of sweat and alcohol and the strong perfume of the women.

And there at the bar, taking a swig from a ten-dollar, watered-down bottle of whiskey, is our local lawman: Sheriff Dan Frisco, posted in Dyea to maintain law and order, courtesy of the Canadian constabulary. He's an older man, gray hair, white handlebar mustache. He's soaked in sweat, either sick or raucously drunk.

"Mr. Frisco," I say.

I take a seat beside him on the stool. I touch his shoulder.

"Dan Frisco," I say again. "It's me, Jenna Renee. You remember me, surely?"

He sets the bottle down, peering at me through bloodshot eyes.

"Jenna Renee," he replies, pronouncing the words slowly, like a child learning how to speak. Then, a spark of recognition. He remembers.

"What the *hell* do you want?" he demands, suddenly angry.

"Dan," I continue, unmoved, "I'm here to report a crime. A murder."

He looks at me, starting at my boots, then bringing his gaze to my face.

"This ain't another one of your wild stories, is it, Jenna?" he asks.

My first instinct is to respond with rage: to demand an apology.

Why does the fact that I am a woman destroy the credibility of my claim?

I contain myself. As always, I am expressionless and still.

"Dan," I say. "Conroy Parker came to our land four days ago. He killed Marilyn and his boys wrecked the place. They took the money, the gold. They burned down the shed *and* the cabin. There's nothin' left."

"Conroy Parker did it, eh?"

"Yes."

"And his whole gang, I suppose?"

"*Yes.*"

"And he killed your aunt. But not you."

"He never saw me. He was looking for me, though. I don't know why."

"How'd you manage that, Jenna? How'd you manage to *survive?*"

Frisco's words are terse and accusatory. He is not listening.

"I hid just outside of the property," I continue. "Mr. Frisco, are you listening to me? Conroy and his boys killed Marilyn Renee and destroyed everything we own. All of it."

I am still calm. The only betrayal of my desperation is my hands: they're trembling.

Dan takes another swig of whiskey.

"Jenna," he says, "what really happened?"

"I'm telling you what really happened. My aunt is dead. Our money is gone. The cabin's destroyed."

"That's really interesting," Dan goes on, glaring at me. "Because I just got a report in this week from Anchorage saying that Conroy Parker was *shot dead*. They've even got the body to prove it."

"That's impossible!" I reply. "He was at my cabin *four* days ago! He killed Marilyn. He took our money—our gold. Everything!"

"Not if he's dead."

"I'm not spinning a yarn! Whoever they shot in Anchorage...it's the wrong man!"

"Because the Anchorage lawmen are making *their* story up?"

"I'm *not* lying."

"I don't care."

"Come up to the cabin yourself. I got the ashes to prove it."

At this, Dan raises his eyebrows.

"I can't get up there for a few days," he says, at last. "I got some business in town."

"I don't have a few days!" I stand up, slamming my fist against the bar. "I don't have *anything left*! Dan, I'm homeless."

"I'm sorry to say that ain't my problem," Dan replies.

Again, the injustice.

"By the time you get to my land," I say, "and come back to make a report, and round up a posse...Conroy will be hundreds of miles from here and I'll never get a cent back. But right now, we still have a chance. There hasn't been a storm in days. His trail is fresh. He can still be found."

"So you're saying I should take you at your word and round up some men," Dan replies, "and go hunting for a man that, according to Anchorage, was shot and buried last week?"

"Yes," I say, firmly. "Only he's not dead. He's alive and he's running free."

Dan hawks a wad of tobacco spittle into a spittoon.

"Jenna," he says. "I'll tell you what: I'll come up to the cabin this week. I'll take a look around. And then we'll talk, once I've seen it with my own eyes. How 'bout that?"

I see it in his face: he's made up his mind. He's humoring me. He may not make it out to the cabin until spring, because he doesn't believe me. By the time he realizes Marilyn really *has* been killed, it will be too late. I'll have lost everything, and Conroy will be gone and free.

"You're a disgrace, Dan Frisco," I say, infuriated. Humiliated. Frustrated. "You're a coward."

He throws his head back and laughs as if I've just told a joke.

"I don't give a damn what you think," he mutters, holding a finger up, signaling the bartender to give him another bottle. "I've run out, Willy. I need another…"

I push away from the bar, walking through the rough and tumble customers, ignoring hoots and hollers as I pass. I push outside, frustrated. It is always the same in this town: no justice, no help. What am I supposed to do now? I have to do *something*. I'm homeless, penniless…

It's not as if I can go after Conroy myself.

Not even one single, crazy gunfighter would do something so outlandish. Conroy has an entire gang of thugs, all of them dangerous and unforgiving. I may be tough, but I'm not stupid. There *has* to be another way. A smarter way.

I curse under my breath and head back to the dogs. They are waiting for me, settled in the snow, resting their tired legs after the long journey. I walk back in the store. Timothy Healy is waiting on a customer, so I wait, picking at the bolts of patterned muslin.

When I come into town, I usually keep the dogs in Timothy's stable, and I give him fifty cents to stay in one of his rooms. I usually let the dogs rest overnight, and then we head home in the morning. Timothy has always made sure I am taken care of when I stay in town, protecting me from the drunken masses of men at the saloon.

Now, I don't even have fifty cents to spend on a room.

Timothy waves me over to the counter. He wraps up the final packages for his customer and sends him on his way.

"I take it you had no luck with Dan, then," he says. "Elsewise you wouldn't be here."

"No luck. He's a drunken disgrace."

"I can't disagree. You should have seen how much help he was when my store was robbed last year." Timothy forces a smile. "That is to say, he was no help at all."

"I can only imagine."

Timothy pulls a piece of paper from behind the counter, jotting something down.

"Here," he says.

I take the paper, squinting at the messy scrawl.

"Jeremiah Black," I read. *"Hayley's Hotel.* What is this?""Somebody who might be willing to help you," Timothy explains.

"Oh? I'm intrigued."

"He's a unique sort of fellow." Timothy lifts a hand, wiping his brow. "Used to be a fur-trapper from the South, found his way here after the war was over. I've known him for a few years. Now he's a United States Marshal."

"A *marshal*?" I repeat. A spark of hope blooms in my chest. "So he's a *real* lawman."

"That he is. He works alone. He's a bit difficult to work with, the way I hear folks talk about him."

"I don't care. I need help."

"He may be your man. You ever heard of the Dublin Robberies?"

"The three Englishmen in the Klondike who were robbed?"

"That's the one. Gunned down and robbed by a posse of six men. Irish prospectors."

I lean across the counter.

"What happened?" I ask.

"Jeremiah Black was the marshal that gunned the Irishmen down," Timothy says. "So they say."

"All six of them? By himself?"

"He's got a reputation. Not the nicest man, from the sound of it."

"I don't want a *nice* man," I reply. "I want a man who will believe me."

"It may be worth your time, Jenna. But I'd be mighty careful. I hear he's an irritable sort."

"How do you know the marshal? Who is he?"

"He comes into town in the winter sometimes," Timothy explains. "Keeps to himself. Quiet man. To be plainly honest, he's a bit off-putting. There are stories about him—rumors. They say he'll do just about anything for money."

"But he's a *United States Marshal.*"

"He is that."

"But can he track?" I wonder.

"Jenna, if he's a marshal, I'm sure he can do just about anything. Why don't you go talk to him? There's a big reward out on Conroy Parker, ain't that right? Something like two thousand American dollars?"

"Something like that."

"Go talk to him. Please."

I bite my lip, looking at the name scrawled on the paper.

"All right," I agree. "I'll go talk to him."

"Good."

"Don't say anything to Dan Frisco about this."

"Honestly?" Timothy smiles. "I never tell him anything."

Four

ayley's Hotel carries a strange odor. I hold my breath when I walk inside, shocked with the scent of must, alcohol and tobacco pipe smoke. The waiting area is dimly lit. A small, wrinkled woman hunches behind the counter, a thick black collar cupping her neck. A wool blanket is wrapped around her frail body.

"Excuse me," I say. "I'm looking for Marshal Jeremiah Black of the United States."

The woman peers at me through half-moon glasses.

"Upstairs," she says.

"Thank you. Which room?"

"Room three. You'll see the numbers on the door."

I nod.

I climb the narrow staircase, into the dimly lit upper level of the hotel. Each step creaks beneath my weight. The upstairs hallway is hollow. Voices and phonograph music echo off the walls. I hear laughter—women, men. More tobacco pipe smoke. I cough, catching my breath.

Room three...room three...

I see it at the end of the hall. Orange lamplight flickers across the wooden floor through the crack beneath the door.

I rap my knuckles against the door.

I hear voices from within: a woman, squealing with laughter. A man, his voice low and gruff.

I knock again.

Footsteps. The door flies open. I jerk my fist backward, surprised. Marshal Black—it has to be. He's tall, dark hair messy and unkempt. The shadow of stubble is on his face, his jaw strong, and his eyes fierce and dark. His nose looks as if it's been broken once or twice. He's older than I had imagined, and taller, too; skin darkened by the sun, pants slung low on his hips, no shirt. Dark, thick hair touches his tight and muscled stomach. His skin glistens with sweat. Drunk, perhaps? I certainly hope not.

"What the hell do *you* want?" Marshal Black demands.

I straighten my shoulders.

"Marshal Jeremiah Black?" I inquire. "You're a United States Marshal, yes?"

Behind him, a woman stumbles through the light, clutching what looks like a tin can of hootchinoo. She slips her head under Jeremiah's arm and stares at me.

"Who's *she*?" she screeches.

She's young—face powdered white like the girls from the saloon, eye makeup running in black streaks down her cheeks, a too-tight red dress corset constricting her chest.

"You said I was the *only one!*" she squeals, throwing the can against the wall.

"Dammit, Trisha!" the marshal growls, pushing her away. "Get out, will you?"

"How could you do this to me?!" the woman continues, stumbling.

She lunges at me, and I take a step back.

I remain still, watching the scene unfold before me, watching as the woman grabs her jacket and stalks to the door. She lifts a hand, intending to slap my face. I move out of her reach and her arm falls to her side, limp, suddenly exhausted. She spits on Marshal Black's boots and curses me. He doesn't flinch—he doesn't even blink.

I have a feeling he's not wounded to see her leave.

The woman stumbles down the stairs, muttering to herself. I stand there, facing the United States Marshal, waiting for the woman's voice to fade away.

"Marshal Jeremiah Black?" I ask, again.

He raises his eyes to mine.

He says nothing, but I know.

"I have information," I say, "about a wanted robber and murderer."

The marshal gives me a long, hard look. He makes a quick study of the buffalo robe, the Levi denim trousers and the seal-skin boots—my dark hair, my dark skin. He shakes his head, apparently disgusted.

"Don't waste my time," he warns.

"Sir," I reply. "I mean no disrespect, but I'm not leaving until you hear what I have to say."

We glare at each other for a long moment. At last, he steps aside, wordlessly motioning me into his room. I step inside. The bed is unmade. The stove is burning hot. A wooden table is stacked with crinkled, yellowing wanted posters. A Winchester pump-action shotgun is propped against the wall—the same model as the one I own.

"So," the marshal says, lighting a tobacco pipe. He takes a long drag. The smoke clouds above his head. "You have *information*, do you? Start talkin'."

There is not an ounce of interest or curiosity on his face.

He is as cold as a stone—as cold as *me.*

"Four days ago," I say, "a man named Conroy Parker came to our land, murdered my aunt, and burned our property to the ground."

The marshal's eyes flick to mine, and he exhales another cloud of smoke.

"Conroy Parker?" he asks.

"Yes."

"I heard he's dead."

"You heard wrong."

He chews on the pipe.

"Go on," he says at last.

"He would have killed me, too, I'm sure of it," I continue. "But I was hiding, outside. He was looking for me—I'm not sure why. He seemed hell-bent on finding me."

"Ever crossed paths with Parker before?" Marshal Black asks, looking out the window—glass bottles chinked with moss.

"Yes. Last year, Parker came to our land and murdered my uncle. Left my aunt alive—I was hiding then, too. They didn't burn anything. Didn't even steal anything. Just killed him and left." I take a step forward. "He mentioned something to my aunt before he killed her—about checking up on my uncle's old mines. I don't know why." I chew on my lower lip. "He took all of our gold, too. Our nuggets and our paper bills. About a thousand dollars' worth."

"You tellin' me Conroy Parker ain't dead?" Marshal Black asks.

"I am."

"That's quite a story, Miss...?"

"Renee. Jenna Renee."

"That's quite a story, *Miss Renee.*"

Marshal Black takes a seat beside the table, breathing another cloud of smoke. I cough.

"Mr. Healy told me you were a United States Marshal," I go on. "Don't you hunt down outlaws like Conroy Parker?"

"Sometimes," he replies.

"Conroy Parker's got a two thousand dollar reward on his head."

"He does. If he's *alive.*"

"I believe he's wanted dead or alive, Mr. Black."

The marshal flashes an irritated look—I take it he doesn't like being corrected.

"You want me to kill him," the marshal says.

"To put it simply, yes," I reply.

58

He throws his head back and laughs. It's so sudden—so unexpected—that I am startled by the sound. His smile is disarming. It makes him look years younger than he must be.

"Spunk," he remarks. "I like that. But like I said before, I heard Conroy's dead."

"I told you—he's alive. Somebody in Anchorage is lying."

"Have you taken this to the sheriff?" the marshal asks.

"Dan Frisco? He's useless. He's drunk. And besides, he doesn't believe me."

"You *are* a woman."

"My sex has no bearing on this conversation!" I slam my open palm against the table. "I can prove that I'm telling the truth. You can come see my cabin—what's left of it. I'll show you my aunt's body. It's burned now, but I can show you."

The marshal rubs his chin.

"I don't work with women," he remarks. "And in the event that you're lying, Miss Renee, you will—"

"I am *not* lying."

He considers this. I can see the wheels turning in his head as he looks at the stack of wanted posters on the table. Conroy Parker is one of the most wanted robbers and murderers in the entire Alaskan wilderness. I'm sure that capturing or killing him would give Marshal Black quite a bit of notoriety.

"How far away is your land?" he asks.

"Four days by dog team—three if we make better time."

"If Conroy Parker *is* alive, he could be anywhere by now."

"I suppose that's where you do your job and track him down."

"I know Conroy. He moves fast."

"You know him?"

"I know *of* him," he corrects. "There's not a US Marshal that doesn't."

"I'll be glad to see justice done," I say.

"I'm sure you will." He doesn't seem sure at all. "Was your aunt your only remaining blood relative?"

"Yes, sir."

"How old *are* you?"

"It's rude to ask a woman's age."

"So it is." He pauses. "I'll have to see the cabin first. If he was there, we can start tracking from your property."

I nod, relieved that someone is listening to me.

"Thank you," I say.

"You have dogs?" the marshal inquires.

"I do."

"Good. We'll take them to your land tomorrow morning. First thing." He stands up, pacing the length of the room. "Be ready, Miss Renee. Sunrise."

"Yes, sir."

"Meet me in front of Healy and Wilson's."

"I will."

A long moment of uncomfortable silence lapses between us. I look down at my hands.

"Renee," the marshal says, studying my face. "That's a French name, I take it."

"Yes," I answer.

"And *you're* French?"

"Of course, Monsieur." I force a small smile, a familiar wave of fear prickling inside me. "Why?"

He raises an eyebrow.

"Just a question, Miss Renee." He opens the door. "Get out."

I stare at him.

"Are you serious?" I ask, blinking. "That's rather—"

"Rude? I know. Get out."

Irritated, I walk past him, avoiding his gaze.

As I step out of the room, I feel his eyes on me. I don't dare meet his gaze again.

I'm afraid he might see right through me. It's illogical, of course, but still...

"Miss Renee," the marshal says, stopping me on the stairs.

I turn.

"Do you have a gun?" he asks.

"Yes," I reply. "Of course."

"Good," he says. "You're gonna need it."

*

Timothy Healy lets me sleep behind the counter at the store.

"Just this once, Jenna," he'd said. "For Marilyn's sake."

We leave at sunrise. I have brought the dogs out of Mr. Healy's stables, harnessed them, checked the sled and made sure my supplies are still accounted for. I stand beside Lincoln and wait. The streets are mostly silent this early in the morning. It is forty below zero. My face is wrapped tight, only my eyes visible through a slit in the material. The minutes drag by, and the marshal doesn't show. I walk up and down the street, shaking my limbs, willing myself to stay warm.

Almost everyone is asleep at this hour, except for a few drunken stragglers stumbling out of the saloon and dancing hall.

I see him.

United States Marshal Jeremiah Black. He wears a long, thick black jacket with a wide-brimmed hat pulled low across his face. All black, true to his surname. He looks as if he has been cut from shadow, a specter of darkness drifting toward me. A silver star is pinned to the breast of his jacket.

I clear my throat and say, "You're a bit late, Marshal."

"This your team?" he asks, ignoring my remark.

He pulls his own wrap away from his face, peering at the dogs. I notice the small bump in his nose, the slight dark circles beneath his eyes, the traces of scarring on his left cheek.

"Yes, these are my dogs," I say. "They're the best team in this area of the country."

"That's quite a claim."

"It's the truth."

He leans down, looking into Lincoln's face.

"Malamute," he murmurs. "Looks more like a timber wolf."

"He's my fastest."

"How long have you been running dogs, Miss Renee?"

"Since I was thirteen."

"Which makes you...?"

"I told you, it's not polite to ask a woman's age."

"So you did." He swings his pack onto the sled, securing it. He slides his shotgun there, too. I suspect that he has more weapons hidden beneath his coat as well.

"I'll drive the dogs from here, Miss Renee," he tells me.

"Very well."

"We can switch off," he continues. "We'll need to. It's damned cold this morning."

"I understand."

When the skies clear and the temperature becomes cold enough to freeze the gates of hell, mushers traveling together take turns mushing the dogs.

"Be good," I tell the dogs. "Run fast today."

As you wish, Lincoln replies, his eyes sparkling. *We will run like the wind.*

I scratch his ears.

"So you're one of *those*," Jeremiah remarks.

"What do you mean?"

"You talk to your dogs."

"Of course. Don't you?"

"I don't have a team at the moment."

I settle down in the sled, pulling a warm fur blanket over my lap for now. The marshal takes his place behind me on the footboards, cracking the whip in the air. The dogs are jittery, hyper. They shake their heads and paw the snow. When the marshal gives the command to run, they bolt forward, straining only for a moment, and then flying up the road, out of the small city.

The dogs run beautifully, and I admit as we move farther out of Dyea that the marshal is an excellent musher.

That shouldn't surprise you, I tell myself. *Mr. Healy said he was a fur-trapper, once. Besides, if he's been a marshal in Alaska for any amount of time, he surely would be familiar with mushing dogs just like the rest of us.*

I focus on the scenery, on the quiet stillness of the country this morning, on the constant and determined rhythm of the dogs' running.

We run the dogs for a few hours. Jeremiah runs beside the sled for a bit, and then we switch off again and *I* run, too. We stop to eat, offering the dogs a small portion of frozen bear meat to keep their strength up. They crunch on snow, gobble up their food and rest in the cold as we pause. The marshal remains standing. He pulls a flask from his pocket and shakes it.

"Frozen solid," he mutters. "Damn."

"Good," I reply. "Drinking is a foul habit."

"Is it, now?" He turns to me, brow furrowed. "What would you know? You don't even look old enough to be married."

"It's none of your business how old I am, Marshal," I respond coolly.

"And it's none of your business if I drink or not."

Silence hangs between us. I look away.

"Are you always this pleasant?" I ask, standing, dusting the snow from my jacket.

"To be honest, Miss Renee, most women find my company charming."

"Most women don't have the brains to know better."

"That's a fairly harsh assessment of your own, sex, ma'am."

"It was meant to be."

He nearly smiles, giving me a long look, and then gazing back toward the horizon. "If we run through the night, we'll cut our journey in half," he says.

"Good. I want to get there as quickly as we can."

I wander into the forest to relieve myself, putting enough distance between myself and the marshal for some semblance of privacy. When I'm finished, I return to the small clearing to see the sled gone, and the marshal already a good distance ahead of me.

I glare at him.

"Wait!" I shout.

The sled is flying away from me. I run to catch it. I stumble through the snow, falling twice in my heavy clothing, slowed by my stiff muscles. The sled is moving too fast—it's fading from view. My heart pounds against my ribcage.

I run until a bead of sweat slides down my face and the muscles in my legs burn from sloughing through the snow, taking deep steps, lifting my feet as high as I can to avoid sinking too far into the ice. In the distance, I see the marshal bring the sled to a halt. He leans against the handrail, leisurely watching as I approach.

"What the *bloody hell* is wrong with you?" I yell.

I lean forward, hands on my knees, panting hard.

The marshal watches me, a hint of amusement on his face. His eyes are sparkling with excitement as he assesses me, crossing his arms.

"You looked cold," he says.

"*So?*"

"Are you cold now?"

I stare at him.

"That is certainly one of the *most*—"

"You're welcome."

I open my mouth and close it again, unsure if I should be angry or grateful.

For a long moment, we stare at each other in the strange, wintery Alaska daylight. He offers the whip to me.

"Your turn," he says.

He steps off the platform and I take the whip. As we continue to travel, I feel him watching me, and I think, *What is he looking for? What does he think of me?*

I can only hope it is not something that will bring me more pain.

Five

The Klondike has a mystery about it. When I first came to the North on a steamship, I could smell the magic in the air. It was the scent of adventure, the seduction of possible wealth, the promise of something new and exciting. I had clung to one cloth bag of belongings, a hat firmly on my head, my small hand wrapped around the rail of the ship, watching as we approached Sitka. It was warm—humid, sticky. Mosquitos the size of small birds swarmed the boat and the banks, drawing blood and leaving red, painful welts that itched for days.

I remember seeing Nathaniel for the first time on the docks; I'd been so relieved to see his face. Familiar, friendly, open. He'd wrapped his arms around me, told me everything would be all right.

"Welcome to Alaska," he said. "Land of adventure and magic."

I believed him.

Today, the wilderness is crawling with adventurous spirits seeking their fortunes in gold. My uncle came to Alaska long before the craze began, a man "ahead of his time," as he always claimed. With the discovery of gold in 1896, people began flooding to Alaska. The mines that Nathaniel owned had produced *some* gold—enough to make him a small fortune, enough to tuck away for future use. He and Marilyn had never intended to stay in Alaska permanently, but they had fallen in love with the land here and so he remained a gold prospector, spending weeks at a time living in Dawson City, managing his business. The rush and craze of the gold boom mostly flowed around me, because I rarely visited the mines myself. Like a pebble in the middle of a stream, the crazed wealth-seekers left our land alone. We were far enough away from Dyea to maintain peace and privacy, yet close enough to run into town for supplies if we needed to.

As I approach the cabin with Jeremiah, I think about the gold, the mines...the Klondike. I think about how it seems that everywhere I go, death follows me like a curse. First in San Francisco, and now in the midst of a wild country.

By the time we pull up to the remains of the buildings, I am tired and numb with cold. It's been a long three days, nonstop running. The dogs sink into the snow, resting. Nothing has changed. Everything still smells of smoke. The supplies I left behind are still here, caked in a layer of ice.

The marshal slowly steps off the sled. He pulls his hat off, his dark hair messy and crooked.

"Welcome to the Renee Estate," I say grimly. "What's left of it."

He swings the Winchester into his arms, holding it close as we leave the dogs to rest.

"Her body is in the cabin," I say. "If there's anything left of it."

Jeremiah nods, his expression grim.

He doesn't look. He walks around the property. He stops every now and then to study something—although I'm not sure *what*—and then returns to what used to be the front steps to the cabin.

"This is where Parker killed her?" Jeremiah asks, his voice low.

"Yes," I reply. "And my uncle, a year back."

"Why didn't he kill your aunt then?"

"I don't know."

"And why did he kill your uncle?"

"I don't know that, either."

"You mentioned something about Conroy checking up on your late uncle's mines...?"

"Yes, I heard him say that. I'm not sure why. It doesn't make sense."

"Parker always has a reason." The marshal pauses. "You said he came here looking for *you*."

"I guess so."

Jeremiah leans on the handles of the sled, tipping his hat back, exhaling.

"Tell me, Miss Renee," the marshal begins. "Where are you from?"

"What do you mean?" I respond.

I am instantly cautious—I cannot help it.

"I *mean*, where did you live before you came to Alaska?" the marshal continues, irritation creeping into his tone. "You didn't learn to speak French in this cabin, did you?"

"No," I admit. "I was born in San Francisco. Nathaniel and Marilyn Renee were my last living family. Nathaniel was my father's older brother."

"And what prompted your immigration to this frozen wasteland?"

I reply, "My family was killed in a ferry accident in the city when I was a child. Nathaniel and Marilyn sent for me. Took me in, raised me as their own. They were good people."

"And then Conroy Parker walked through your door," the marshal murmurs.

"That's about the size of it," I agree.

"You've lived here for how long, then?"

"Five years. Almost six."

"Ah, so that makes you eighteen."

I don't confirm my age.

He rests his hand on the shotgun

"Look, Conroy will head north, and then he'll go west toward Anchorage. Chances are, if he's taken your gold and your money anywhere, it's going to be there."

"Why Anchorage? It's hardly a boomtown. They barely even fish there."

"Conroy Parker doesn't work alone," the marshal explains, frowning. "He's partners with a man named Matthias Cooper; Cooper owns a mining company in these parts. The man's richer than God.

He's got a monopoly on most of the gold fields down at the Klondike and all of the Yukon these days."

"I know who he is," I reply. "Everyone around here does. Nathaniel used to talk about Cooper Mining quite a bit."

"Cooper is a snake."

"And Conroy *works* for him?'

"Yes."

I exhale. "So…it's not just Conroy Parker. It's much more than that."

"Yes. In fact, it ain't uncommon for Cooper Mining to buy up small mines after the owner dies." He leans forward. "Personally, Miss Renee…I think Cooper Mining is paying Conroy Parker to kill prospectors so that they can strengthen their monopoly over the Yukon."

I stand up, heart beating, a revelation striking me like a lightning bolt.

"Then do you think Matthias Cooper paid Conroy Parker to come here and kill Nathaniel?" I ask, eyes wide. "God, wouldn't that make sense? Cooper hired Parker to kill Nathaniel so he could seize the mines!"

Jeremiah knits his brow.

"It's possible," he agrees. "Who owns Nathanial's mines now?"

I stare at Jeremiah.

"Cooper Mining," I whisper. "Marilyn sold them the mines after Nathaniel was murdered."

The marshal nods.

This knowledge stuns me. It means that Nathaniel was not killed randomly, but methodically. That his death was meant to look like a murder by highway robbers, when it was, in fact, a hit ordered by Matthias Cooper, gold god of the North.

This changes everything.

"But...why would Conroy Parker come back and kill Marilyn?" I ask. "It doesn't make sense. The mines already belong to Cooper now. Where was the purpose in it?"

The marshal walks up to the ashy, charred remains of the cabin.

"It's possible," he says, "that Parker killed Marilyn Renee because Cooper didn't realize Nathaniel had a family, and he wanted the witnesses to Nathaniel's murder eradicated. It's also possible that Parker did it for fun."

"For *fun*?"

"Conroy Parker has a reputation for a reason. He's unpredictable."

"But I'm still alive."

He answers, "Yes. And he knows it."

Jeremiah stops, kneeling in the snow, studying the footprints.

"All he took was the gold and the money?" he asks. "No dogs, nothing else?"

"Nothing. He burned everything else."

"We'll have to leave first thing tomorrow if we're going to pick up his trail."

"We have plenty of supplies," I tell him.

"Let's hope so. Winter's far from over."

"Marshal—what are we going to do when we actually find Conroy?"

"Kill him."

"He's got men with him."

"I'm a United States Marshal for a reason, Miss Renee." He points to his face. "And it ain't just because I got a pretty face."

A joke?

This coaxes a surprised smile out of me.

"You mentioned Anchorage, before," I say.

"Cooper Mining has based one of their biggest ports there," the marshal replies. "Of course, there's one in Dawson City, too. I'm betting that Conroy is headed to Anchorage. He always does this time of year."

"Anchorage is hundreds of miles from here! It will take us all winter to get there!"

Jeremiah answers, "I'd like to catch Conroy before he gets that far."

"And if we don't?"

"One day at a time, Miss Renee." He stands up. "Do me a favor."

"Yes?"

"Call me Jeremiah."

***

Night comes quickly. The temperature is deadly cold. We make a small camp on the edge of my family's property, huddled inside a double-tent, the small stove burning for warmth. I am wrapped in my familiar buffalo robe and blankets. Marshal Jeremiah Black is sitting across from me, silent and stony.

Despite our clothes and the stove and the tent, it is still freezing. It's the kind of cold that creeps into your bones and makes you ache. The kind of cold that makes your teeth hurt, that makes you want to die if you're exposed to it for too long.

The secret to surviving the weather here, Nathaniel always told me, is to learn to be patient. To take it slow, to hunker down, and to wait it out.

I watch Jeremiah through the slits between my blankets, studying his bold, rough features, his calloused hands, the way his dark eyes stare into the sides of the tent, ignoring me.

I drift into an uneasy sleep. I dream about Marilyn. I see her reaching her hands out to me, blood filling her mouth, bathing her body. She's screaming for help, and I can only stand there, motionless, rooted to the spot as she is consumed by the curtain of red. I hear Conroy Parker's malicious laughter, and I am taken back to Nathaniel's murder. I see him being dragged behind the shed, his dead body thrown into the back of a dog sled, Marilyn weeping...

I wake, feeling suffocated.

"Marshal Black?" I whisper. "Jeremiah?"

He's gone.

Jeremiah has vanished from the tent. Why would he venture out into the cold?

I crawl out of the pile of blankets and take a deep breath, steeling myself for the frigidity that is sure to meet me outside. I slip into the night air.

I look around, past the dogs sleeping in the snow, past the fence surrounding the property.

Jeremiah is nowhere to be seen. Sudden fear strikes me. Perhaps he's fled—decided he wants nothing to do with me and the chase for Conroy Parker. I squint through the darkness and shoulder my Winchester from the tent. I make sure it's loaded, and I follow a pair of boot-prints leading away from the tent, behind the ruins of the cabin.

I tighten my grip on the gun and march forward, walking toward the edge of the trees, balsam and spruce and stunted pine.

"Jeremiah?" I call quietly.

No answer. I peer into the trees. Nothing but shadows.

"*Jeremiah Black*!" I say again—this time a demand, not a question.

A gunshot cracks through the night air. The shot is shockingly loud. I drop low, into the snow. The dogs scream and howl, suddenly awake and agitated. My ears ring. The bullet just missed me. It has wedged into the tree beside my head.

I bring the heavy shotgun up into my shoulder, searching the darkness for any signs of the gunman who nearly killed me. A dark figure moves across the snow. I pull the trigger on the shotgun. It kicks like a mule, slamming against my shoulder, the shot ripping through the quiet of the woods. The dark figure dances aside. My shot misses him. I curse the darkness and my cold, stiff fingers.

The man raises his hand—he's holding a revolver. A Colt, perhaps.

I am going to die.

The thought flashes through my head—instantaneous, quicker than a blink. Someone grabs me from behind and throws me aside just as the figure takes a shot with the revolver. The bullet goes wild. Another miss on the gunman's part.

"Stay *down!*" Jeremiah hisses in my ear.

"Marshal?" I gasp. "I thought—"

But he is already up, gone. He runs across the snow, slamming against the shadowy gunman. The man curses and screams. I hold the Winchester into my shoulder again, ready to use it if I need to. Jeremiah flips the gunman onto his back, pressing his heavy boot against his chest. I take a few steps closer, looking at his face.

"Oh, God," I breathe.

The gunman's face is bleeding like a stuck pig, a bronze badge pinned to his chest.

It's Dan Frisco.

Six

Jeremiah ties Dan Frisco's wrists above his head, knotting the rope around a tree branch. I stare at him, slathered in sweat turned to ice, blood spurting from his mouth and nose. Jeremiah casually balances his shotgun against his shoulder. He betrays no expression—just a calm, cold undercurrent of calculation.

"Dan Frisco," Jeremiah says. "Fancy findin' you out here."

Dan grunts. His handlebar mustache is soaked in blood.

"You tried to kill me," I say, shivering. "Dan. What the *hell* were you—"

"I know what you are," Dan interrupts. He is sober—I've never seen him this way. "Don't think I'm stupid. They *told* me what you are."

I stare at him.

"You're a goddamned savage, is what they say," he spits.

Jeremiah grabs Dan's collar, bringing him to his face. Dan chokes and coughs.

His face turns blue.

"*Who* says?" Jeremiah growls. "You realize you just tried to kill an innocent woman? I can see you hang for that."

He pushes Dan backward. His wrists strain against the rope. Dan winces.

"*Who sent you*?" Jeremiah demands.

Dan replies, "What makes you think I was sent, *Marshal*? I was just doin' my sworn duty, tryin' to investigate a reported murder…and wouldn't ya know it—I come stumblin' upon a couple a people in the dark. So I shoot at them to defend myself. Had no choice, as you can see."

I look to Jeremiah, who takes a step away from Dan. He seems monstrously powerful compared to the short, bloody man tied to the tree.

"I don't understand," I say. "You said you didn't believe me."

"He changed his mind," Jeremiah interrupts. "Because *Sheriff Frisco* here is on Cooper's payroll. Am I right, Sheriff? I figured you for a sniveling weasel from the moment I met you."

He presses the barrel of his shotgun against Dan's throat.

"I think it's safe to assume that Dan couldn't have you spreading rumors about Marilyn being killed by Conroy Parker, when Parker is *supposed* to be dead," Jeremiah says.

Dan Frisco sneers, "You think you got any right to come rollin' into my town and makin' your own justice, Marshal? This is *my* country out here."

"This is Cooper's country."

"Even so. You got no idea what kind a' fire you're messin' with."

"I think I do," Jeremiah replies.

He cocks the hammer. Dan flinches.

"All right, all right," Dan says, his voice quivering. "So, I sometimes get some personal requests from Matthias...a personal favor here and there, ya know. It pays the bills, as they say."

"It pays for the *whiskey*," I mutter.

"I can get you in on a deal," Dan continues, lighting up, as if he's just pulled a rabbit out of a hat, expecting us to be dazzled. "You forget about this, Marshal, and I'll make it worth your while. Swear to Mother Mary I will."

"I'm going to kill you," Jeremiah responds coldly.

Quiet. Jeremiah and Dan stare each other down. It's unsettling, despite the fact that I am nothing more than an observer.

"Cooper'll come for ya!" Dan exclaims, eyes going wild. "If you kill me, he'll hunt ya down like an animal and kill ya—and he'll take the girl. He *wants* the girl."

"Good," Jeremiah answers. "Saves me the trouble of having to track Conroy and his boys down—they'll come straight to me."

Dan's breathing quickens. I can see his panic growing.

"You won't get away with it." He leans forward. "I'm a sworn lawman! If anyone finds out you killed me, they'll take away your badge, Marshal."

"What makes you think they'll find out?" Jeremiah asks. There is no mirth in his tone. Only confidence. I wonder if he's bluffing.

"Jeremiah," I say. "Just leave him here. That's punishment enough, don't you think?"

Jeremiah ignores me.

"If Conroy finds out it's *you* who's hunting him down with this redskin bitch," Dan spits, "he'll peel the skin right off your bones. You know I'm right."

Jeremiah strikes him again, eyes sparking with anger.

"Watch your *mouth*," he says, slowly, fingers fisted.

"You can't *do this*!" Dan begs. "I'll give you anything you want. Anything!"

Jeremiah slams the stock of his shotgun into Dan's head. His eyes shutter, his body goes limp. The two of us stare at Dan for a moment before I break the silence.

"You're not going to kill him, are you?" I ask.

Redskin...redskin...redskin...

I swallow the fear rising within me.

Who could have possibly told Dan Frisco about my Cherokee mother? Nobody knew—not a single person. Marilyn suspected it, but never said a word, and neither did Nathaniel. There is nobody left in this world who knows the truth.

"Marshal—" I begin, but he cuts me off.

"Jeremiah," he says.

"*Jeremiah.* Are you going to kill him?" I ask again.

"I don't have to. The wolves will take care of it." Jeremiah digs through Dan's pockets. He pulls out some bills, a knife, and a folded-up piece of paper. "Well, look at this."

He unfolds the paper. It's an advertisement for Cooper Mining.

WANTED

Strong and Able-Bodied Men for Employment at the Cooper Mining Company. Pay is $20 per week, lodging included. See Cooper Mining Office to apply. 1256 Dungee Avenue, Anchorage.

"Very fortuitous," Jeremiah remarks. "We've got ourselves an address."

"But Dan Frisco?" I whisper. "Shouldn't we turn him into the constabulary?"

"To *who*, Jenna?" Jeremiah replies. "Dan's the only lawman stationed out here, besides marshals like me. We'll let the woods do their justice."

He shoves the paper into his pocket.

He's right. To turn Dan in, we'd have to trek into Skagway, a larger boomtown just beyond Dyea, and that would take at least four or five days. We can't afford that kind of a delay if we want to catch Conroy Parker.

"Get the dogs ready," Jeremiah advises. "We're awake. We might as well get going."

I nod, intending to do as he says.

Then, "Jeremiah, Dan said that when Conroy found out it was *you* hunting him, he'd kill you… Does Conroy know who you are?"

Jeremiah doesn't reply.

"*Jeremiah*," I insist. "Kindly do me the favor of answering my question, please."

He tips his hat back.

"I'm a United States Marshal," he replies, raising an eyebrow. "Of course Parker knows who I am. I've been hunting that son of a bitch for the last four years. Haven't had much luck yet. And now you…" He shakes his head. "Come on."

I head back to the tent, slowly gathering our supplies and comforting the dogs—they are agitated and upset. The gunshots have disturbed them. They know as well as I do that gunshots bring death, and they fear the metal weapons of man more than they fear being hunted by the wolves.

I watch Jeremiah silently drag Dan Frisco's unconscious body through the snow, toward the woods behind the cabin. He disappears into the trees. Lincoln pricks his ears and looks at me, tilting his head.

"I'm sorry," I sigh. "Don't you worry. We'll take care of each other."

He bows his head, resting his chin on the straw.

We're ready to run, Jenna. Just give the word.

He watches me as I load the sled. I do not doubt that he knows where we are going, and why. The dogs have always held a sense of infinite wisdom and understanding, which is why I was drawn to them in the first place. They never asked *why*. They didn't need to. They understood. They sensed more, felt more and knew more than any of us, and it was their instinct that had driven me to trust them when we ran in the woods as a child, and then a woman.

I hear Jeremiah returning. His is a dark figure against the white, hat pulled low.

Dan Frisco is not with him.

***

We leave for Anchorage. My heart aches, leaving the land behind, even if it is nothing more than ashes. It is so numbingly freezing that the marshal—*Jeremiah*—and I take turns running behind the sled every few minutes. The motion is helpful, I find, in forgetting my troubles. To lose one's self in physical movement is a wonderful escape.

The air is still. I do not trust it for a single moment. Winter here can turn savage in an instant. Even the calm can kill. We are bound to hit another storm soon. One can only travel so far without experiencing the discomfort of a blizzard or snowfall in this country.

As we journey, I feel nothing but aching, detached hatred toward Conroy Parker and the man who pulls his strings, Matthias Cooper. Why did my family have to succumb to their wrath? Haven't I suffered *enough* loss?

When we stop to feed the dogs, I ask Jeremiah,

"What exactly *did* you do with Dan Frisco?"

He looks across the snow, hat pulled low across his face.

"Justice," he replies.

"So you did kill him?"

"I told you. The wolves will take care of him."

The twilight sun shines against the snow. I squint. I check each and every dog on the team, rubbing their heads, scratching their ears, gently offering murmurs of encouragement. Jax and Duke growl softly as the wind picks up, no doubt smelling something in the air that I can't. My girls are stoic and lovely in the morning light. Ella runs just behind Lincoln; they are mates, in a way. The two of them are the parents of five of the dogs on the team: Dasha, Gnat, Moscow, Kip, and Buck.

I have no doubt that the litters of any of their offspring would fetch a high price on the dog market...not that I could ever have the heart to sell them. These dogs are my family, and it would kill me to part with just one. Together, we make a cohesive, single unit. To remain intact, we must stay together...always.

We run the dogs for a few more hours, into the empty wilderness. There is nothing out here—nothing but the occasional outpost or campsite, nothing but the lingering scent of wolves on the week-old snow, nothing but the jaw-dropping loneliness of the land. It is an uneventful first day of travel, and I am grateful for it.

We tie the dogs down for the night. I light the Primus and cook up rations of beans and cornbread, boiling water for hot tea. It is a trick to boil the snow—it is almost too cold. Yet I manage all right, and Jeremiah and I crawl into the tent, sealing the opening, warming our hands by the small stove. We drink our tea and eat the hot food. For a moment, we simply enjoy the warmth in silence.

I take a bite of beans and study Jeremiah's face. I am still unsure how old he is...he could be twenty and five years of age, but he could also be forty. The scars and rough expression he carries make it difficult to tell.

"Where are you from, Marshal...*Jeremiah*?" I ask amiably.

An attempt at conversation; an attempt at uncovering the mystery of who this gruff marshal really is.

"Far away," Jeremiah replies, staring down at his food.

"Oh, come now," I press, curious. "For the sake of conversation....?"

Jeremiah sighs and takes the last bite of food. He wipes his mouth on his jacket sleeve, gulps the tea and rests his arms on his knees.

"I'm from the South," he says.

"Where?"

"South Carolina."

"So far away!"

He takes another drink.

"Where's your family?" I ask.

He doesn't answer.

"What brought you to Alaska?" I continue.

"What do you *think*?"

"Gold," I sigh. "Everyone comes for the gold."

"And that is where you'd be wrong, Miss Renee."

"Gold didn't bring you here, then?"

"Oh, it brought me here," Jeremiah replies. "But it ain't why I stayed."

"Why did you stay?"

He doesn't say.

"Nathaniel came to Alaska before gold was discovered in the Klondike," I sigh. "He was always a man ahead of his time. He came for adventure. He suspected that there was gold here, long before anyone else did."

"But you didn't come for gold," Jeremiah surmises. "You came to survive."

I shrug.

"How did the ferry catch fire?" Jeremiah asks. He takes his hat off, sets it on the floor. His hair is covered with a thick, patterned neckerchief. It appears to be something an Inuit would wear.

"The ferry," I repeat dully. "The ferry that killed my family?"

Jeremiah doesn't move. He waits for me to speak.

"No one is sure," I say, quietly. "It simply *happened*. Some say it was an accident. Some say the boiler exploded. I suppose we can never truly be sure, because the ferry itself sunk to the very bottom of the bay."

"Your parents were French?" Jeremiah asks.

"Yes. Jacques and Louise Renee. And my brother, Daniel."

"You were fortunate to have kin in Alaska. Most children like you would have ended up on the streets or in the poorhouse...or worse."

I say, "I know."

I pull my knees to my chest, holding the hot tea beneath my face, soaking in its heat.

"And your family?" I ask. "What tragedy has befallen yours?"

"Why do you believe that there's tragedy involved?"

"Because you carry it in your eyes—just as I do."

Jeremiah raises an eyebrow, rubbing his chin.

"My father," he says slowly, "went north to join the Union Army during the war...he believed President Lincoln was a great man, and he was fully devoted to fighting for the cause of the Union from the day the war broke out. My mother and two brothers and I were meant to follow soon after, to meet father behind Union lines."

"What happened?"

"Father was killed by Confederate soldiers before he even had a chance to fight," Jeremiah replies. "It was an ambush; he never stood a chance."

"And the rest of your family?"

"Mother took to the bottle. Drank herself to death—died a year after I was born."

"I'm so sorry."

"She was a fool."

"Heartbroken, most likely. And your brothers?"

"One died of tuberculosis, another was killed by Confederate sympathizers in our town after the war. They'd heard of my father's defection to the Union and killed Jonathan one day on his way home from church: in broad daylight. Left him hangin' in a tree."

I stare at him.

"That must have been horrible for you," I say.

"I was ten."

"What did you do?"

"I had no one else. I ran to Texas."

"Texas!" I exclaim. "How did you get there?"

"After the war—and toward the end of the fighting, before Lee surrendered to Grant—people started leaving. They saw the writing on the wall. They knew defeat was coming...and so they left. I hitchhiked all the way to Texas, bouncin' from one group of travelers to the next."

I watch him in the firelight, amazed—an orphaned ten-year-old boy, traveling across the country...and *alone*! How must he have felt?

"What then?" I ask, leaning forward, enraptured by his story.

Jeremiah stands up.

"I'm gonna check the woods," he says. "Make sure we're not being followed."

"But—"

"Goodnight, Miss Renee."

He slips outside, his expression taut, and the conversation is over.

I frown, irritated by his brusque rudeness. I wonder, too, what the rest of the story is. Is it too painful to relay? Or is it something he's ashamed of?

If Jeremiah was only an infant when the war ended...that puts him at thirty-three years old.

So old!

By the time Jeremiah returns from the woods, I am drifting off to sleep, where I dream of a young boy running from the aftermath of war, searching for peace and belonging.

Seven

Smoke.

I smell it long before I see it. I am just finishing feeding the dogs as the tip of the twilight crests over the mountains—almost seven in the morning—when I notice the scent of burning wood.

"Jeremiah...," I say.

"I smell it," he responds.

I look toward the spindly, leafless trees surrounding us. I spot it: a thin tendril of black smoke in the distance, joined by several monstrous billows. Jeremiah grabs his shotgun and says, "Stay with the dogs."

"I'm coming with you," I reply.

I tie the team up and follow Jeremiah through the trees, crunching through the snow.

"I told you to stay behind," he commands, stopping.

I barely manage to stop myself from colliding with his broad chest.

"I'm *coming*," I say.

He glares at me. I glare back.

We keep going.

We come to a small clearing amidst the trees. There is a cluster of four log cabins—miner's cabins, from the looks of it. They are ablaze with fire. Two dead men lie on the ground. I blink through the acidic smoke.

More bodies. At least a dozen, mostly women and children. I clap my hand over my mouth, horrified. I see the corpses of little girls and small boys. I see a dead woman clutching a deceased infant to her still chest. Blood is everywhere; it stains the snow, runs in frozen rivers from the bodies lying on the ground.

"What happened here?" I breathe, trembling.

Jeremiah raises the shotgun. I stay beside him.

I see the marks of fresh footprints and sled marks in the snow.

"Men," I say, kneeling and tracing my finger along the prints. "Six of them, at least…strong men, too. Look at the size of their feet— they're all very tall. They were here an hour ago. Maybe more."

I stand, facing Jeremiah.

"You can track," he states, looking surprised.

"Nathaniel taught me well," I explain.

"What else can you do, Miss Renee?"

"I suppose you'll find out."

We step into the smoldering settlement.

"Do you think Conroy did this?" I whisper.

Jeremiah doesn't answer. We keep walking. I almost stumble over a dead woman lying face down in the snow. The last cabin in the clearing is burned to the ground; made of brittle pinewood, it must have ignited like a torch. Just beside the cabin, there is a small metal vault, roughly the size of a wine barrel. The vault has been broken, and the contents are gone.

The blackened remains are almost a mirror image of my cabin.

"I don't think this was Conroy," Jeremiah replies.

"How can you say that?" I whisper. "He killed everyone and burned the cabins."

"Yes, but there were six men. You said Conroy had nearly ten with him at your cabin." He points to the blood in the snow. "Parker usually burns his bodies or takes the dead to be buried. These folks ain't been given that dignity."

"I don't know that I agree, Marshal. Conroy is cruel and—"

"And I know his patterns, Jenna." Jeremiah fixes me with a stern gaze. "I *know*."

I see the death around me and I feel the insurmountable devastation and injustice of the loss of my adoptive parents again. It's crippling—like a blow to the chest, like a bullet to the heart. I gasp for breath and then straighten up.

Gather your wits, girl.

"If it's not Conroy Parker who did this," I say, "then who do you think—"

"I don't know."

Bang!

A gunshot cracks through the air. It's sudden—unexpected.

All I can think is, *Again? Weren't we shot at last night, too?*

Jeremiah's hat sails off his head, tumbling to the ground. He drops to the snow. I roll behind a mound of rubble. There is a hole in the center of Jeremiah's hat.

I look back toward the woods.

A figure moves through the trees, ghosting like a shadow around the settlement. Another gunman—and I know this time it is not Dan Frisco. The gunman takes another shot at us. I duck my head. Jeremiah twirls the shotgun up into his arms, fitting it into his shoulder. He squeezes the trigger, and the shot shatters the air. The gunman goes down with a broken scream. Jeremiah hoists his shotgun over his shoulder and runs forward. I follow, breathless.

It's a young man—practically a child. Baby-faced, pale, white-blond hair. Jeremiah's bullet has pierced his heart. Blood oozes through his shirt, onto his jacket. His eyes are wide open. He's dead—a small revolver lies in the snow beside him.

"He's only a boy," I murmur.

Jeremiah kneels beside the body.

"Cooper Mining," he says.

He holds up the boy's lifeless fingers. He turns his hand. On the underside of his wrist, there is a brand mark: CM.

"I don't understand," I say.

"Cooper Mining," Jeremiah explains, "has taken to branding some of their labor force. This was their handiwork. Had to be. You've never seen this boy, have you? Was he at the cabin when Parker shot your aunt?"

I shake my head. No.

"Look at the tracks again," Jeremiah continues. "See how they move around the camp? There are no signs of a real struggle. Clearly, these men were employed by the company and supplied with plenty of weapons. But now look to the cabins. What do you see?"

I study the burning frames.

"Oh, *God!*" I gasp.

Scalps.

Scalps have been strung up just behind the cabins, in the trees.

"Indians?" I say.

"It's meant to look that way...but anyone who knows *anything* would know—"

"That the natives here don't scalp their victims," I finish, exhaling. "The Inuit and the Tlingit and the Chilkat are traders. I don't believe I've ever heard of a single person being killed by the natives in this area in years. The only deaths Nathaniel ever talked about were the men who attempted to climb over the Chilkoot Pass without the Chilkat peoples' permission."

"You catch on quick, Jenna," Jeremiah says, standing. "I'm guessin' this boy and whoever was with him didn't know what the hell they were doing."

"But why kill these people?" I wonder. "Why even try to frame someone else?"

"The most likely explanation?"

"Cooper Mining."

"Cooper Mining has a history, Jenna," Jeremiah says, nodding toward the settlement. "Towns like this—sitting close to gold mines or streams thought to be filled with nuggets—end up getting torched or bought out...and I'm sure you got a pretty good idea a' who buys the land after."

"Cooper Mining," I say again.

"Right. Cooper Mining kills their competitors, to put it nicely."

"Why blame the Inuit or the Tlingit?"

"Because it's so damn easy to blame them, isn't it?" Here, Jeremiah looks grim. "Come on."

"Where?"

"We're going to burn the scalps."

I blink, taking a step back from the dead boy.

"But what about this boy?" I ask. "This…*child*?"

"If he didn't want to die, he shouldn't have shot at us."

"But he's only—"

"*Jenna,* you understand the law of the land out here. I don't have to tell you."

I nod numbly.

He seems satisfied with this, and then he begins trekking back through the snow, toward the settlement filled with death, destroyed by Matthias Cooper and his utter greed.

I am sorry for your deaths, I think, looking toward the corpses. *May you rest in peace.*

***

We leave the settlement with a message. The scalps are discarded and we lay the bodies to rest just outside of the camp. Jeremiah takes the black charcoal from the destroyed cabins and writes on the stones just outside the clearing:

COOPER MINING: KILLED THEM FOR GOLD.

We trudge back to the team, where the dogs are anxiously awaiting our return. Lincoln wags his tail and jumps up as we come through the trees.

"They were worried," I say. "Poor darlings."

I kneel down and rub Lincoln's head, kiss his nose.

"Let's go," Jeremiah replies. "That boy wasn't alone. Best not to linger in one place too long – I'd prefer to surprise *them*, and avoid gettin' shot in the back."

I cannot disagree.

I take my place on the sled and Jeremiah runs behind us. He keeps the shotgun strapped across his back, within easy reach. My gloved hands clutch the runners and the whip. As the dogs pull and we move again, every shadow—every tree and stump and hill— seems to hold a dark secret. I am suddenly afraid of the unknown, afraid of the men who came to this place and killed so many innocent people.

The dogs sense our apprehension. They know, as they always do. They run faster than usual, fiercely concentrating on driving the sled through the snow at a breakneck speed, full of spit and fire and determined to catch the wind itself. As we journey, I think about the dead bodies and the scalps, the sloppy framework. Why, I wonder, do people always blame people like mine for killings like this? Surely there is enough blood on *both* the hands of the white man and the so- called savages.

When I was a child, Mother had gone to extremes to protect me from abuse. She told me Cherokee stories and legends. Told me about life in the plains, about Grandmother and Grandfather, whom I had never met. She told me to keep the stories close to my heart. To remember who I was, but to tell no one.

"Hold your head high," Mother would say. "We are just as good as everyone else, but most people won't understand that. You must never speak of the Cherokee. Remember, you are only French, now."

To city people, being Cherokee was interesting—a fascinating, exotic background, but nothing more. Native people were regarded as little more than cattle, perhaps good for hard labor at the very most. Mother was meticulous in maintaining her image of a Frenchwoman, and Father only reinforced the picture. He was boisterous and fun-loving and would do anything to protect Mother and me.

When I was nearly six years of age, I remember standing on Market Street one day, watching the steady ebb and flow of the crowd, listening to the gentle *clip clop* of hooves against the ground. It was a warm day, the ocean breeze was fresh and invigorating. I'd been impatient, waiting for Mother to finish her shopping...

I stole across the street, wanting to pat the nose of the horse tied to the post just outside of a fruit stand. I placed my hand on the horse's velvety nose and looked into his kind face.

Hello there, *he said with his eyes. You are young and curious.*

I remember laughing. I'd always been able to imagine what animals were saying—Mother called it the Gift, something Mother Earth had bestowed upon all members of her family. It was, of course, a secret.

A rough hand removed my fingers from the horse's nose. A man shoved me backward—tall, gray-haired, and pale-white. He wore a black suit with a matching stovepipe hat. I hit the ground on my side. I felt my hand tremble with pain—sprained, perhaps.

"Stay away from my horse, injun," *he spat.*

I stared at him, terrified. I'd never been the subject of ill-treatment before. This was the first time. A tear slid down my cheek, and then my mother was there. She picked me up, swept me into her arms, her blue skirt swishing across the dirt.

"Have you no sense of decency?" she demanded, eyes flashing. "She's only a child."

"Savages killed my father," the man gritted. "I have no love for your kind."

"We are French!" she screamed. "How dare you!"

She turned on her heel and we flew down the street. By the time we reached home, she was crying.

"Mother," I said. "It's all right, Mother. I'm fine. I promise. See?"

I forced a smile.

Mother laughed through her tears.

"My darling Jenna, my sweet bird," she said. Her waist-length black hair was braided down the center of her back. "Come here, my love."

I crawled into her lap. She held my head against her soft chest.

"What's wrong with our kind, Mother?" I asked.

"Nothing at all," Mother replied. "We are all humankind, Jenna."

"What is a savage?"

"Never you mind, child. There is nothing wrong with you." She sighed. "Do you understand, now, why we must never speak of the Cherokee?"

"Yes, Mother."

She slowly began braiding my long, glossy black hair.

"Sometimes, I feel different," I whispered.

"Because you are *different." Mother smiled. "And that is a wonderful thing. You are my child, a daughter of the Earth. Someday you will see how special you are."*

My mother had great pride in her heritage. I never knew any family other than Nathaniel and Marilyn—relatives on my father's side—but I had heard stories of Mother's family. Her grandfather and grandmother had been forced out of their home due to the Indian Removal Act of 1830—better known these days as the Trail of Tears. My ancestors were forced to give up their land to the federal government and move west. My grandparents were only children at the time. Their entire family perished during the journey.

Regardless, Mother carefully guarded her past.

"I was born in Oklahoma," she'd say one day. The next, she'd tell me that she was born in Canada. "Your grandparents," she swore, "eventually perished of a broken heart. They never recovered from the loss of their land. I never saw Papa smile—not once."

Mother found her way to Texas at some point, and that's where she met my father. They married and came out west. It was as simple as that...but Mother fiercely clung to the native traditions her parents had instilled in her. She believed in the spirit world, in the animals, in the Earth itself. She passed those traditions down to me. It wasn't superstition or silliness. It was belief, spirituality, peace of mind, and subtle wisdom. More than anything, I longed to be like my mother, and after she died, I lost a piece of myself.

Now, standing on the sled as the dogs run and the wilderness sings around us, I think of her. I think of Mother, and how she might have handled this situation. I think of what she would make of the Marshal Jeremiah Black. I think of how much I am like her, and that, at least, gives me a sense of peace and pride.

If I am even a little like Mother at the end of all of this, I can die content.

But I would prefer not to die at all.

***

We travel at a steady pace, resting the dogs off and on, eating the rations sparingly. It is roughly an 800-mile journey to Anchorage from my cabin. At this current pace, we will not reach Anchorage for weeks.

"We simply can't get to Anchorage fast enough," I tell Jeremiah.

"I'm well aware," Jeremiah replies.

"My dogs can cover many more miles than what we're running now." I point to Lincoln. "I've run this team forty to sixty miles a day before."

"We'll need them for a return journey," Jeremiah points out. "It's best not to push them too hard."

"But Anchorage is so far away and—"

"We don't need to *get* to Anchorage, Miss Renee," Jeremiah interrupts. "We merely need to catch up to Conroy. That is all."

If we do indeed resign ourselves to chasing Conroy Parker all the way to Anchorage, I imagine winter will be over and melting away, making the dogs' job harder. It is much more difficult for a dog team to pull a sled over slushy snow than the frozen, packed ice we glide across today. Their paws are much more likely to be injured on rocks and gravel. I learned this the hard way as a fifteen-year-old musher, attempting to run my team through a mud patch on the way back from Dyea. My lead dog at the time—a malamute named Dexter—sliced his foot open on a sharp rock, and I had to carry him on the sled while the rest of the dogs pulled without him. Dexter's wound became mortal by the time I got back to the cabin. A few days later, he died. Not even Aunt Marilyn's medicinal remedies could save him. The infection had already entered his blood.

I was heartbroken, yet it taught me an important lesson: listen to the dogs.

I had ignored their apprehension and pushed them through the mud despite Dexter's hesitation. After losing him, I realized that I had to trust the dogs, just as they trusted me. We would guide each other.

We are making camp on our second day when I hear the wolves.

Lincoln sits up straight. The hair on his back stands up. He growls low in his throat. The wolves must be miles away, but their sorrowful refrain echoes through our small camp. The temperature is dropping, and I scramble to erect the tent alongside Jeremiah, lighting the stove and pulling the blankets from the sled. Once the dogs have been fed, they settle into their regular spots and I crawl into the tent. I study a faded old map of Nathaniel's in the waning light, tracking our progress.

"Nathaniel drew this up last year, shortly before his death," I mutter. "But there's not much detail to it."

It is marked, *Alaskan Gold Fields, 1897: Routes Indicated By Dotted Red Lines. Gold Districts Are In Red.* It does not show the myriad of musher's trails and old native paths carved into the land. I pull out another map—yet one more that Nathaniel drew himself—and study it. Here, he marked the dozens of trails and pathways he used when he was alive—shortcuts into trade outposts and ports, switchback trails into the Klondike and passageways around frozen lakes.

Again, the wolves howl. They sound closer this time.

Jeremiah looks up. He is leaning on his side, casually warming a pot of coffee by the fire of the stove.

"I believe we're being hunted," Jeremiah remarks, unconcerned.

I lower the map, peering at him in the dim light.

"Hunted?" I repeat.

"Yes. Haven't you noticed? The wolves are roughly ten or fifteen miles away from us at all times." He glances up at me. "They're tracking us—keeping their distance. Watching."

"If they wanted to kill us," I say, "I'm sure they would be circling us already."

"Do wolves *always* follow you like this?"

"I *have* heard that wolves hunt sled dog teams," I say. "Easy prey, I suppose."

"Possibly, but I've never been followed for such a long period of time before."

"I suppose it's a coincidence, Marshal. If the wolves wanted us dead, I'm sure we'd be dead."

I don't tell him about the wolves that nearly killed my team and me on the way back from Dyea right before Marilyn was murdered. I don't mention how I looked right into the eyes of the alpha and lived to tell the tale. I don't bring this up, because Jeremiah will think I'm crazy, and because it is something only I can understand.

Still, the team is uneasy as they listen to the distant cries of the wolf pack. I notice that Jeremiah keeps his shotgun close, despite his nonchalance. I slowly sink into a light sleep.

"They hunt, we hunt," I whisper. "It's the way of the wild."

If he's listening, Jeremiah says nothing.

"We are hunting Conroy," I go on. "The wolves are hunting *us*. It's only fair."

I open my eyes, slightly. Jeremiah is watching me, a curious expression on his face. Our eyes meet, and he looks down, tasting the coffee. As he does, I notice a leather cord peeking out from the folds of his jacket. The cord hangs around his neck. Small feathers and birds are affixed to it, flashes of color and beading.

"I like the charms," I whisper, smiling a little. "It looks like something my mother would have made."

"Your mother made jewelry, did she?" he asks, raising an eyebrow.

"Yes," I say, realizing I revealed too much information. "She did."

"This," Jeremiah goes on, "was given to me by a woman back in the States. An Indian from the plains in Texas."

"Really?" I ask, feigning awe. "How interesting!"

"Interesting indeed." Jeremiah takes another drink of coffee. "I believe you said your parents were French immigrants, Miss Renee? Ain't that right?"

"Yes," I say.

"Funny. Dan Frisco seemed to think you were a redskin."

A heavy, horrible silence settles inside the tent. I swallow a lump in my throat and respond. "Dan Frisco," I say carefully, "is a drunk and a liar."

Jeremiah looks at me for a moment longer, and then he says, "The woman who gave me this said it would bring me luck."

"I see. And has it?"

"Well, I ain't dead yet so I reckon it's done its job so far."

More silence. I feel exposed, as if I have laid bare my darkest secret. I can see by the look on Jeremiah's face that he suspects me— he suspects my story, suspects my truth.

Anxious to avoid being found out, I change the topic of conversation completely.

"Have you been with many women?" I ask, resting my head against the blankets. "You seemed to be enjoying the company of that blonde in Dyea."

"Trisha?" Jeremiah asks, surprised. "Hardly. She owed me a favor, that's all."

"What kind of a favor?"

He shrugs, and I understand.

"That really *is* disgusting," I remark. "There are millions of perfectly respectful young ladies in the world who I'm sure would be more than happy to marry you, Marshal. You'll never find one if you spend your time with women like *that*."

"And I suppose you're the expert on matters of love, then?" Jeremiah asks, amusement flashing in his eyes. "Tell me, *Jenna*, what sort of a woman do you think I should take for a wife?"

"Someone with the temperament and patience of an angel," I reply. "Someone who can cook well and someone who does not mind the fact that you roam about the wilderness for weeks at a time, hunting down outlaws."

"In other words, I should marry a saint," Jeremiah responds.

"Quite frankly, yes."

Jeremiah throws his head back and laughs. It's the most genuine thing I've seen him do since we met. He looks younger when he smiles, more at ease. The hardness and cold composure flickers away and I see past the scars and the age and the worry in his face. Perhaps he notices my observations, because he stops laughing and tilts his head, searching my face.

He leans forward, his arms on each side of me, his broad chest nearly pressed against mine. He smells of coffee and fresh snow, of cigar smoke and gunpowder. His face is close, his breath is warm on my cheek. He seems so young and careless in this moment; like a young boy playing a game, working out the best way to win.

I open my mouth to speak, but think better of it. I am speechless, held there not by force, but by the sudden closeness of Jeremiah's body.

"I am not the marrying type," he says, quietly.

He touches my lip with his finger. My skin burns hot where it rests, and I am stricken with the desire to press a kiss against his hand and rest my cheek against his shoulder.

I shake myself. What am I thinking? I hardly know this man!

"You're a womanizer," I say, smiling lightly, leaning away from him. "A snake-charmer."

The moment is broken then, and he pulls away, as if waking from a dream.

"I'm going to walk a circle around camp again," he says gruffly, grabbing the gun.

"Didn't you just—"

"Goodnight, Miss Renee."

I say nothing, and he vanishes into the darkness, leaving me alone in the tent. I pull my blanket over my shoulders, chewing on my lower lip, tasting the place where Jeremiah's rough finger touched me.

I will make it through somehow, I tell myself.

I hope I am telling myself the truth.

Eight

I run through the forest. The sky is black, starless. Only the moon—white and pale against the darkness—guides my steps through the woods. I hear the howling of the wolves as I move, bare feet treading across snow and twigs and rocks. I am silent and swift, as fluid as the wind. Yet I cannot outrun the wolves. I feel their presence in my blood.

At last, I break out of the woods and come to a clearing. The ground drops off into a cliff, shearing into the vast, freezing water of the Bering Sea. I am trapped. There is nowhere to go.

I turn and face the forest, and there is the pack. They converge around me, stoic and snarling. The alpha emerges from the midst of their ring, his eyes liquid gold as he peers at me. I am still. I am a statue. His eyes are ancient, and when he looks at me, I feel as if I am thousands of years old, filled with infinite instinct, threaded to the wilderness, rooted to the land like a tree.

"Show me the way," I whisper. "Show me how to survive."

The alpha prowls toward me.

I drop to one knee and lean my arm on my right thigh. I look down at a pistol on my belt. If I am going to use it, now is the time...

The alpha is here. He is inches away from my face. I see the tips of his white fangs peeking out from behind his lips—smell his breath: the breath of running and blood and the hunt. I drop my hand, ashamed. The alpha looks at the weapon.

Weapons of fire**, he says with his eyes. **Weapons of destruction.

I say nothing.

To survive, you must follow the path that has been set before you.

I stare at him.

"Are you hunting us?" I ask. "Are you going to kill us? Are you going to kill my dogs?"

The alpha sits down, snorting. White puffs cloud around his nose.

I do not hunt your kind. I guide them.

I do not understand, but I know better than to admit this. I stay there, unmoving. The pack sits around me, and the alpha tips his head toward the sky. He releases a mournful howl, and his pack joins in. It is a chorus of music, a symphony of the wild. I feel my heart rise in my chest, and for a moment, I am one of them. I am intertwined with the pack, and I feel weightless.

I must follow the path, I think.

I wake up.

I jerk awake, sunrise coming sudden and early through the canvas tent. Lincoln's head is resting on my chest, and he huffs—clearly offended—when I sit up without warning. Jeremiah is already outside, moving around, readying the team.

I crawl outside.

"Is everything all right?" I ask.

I am awake, but my dream continues to flash through my mind.

I feel the wolf...I *am* the wolf.

Jeremiah stands up, dusts off his trousers, harnesses the dogs.

"Let's go," he says. "I'll get the tent. You finish the dogs."

"All right."

I hike into the woods and relieve myself, returning to the camp. Jeremiah has packed everything up already by the time I return. Kip—my most gentle female dog—wiggles her tail and smiles as I rub the soft fur between her ears. Her white face is offset by a black spot around her left ear. Her eyes are brilliantly blue. Besides Lincoln, she is my favorite dog; she is sweet, loving and unendingly loyal.

Let's run! She laughs. *We're ready!*

"Do you ever hear what they're saying?" I ask Jeremiah.

"What the hell you goin' on about?" he replies.

"The dogs! Do you ever look at them and feel that you know exactly what they're saying?"

Jeremiah tosses me the whip.

"You drive them first today," he says.

I sigh, and then we are on our way again. The dogs run and I dissolve into a trancelike state and try not to think about everything in my life that has gone wrong, and Jeremiah jogs along behind us.

And then I see it again: more smoke. I sit up straight and yell, "Jeremiah! Smoke!"

"I see it!" he replies.

A cold chill settles into my bones. I do not want to see the same kind of death and destruction that we witnessed in the settlement outside of Dyea...the savagery was unimaginable, and I am not sure I could stomach cleaning up the dead again.

"I say we avoid it!" I exclaim, over the sound of the running dogs and the slushing snow.

Jeremiah doesn't answer me, but he doesn't disagree. I wonder if it's because he feels the same way about facing another bloody scene...or if he, too, is afraid of what the smoke might bring for us.

I exhale and focus my eyes on the horizon. Lincoln suddenly rears up and veers left. The snow disappears beneath the dogs, opening into a chasm. The sled lurches sideways. I tumble out of my spot and feel myself falling, falling. I keep tumbling—down, down, down.

The dogs yip and whine as I fall. I see the entire sled slide past me, twisting and turning, smashing against rocks. My mind is reeling as I spin—the last time I checked, the horizon was flat. Where did this cliff come from? I don't understand...

At last, I stop falling. I land on my chest, my face pressed into cold snow. I taste blood in my mouth. I feel it running hot and sticky down my face. The team is howling and crying. The sled is smashed to pieces near my head. I see Jeremiah slowly pulling himself to his feet, a bloody gash split across his forehead.

I peer through blurry double vision, coughing up dirt and more blood. I sit up, dizzy. I look toward the sky. A slope of nearly one hundred feet stretches between me and the ground above. A cliff, completely hidden by the snow. Even Lincoln didn't see it coming.

Lincoln! The dogs!

The shock of the fall ebbs away. I turn my attention toward the dogs. They are twisted and trapped in their harnesses, the lines knotted between them. I crawl to them. Kip lunges at me and I catch her, hold her against my chest. She is unhurt. Thank God. I check the rest of the team—everyone seems fine, but Lincoln is shaken. He sits still in the snow, staring at me, as if embarrassed that he led the team over a cliff; as if he is aware that he almost killed us, almost doomed us all.

"It's okay," I tell him, stroking his head. "It's not your fault."

I am sorry, he says with his eyes, glittering with sadness, with disappointment.

I kiss his nose.

Jeremiah limps toward me.

"Are you hurt?" I ask. "Jeremiah—are you okay?"

"Fine," he replies, gruffly. "Well…damn."

The sled is ruined. There's no two ways about it. The runners are splintered, the body of the sled has snapped in two. The rations and supplies are scattered everywhere. I sit on my knees in the snow, taking a good look at our surroundings. I realize that not only have we fallen to the bottom of a steep chasm, but we are sitting on top of a frozen stream. Beneath my feet, I see the ice—thick and slick. The only way out of the chasm is to follow the stream...going back up the slope is out of the question. It's too steep, and we could never haul the supplies up such a grade anyway.

Grim realization sets in: without the supplies, we'll die.

Without the sled, it will take us days to reach the nearest settlement or town. Without the sled, we are nothing. We can only carry so much on our backs—not enough to keep us alive. Not out here.

"We have to bring the food," I say. "Everything we can. The sled is useless now. We can keep the dogs harnessed and tied. We'll have to walk to the next outpost or settlement....whatever comes first, I guess."

Jeremiah kneels beside the broken sled. Two bags of food for us—two bags of food for the dogs. Both fairly heavy; tolerable on a sled being pulled by a team of ten, but almost impossible to carry on your own back...to say nothing of the canvas tent and the wood stove.

"Come on," Jeremiah instructs.

"You're bleeding," I say. I stand and press my palm against his forehead. I grimace and pull a handkerchief out of my coat pocket. I hold it against his wound, concerned.

"It's fine," Jeremiah says.

He pushes my hand away. He keeps the handkerchief.

My hands are trembling slightly from the shocking suddenness of the fall—the near brush with death. Jeremiah and I work together in silence, untangling the dogs, unknotting the lines. We tie the lead gang line around my belt, and this alone is enough to hold them in place. We set to work dividing the supplies into smaller bags and barrels. Jeremiah takes an extra line from the sled, using it as a load harness for the dogs. He attaches small loads of supplies to the backs of each dog. I have to admit, the marshal is resourceful, if not the friendliest conversationalist. I am grateful for his help, at the very least.

The dogs like the weight on their backs—it makes them feel as if they are working again, as if they are pulling the sled. It gives them purpose and they love it. Even Lincoln seems to perk back up as I tie packets of pounded meat to his back.

I'm ready to go again, he says. *I'll make up for this, I promise.*

I pat his head. Poor dog—Lincoln, as the wisest and oldest, takes responsibility for everything the team does. I whisper into his ear, telling them that this isn't his fault, and that we are all okay. I don't know if he understands what I am saying, but he licks my chin, and that is enough for me.

"Where's the nearest settlement?" I say aloud, reaching for the map.

"I know a place," Jeremiah replies.

"Where?"

"An old friend. He's not far from here. Maybe fifteen miles out."

"That will take us two days with this load."

"We'll make it."

I look at the remains of my precious sled. It pierces my heart to see it destroyed—I remember when Nathaniel purchased it for me. He'd bought it while on a business trip to Sitka. At the beginning of winter, when the snow was gentle and soft, before the freeze began to set in. He'd arrived at the gate of the cabin with the most beautiful sled I'd ever seen.

"Happy birthday, Jenna," he said. "This is your sled. Protect it and use it well."

I'd been elated. It was the most elaborate gift anyone had ever given me.

And now it is destroyed, just like Nathaniel.

***

Without the sled, our progress is slow. The dogs cannot run. This frustrates them. They toss their heads. Kip snorts and throws me a disdainful look—as if this whole mess is somehow my fault. Lincoln walks at the front of the line, quiet and guilt-ridden. Jeremiah thinks I'm crazy to see sadness or blame in Lincoln's face...but I know I'm right. The dogs feel more and know more than most would like to admit. To humanize dogs is to vilify men.

I struggle under the load on my back. I trod through the snow, shoulders aching, face numb from the cold. The wind is picking up, cutting across my vision. I pause to wrap my scarf tighter around my mouth and nose. Jeremiah walks out front beside Lincoln, unwavering. He occasionally glances behind his shoulder to make sure I am still following him—that I have not frozen stiff—and keeps moving.

We push onward. I follow Jeremiah because he knows somewhere we can take shelter. We were only able to take a few days' worth of supplies from the sled. The amount of rations is meager compared to what we started with—even with the dogs hauling some of it on their backs.

I do not know of any settlements or trade outposts in this area—this is largely unknown territory to me. Whenever I have run the dogs, I have always taken them south, toward Juneau or Skagway. Nathaniel and I once took the team all the way down to Hazelton, chasing a runaway member of the team. It had been Gnat, our then-unexperienced husky pup, who ran away, and we were determined to get him back. We tracked him all the way to a fur trader camped in the woods, on the cusp of one of the worst blizzards I'd ever seen.

Gnat had been confused and afraid. The fur trader had found him wandering in the snow, alone and hungry. He'd taken care of him, and Nathaniel had given the man nearly one hundred American dollars to take Gnat back.

Now, Gnat walks just on Kip's left, behind Lincoln. He has become one of my most reliable dogs, as well as one of the sweetest. Gnat never fails to greet me with an affectionate, slobbery kiss on the chin.

"Did you hear what I said?!" Jeremiah shouts above the wind.

"Sorry?" I say. "I can't hear you!"

"There's a *storm* blowing in!"

"Obviously!"

My eyes rove the horizon. Dark, purplish-gray storm clouds amass over the tips of the mountains. The wind is gaining strength. I stop dead in my tracks, my thoughts drifting back to the blizzard that nearly killed Nathaniel and me on our journey to rescue Gnat...

"Storm's blowin' in, Jenna," Nathaniel muttered. "We'd best hunker down and wait it out."

"It could last for a week!" I countered.

"Better to wait it out than try to cut through it. Too risky."

I was afraid, then. Of the cold, of the emptiness, of the barren wilderness of the tundra. I was barely fifteen years old, and this was the farthest I'd ever gone with the dogs and with Nathaniel, into the unknown abyss of the arctic chill.

We took shelter in a cave burrowed into the side of the hill, surrounded by snow. The wind screamed and howled. The temperature was abysmal—forty below zero. We kept warm by huddling close to the dogs, keeping the stove going, slowly eating bits of meat to keep our energy from plummeting. I stayed still, wrapped in blankets and coats, my head pressed against Kip's fur, listening to the tap-tap-tap of her heartbeat. We were miles from home, completely alone, trapped by an unforgiving winter storm.

My fear left me. It disappeared with the presence of the dogs, with their calmness. They did not fear the storm, and so neither did I.

"We've got to hunker down!" I say, shouting at Jeremiah from my place at the back of the line of dogs. "If it's a storm, we need to get out of the open and to shelter!"

Jeremiah nods.

"Well? Any ideas, Marshal??" I demand, running to catch up with him. "Marshal—"

"*Jeremiah!*" he thunders. "I told you. Call me *Jeremiah*."

"I'm sorry! *Jeremiah*, we should take shelter!"

"Thank you for stating the obvious, Miss Renee."

"Someone has to."

He stops walking, peering at me through the slit in his head wrap.

"I know a place," he says at last. "We can wait it out."

"Where?"

"Just trust me. I know it's a difficult thing for you to do."

I roll my eyes, intending on slinging a stinging retort...but I think better of it.

I lead the dogs out of the open, toward the woods, following Jeremiah. We burrow into the maze of trees. Jeremiah finds a small outcropping of rock jutting up from beneath the snow and dirt. I step closer, seeing a dark slit in the side. Jeremiah kneels beside it—it seems big enough to fit through.

I take a step forward.

"A cave?" I ask.

"I'll go first," he murmurs.

I stare up at him, but he does not look at me. He lights one of the lanterns and slips inside the crevice, disappearing for a moment. The wind is beginning to scream. My hair and scarf are whipping wildly around my head. The dogs are agitated, barking at the quaking trees, at the noisy weather rolling through the otherwise silent wilderness.

Jeremiah reappears.

"Safe," he says simply. "Come on."

I lead the dogs inside. They follow me without hesitation. I feel my way through the darkness, stepping into a cavernous room. It is tall and narrow. Jeremiah's lantern throws shadows against the walls.

"Wow," I say. My voice echoes. "This is a wonderful hideaway."

Jeremiah sets the lantern down. The dogs make themselves comfortable. I touch the cavern walls—slick with ice. The rock itself is frozen, but at least we are protected from the wind.

"By my reckoning," Jeremiah says, "we've got enough food to last the storm out."

"The cave will get colder as the storm does."

"We'll wait it out."

He is firm.

He sets to work lighting the wood stove. We huddle close together to stay warm.

"It's almost easy to forget why we're out here," I say. "I haven't thought about Conroy Parker since the sled broke..."

Kip sets her head in my lap, peering up at me through clear blue eyes.

"Ah, don't worry," I tell her. "We'll be okay."

More silence.

"Who is this *friend* of yours?" I ask Jeremiah, stroking Kip's head. "Where does he live?"

"He runs a lodge at the bottom of the Chilkoot Pass."

"The Chilkoot?"

"Yes, you've heard of it, of course?"

"Who hasn't? The Golden Staircase, so I hear."

"Thirty-three miles of trail. It's no picnic, Miss Renee. Have you ever traveled the trail?"

"No," I admit. "I've always wanted to."

The Chilkoot Pass is a thirty-three mile mountain pass that cuts into the Klondike Gold Fields. I've heard of people who have died on the pass during the winter. It can be unforgiving. There are multiple tiers to the pass itself—several mining camps, a deadly and steep section of the trail called the *Scales*, and on the other side, a series of small, frozen lakes.

"The Chilkoot," Jeremiahs says, "truly belongs to the Tlingit...there was a time when anyone who even tried to travel over that area of the mountains would never have been seen again. The Chilkat people didn't take kindly to trespassers."

"I've heard stories," I reply. "It's not the pass that's so hard...it's the cold."

"Truth be told, the Chilkoot Pass is one of the easier paths in this part of the country."

"I've heard that, too. But the Chilkat and the Tlingit...they allow travelers to pass over their trails, now," I go on. "What changed their minds?"

"Money," Jeremiah snorts. "They charge travelers by the load. Wouldn't you?"

I smile in the dim light.

"I can't say I wouldn't," I tell him.

The storm rolls in. I feel it in the ground, hear it outside in the wind, taste it in the air. I huddle in around the dogs, soaking in their warmth, taking comfort in their nearness. Jeremiah remains apart from us, closing his eyes, quiet and aloof. I wonder what he is thinking, and whether or not we will find Conroy Parker and Matthias Cooper, and if we will bring them to justice for what they did to my family.

Nine

The storm bites. It is cold and strong and unrelenting. I don't leave the comfort and warmth of the small cavern. We preserve the lantern and spend most of our time sitting in the darkness, by the glow of the stove light, waiting for the weather to pass. We eat small bits of food at a time. The dogs fall into a trancelike state of hibernation, needing no food or movement to stay alive. I stay curled up on the floor, using as little energy as possible. I can hear Jeremiah breathing. Every small movement he makes is achingly loud in the small space. We survive the storm by conserving our energy, just as the Inuit people do.

I wonder, too, if this storm has slowed Conroy Parker's progress like it has ours. Is he hunkered down somewhere with his gang, waiting out the storm? I trust Jeremiah's tracking skills, but what if we are headed in the wrong direction? What if we arrive in

Anchorage—over 800 miles of raw, rigorous journeying—and Parker is no longer there?

Every possible situation of failure runs through my head as we remain huddled in the cave.

At last—perhaps days since we crawled inside—Jeremiah stirs.

"I'm going out," he whispers. "Sounds like the storm's over."

I don't hear any wind. I don't taste the clear and crisp flavor of snow in the air.

"I'll come with you," I offer.

"No," he commands. "Wait."

His boots crunch against the dirt. Footsteps—fading. He is gone, and I wait with the dogs in the darkness, my hands buried in the warmth of both Kip and Lincoln's generous fur coats. Eternity passes by. I am irritated that I am not out there with him, but I trust him to come back.

I have to trust him. I *have* to.

It is not easy. Part of me says, *Jenna, this is a fool's errand. Go back to California while you still can. Go to Dawson City or Skagway. Find a job and save enough money to board a steamer. Leave all of this behind you and start over!*

No. I will see this through. I will find Conroy and Cooper Mining and I will do it with Marshal Jeremiah Black, because he is a sworn lawman who has promised to help me, and because I am not leaving Alaska without vindication.

I am *not leaving* without justice.

Time ticks by. It has been too long. It is no longer impatience that is eating away at me—it is something else. Worry? Suspicion? I rise to my feet and tell the dogs, "Stay here. I'll be back."

They know. They obey.

I feel my way to the slit in the rock, slipping through the small opening, into the clear gray of a post-storm landscape. The trees, the ground—everything is blanketed in a carpet of fresh, crisp snow. It smells like heaven. I take a deep breath, blinking in the winter twilight, harsh after spending so much time in utter darkness.

I look through the maze of trees, of branches piled with snow and ice. It is sunrise, late morning. The clouds have cleared. I see Jeremiah's tracks leading away from the cave, into trees. I follow them.

I stop.

I stare straight ahead. The hairs on the back of my neck stand up. My heartbeat quickens.

I am being watched. I can feel it.

I turn, slowly, searching the trees. Too many shadows, too many hiding places.

"Jeremiah?" I say quietly.

I don't think he is watching me. His tracks lead far away from the cave.

Why?

I feel as if I am being hunted by an animal—prey for some large beast. I know instantly that it is not the wolf who hunts me. The pack has been miles behind us ever since the storm. I kneel down, trying to make myself appear as harmless as possible.

If it is a bear who is hunting me, I am dead already.

Still, I hear nothing. But I feel.

I am not being hunted by a bear, I realize. *It is man.*

My long black hair touches the white snow when I'm on my knees. I feel like a blot of ink on a piece of white paper—out of place and painfully exposed.

"I know you're watching me," I say.

My words are rough but quiet. I see a flicker of movement up ahead. I lift my chin, remaining stoic and unmoving.

There he is.

It *is* a man, his skin and hair as dark as mine. He wears thick pants and a fur jacket, a cap pulled firmly over his head. He carries a gun on his back, but his hands are empty. I look into his face, and I see someone who looks like me. Someone familiar.

I slip my hand into the pocket of my coat, gloved fingers brushing against the metal of my hammerless Smith and Wesson.

"I am sorry to have frightened you," the man says. His voice is heavily accented. He moves forward—graceful and silent, like a deer picking its way through a maze. I watch him, fascinated with both his appearance and fluidity. Behind me, more men emerge. I inhale sharply and stand up, lifting my pistol into sight.

"Don't come any closer," I warn.

"Please," the man replies. "I mean you no harm."

I look on the left—three men. On the right—four men. They are as dark and quiet as the one talking to me. He is the oldest. Long, deep wrinkles cut down the middle of his face, framing a smooth, wide nose. His hair is gathered into a long ponytail on his back, threaded with trinkets and feathers.

"Who are you?" I ask.

"A friend," he replies.

"Where's the man I came with? The United States Marshal?"

The man smiles.

"Jenna," he answers. "Jeremiah Black is fine. He is waiting for you at my settlement. I have come to bring you back with us."

"How do you know my name?" I demand.

"Jeremiah Black sent us to escort you into our settlement."

"Prove it."

Again, the old man smiles.

"He said you would say that." He chuckles.

He reaches into his pocket and holds a leather cord before my face—Jeremiah's.

I slowly lower the hammerless.

"My name is Aguta," the old man says, opening his hand. "You are safe with us."

"Jenna Renee," I say, simply.

There is something about him that feels safe. Something wild and uncertain...but *safe*. I walk into the cave and gather the dogs and supplies. I bring them outside, and they, too, blink in the light. I look at the silent young men gathered around the one who calls himself Aguta.

"Come," Aguta says. "Follow us."

I haul my pack over my shoulder and walk behind the men. It is surreal to come upon people in the middle of such barren territory. I feel as if I'm trudging through a dream. The dogs are happy to be moving. They growl a little, bark a little. They long to run, to push their muscles. But we do not have a sled, so they must walk at my pace.

Of all the dogs, Gnat is the most irritated at the lack of running. He throws me a dirty look every few moments, as if all of this is somehow a punishment for dragging the sled over a hidden cliff and almost killing us all.

Well. Perhaps it is.

"You're a friend of Jeremiah's?" I ask Aguta, breaking the silence.

"A very old friend, yes," he replies, nodding. "You?"

"He's helping me find someone."

"I see. He's working."

"Is Jeremiah all right? He left the cave and didn't come back and I thought—"

"He is fine, I assure you," Aguta says.

We walk for a few more minutes in silence. We break out of the trees, into the open. The storm has left the world clean and smooth in its wake. Alaska is a blank canvas, waiting for the paint of spring.

"How do you know the marshal?" I ask, pressing Aguta.

"I have known him for many years," Aguta replies. "You are very curious, I see."

"I have a right to be," I say. "He keeps secrets. I can see them in his eyes."

"They are his secrets to keep."

More silence. Then, "Your mother, she was Cherokee?"

I stare at him.

"No," I lie. "French."

"My mistake, ma'am," he says, shrugging.

Rattled, I focus my attention on the dogs.

"My mother was Inuit," Aguta says. "My father, Chilkat. I belong to the land here."

"What is your settlement like?" I ask, changing the subject.

"We are a trade settlement," Aguta replies. "We carry supplies to and from mining outposts and boomtowns. We lodge travelers on their way through to the pass. We also sell and breed dogs."

He turns a hungry eye toward my beautiful team.

I make a note to keep my dogs away from Aguta.

"Ah, so *you* are the friend Jeremiah was referring to," I remark.

"Yes," Aguta explains.

Silence. Boots crunching against fresh snow.

Beautiful snow for running the dogs...

"Your uncle was Nathaniel Renee, a prospector," Aguta continues. "That is what Jeremiah tells me."

"Did he also tell you that Nathaniel was murdered?"

"He did."

"Have you seen anyone traveling through here—Conroy Parker and his men, maybe?"

Aguta lowers his head.

"We will discuss Conroy Parker in camp. Privately." His words are clipped and commanding. He does not wish to discuss this while there are others around to hear—I can see that from the way his eyes dart to the men walking with us.

I don't press him.

I see it: the settlement, a cluster of buildings built into the trees. Smoke streaks into the sky from the fires burning around camp. A few men are gathered outside. Everywhere, there are dogs. Dogs tied to posts, dogs harnessed to sleds, dogs coming and going. Some are calm, some are vicious. Some are missing ears and some have fur matted with blood.

This, I think, *is the life of a dog on the trail.*

It is much different than the life I have given my team—warmth and comfort, the opportunity to rest when they are tired. Always fed, always loved. Most of the dogs I see here would bite your hand off if you so much as took a single step toward them.

The camp smells of burning wood and livestock. When Aguta and his men arrive with me, those who are outside stare. They stare at my team: clean and strong, thousands of dollars' worth of dogs.

I lick my lips, nervous.

Most of the camp is asleep, and I hold Lincoln's harness with my gloved fingers, helping lead the team through the snowy road carved through the plot of cabins. I feel the tension in my body; have I been tricked? Is Jeremiah here at all? Is Aguta merely bringing me into the settlement to steal my dogs and kill me?

Fear clutches at my chest.

What have I done? Why did I trust Aguta? Why did I trust the false sense of safety he exuded? Am I out of my right mind? My breath quickens, and I anxiously search for an escape.

The dogs sense my agitation and begin to toss their heads, worried. Lincoln growls low in his throat, licking my hand. I look down at him and back at Aguta. The old man is watching me, and then I see Jeremiah step out of the last cabin in the row. He is wearing nothing but a shirt and pants, boots crusted with mud. No jacket. He's smoking a cigar—a bottle of bourbon in his right hand.

I exhale.

Relief.

I am actually relieved to see him.

"You made it," he states, leaning against the wall.

"No thanks to you," I reply, sharply. "You could have come back for me yourself. You could have told me where we were going."

Jeremiah is untouched.

"My men will take care of your dogs," Aguta assures me. "Please, come inside."

I don't move. I don't trust anyone with my dogs.

Jeremiah sees the distrust in my face and he says, "Jenna. They'll be fine. Trust me."

Trust me.

I exhale.

I step away from Lincoln and climb the steps to the cabin, stopping inches away from Jeremiah's face.

"You've been drinking," I mutter, disapproving.

"It helps with the cold," he replies, nonchalant.

Jeremiah opens the heavy door and I step inside a large, single-room cabin. There is a stove. The windows are made of rows of glass pickle jars. One long table runs the length of the wall. A young and beautiful woman—probably Inuit or Chilkat, like Aguta—gives Jeremiah a furtive glance as she sets plates on the table. She carries a child on her back, in a small basket. My mother would have called the child a *papoose,* and the woman a *squaw.*

"My wife," Aguta says, but he does not offer her name.

I smile at her. She nods, her black hair braided tightly against her scalp.

"Please," Aguta goes on. "Sit. Rest."

I slowly sit on the wooden bench, shrugging off my heavy buffalo jacket, warming my stiff fingers by the stove. Jeremiah doesn't sit. He stands beside the stove, taking one long swig after another.

"Why didn't you tell me where you were going?" I ask. "Why didn't you come back for me yourself?"

"We were closer than I thought," he replies, but I sense that he is lying. "Aguta offered."

I glare at him.

"So...you are looking for Conroy Parker," Aguta says, breaking the tension between us. He sits at the table. "A mission of justice? Or vengeance?"

"Both," I reply.

"I see."

"Have you seen any signs of Conroy recently? He rides with almost ten men and—"

"I know," Aguta interrupts. "I am well acquainted with Conroy Parker."

He trades a glance with Jeremiah. Jeremiah looks away.

"The marshal has been tracking him," I go on. "He thinks Conroy's going to Anchorage to meet up with Matthias Cooper of Cooper Mining. The sheriff out in Dyea was on Cooper's payroll. It seems that everyone is corrupt out here."

"Corruption is a matter of perception," Aguta replies hoarsely. "Some towns function perfectly well without law. They make their own and abide by it."

"Not in Dyea."

Aguta responds, "Tell me, how many mines did your uncle oversee?"

"Nathaniel? He was the lead prospector for six small mines outside of Dyea."

"Any luck?"

"He found enough gold to make a living."

The squaw sets two bowls of steaming stew on the table.

"Thank you," I say.

I grasp a spoon fashioned from a piece of tin. I taste the stew: venison and potatoes. Strong and gamey flavors. Jeremiah sits beside me to eat.

"Three days ago," Aguta tells me, "Conroy Parker came through this settlement."

I almost spit my stew out.

"Here?!" I exclaim. "*Why?*"

"Why does he go anywhere?" Aguta shrugs. "He and his men were on their way over the Chilkoot Pass."

"But the marshal said that Anchorage was the most likely—"

"I know what I said," Jeremiah snaps, frowning. "Things change."

Aguta continues, "I believe they were going to meet Matthias Cooper. He is in Dawson City."

"Are you certain? How can you be sure?" I ask.

Internally, I am screaming, *What if we hadn't stopped here? What if we had gone all the way to Anchorage, only to find nothing? Hundreds of miles of running the dogs—only to emerge fruitless and disappointed?*

In this moment, I feel a deep gratitude for knowing Marshal Jeremiah Black, and that he was wise enough to bring us here.

"Matthias Cooper and his men came through here two days before Parker did," Jeremiah cuts in. "Aguta says that Matthias has been traveling with twenty or so men, prospecting new areas to mine. It wasn't Parker who killed that settlers we came across: it was Cooper's own boys. I was right."

"And they went over the Chilkoot Pass?"

"They did. Conroy Parker is following Matthias in."

"So we're close!" I exclaim. "Only three days behind them! We can catch them!"

I set the spoon down, the stew forgotten.

"Conroy Parker is carrying my gold and all of my money with him," I say. "If we can catch him on the pass—"

"Jenna," Jeremiah interrupts. "Don't be rash. We can't confront Conroy Parker directly. We have to set a trap—take him by surprise."

"I thought you were dangerous," I snap. "I thought you had a *reputation*."

"For good reason," Jeremiah growls. "We have to be smarter than Conroy."

"So how do you propose we do it?"

"We follow him over the pass. Stay behind—don't let him know we're on his trail. If he gets suspicious, we don't have a chance."

"And then?"

"I don't just want Conroy Parker dead, I want Matthias dead, too. To get rid of a symptom, you have to cure the disease. Cooper is the disease, Jenna, and Conroy Parker is the symptom. We have to wait until we make it over the pass; follow Conroy. He'll lead us straight to Matthias."

Again, he and Aguta share a glance, and I stand up, flushed.

"What are you not telling me?" I demand. "There is something about Matthias and Conroy that both of you know—I can see it on your faces. *Tell me.*"

We face each other. I can smell the bourbon on Jeremiah's breath.

"Tell her," Jeremiah grits.

He turns away, staring at the stove.

Aguta sighs, and he makes a motion. The squaw bows her head and hurries from the cabin, leaving us alone. I look from man to man—younger to older. Aguta folds his arms across his chest and says, "Matthias Cooper is not a man to be trifled with. Many years ago, he slaughtered most of the Chilkat people who settled near this pass, including my family. He sought to take our gold and our women, and my father refused. Cooper's response was to kill everyone. I survived only because I was gone—away on a hunting trip. When I returned, my wife and children were dead, along with my father. The cabins were burned. The dogs and young women had been taken."

I look at Jeremiah, at the way his teeth are gritted together, at the way he stares into the stove—into nothingness.

"The only other survivor," Aguta goes on, "was Jeremiah."

I fold my hands together, aware of the magnitude of this revelation.

"I was young," Jeremiah says. "This was my home, back then."

"I found Jeremiah in Sitka, shortly after he came to this place, seeking refuge after the war between the States," Aguta explains. "I offered him a job running dogs, caring for them. Took him back to my settlement. It was good work, and it kept him away from the troubles of living in town."

Some things are beginning to make sense at last: Jeremiah— the young, orphaned son of a dead Union soldier and a drunken mother; sibling to two murdered brothers. A runaway, searching for a better life. Abused and forgotten, starving, terrified. Somehow, finding his way to Alaska; Aguta, taking pity on the young boy and raising him as his own, and Matthias Cooper destroying the life Jeremiah had carved out for himself here, Conroy Parker as Cooper's right-hand man.

The marshal's eagerness to help me find Conroy Parker was no coincidence....

Jeremiah Black wants his vengeance, as well.

We are alike. We are the same.

This knowledge both thrills and shocks me.

"You want him dead as badly as I do," I murmur.

So, I finally understand. It is not just Conroy Parker we are chasing anymore. It is not just reward money or a job to Jeremiah. It is the destruction of both Conroy and Matthias. Both of them must be found...and killed? I shudder, wondering if I will have the guts to watch Jeremiah do the deed. With Conroy, it is different. He's wanted dead or alive. Killing him is an act of justice, sanctioned by the shaky structure of law in this land. But Matthias? He is a high-profile businessman, well-known for thousands of miles. Some say he's richer than God. What penalty will we have to pay for his death? How can Jeremiah kill him? He's a sworn United States Marshal. He must have a good reason to kill him, because we don't have much evidence against Cooper...other than what we have heard.

I will be content with nothing more than a peaceful life, I tell myself.

But it's a lie. I want justice more than anything else—more than what is right or what is attainable. More than the gold or the peace of mind. I want retribution for everything that has been taken from me, and in this, Jeremiah and I understand each other at last.

***

The sun sets. Our bellies are full and we are warm. The dogs are being kept in a pen in the center of camp. I visit them to make sure they are safe, but I'm beginning to warm up to Aguta. I understand now that this old Inuit man is like a father to Jeremiah, and I can see the lifestyle of these people in him. I see it in the way he walks—quiet and swift, like a deer. I can hear it in his voice, soft but firm. He was shaped by Aguta's tribe and by the rough and tumble wilderness of this barren place.

I do not say any of this out loud, however. Jeremiah is still aloof as ever. I find him sitting in the back of the largest cabin. It is smoky inside. Young Inuit and Chilkat women are dancing, laughing drunkenly. It smells of booze and pipe tobacco smoke. I wrinkle my nose and push my way in. Someone is playing a fiddle in the corner, on top of a table. The ceiling is high and vaulted. The windows here are not made of jars—they are sealed with tanned deerskin pulled taut across the openings.

There is food on the table. There is alcohol everywhere. Most of the men are drunk, laughing loudly, raising glasses or bottles and joking with each other, talking in a language I do not understand.

I push my way through the crowd, moving toward Jeremiah.

I stop.

A beautiful young Inuit woman is sitting beside him on the bench. His arm is draped around her, and he is sharing his drink with her. She whispers something in his ear. He smiles.

I feel angry—betrayed. My heart thunders against my chest, and I realize, vaguely, that I am jealous. This infuriates me, and I force myself to remain still and expressionless, ever the most unreadable person in the room.

The fiddle music becomes soft and slow, and many of the young women retreat into corners with their male partners, giggling and talking in low voices. I feel out of place—and utterly alone. I approach Jeremiah and cross my arms over my chest.

"Marshal Black!" I state, holding my chin high. "What on *earth* do you think you're doing? We have business to discuss, and yet here you are, drinking!"

Jeremiah looks up at me through the smoke and the firelight. The woman is much drunker than he is; she hardly notices me, nor does she understand English. She fixes me with an amused expression and burrows her face against his chest.

"Jenna," Jeremiah says, shaking his head. "Now ain't the time to get high and mighty with me. You've got your fair share of vices, I'm sure."

"My *vices* are few and far between!" I snap. "I'd like to discuss our next move, Mr. Black. Conroy Parker is just out of our reach! We need a plan!"

He considers this.

"All right. Tomorrow," he says. "We'll leave in the morning. Satisfied?"

I glare at him. I grab a glass from the table and pour myself a generous amount of whiskey. It smells strong and bitter. I sit down beside him and drink the entire glass in one shot. It is fire in my throat. My eyes water and I fight the urge to gag. Jeremiah watches me, an amused smirk tugging on the corners of his lips.

"Speakin' of vices," Jeremiah says. "I never figured you for a drinker."

"I'm not."

"Then what are you doing, Jenna?"

"Joining you," I say. "That's what business partners do, isn't it? Drink together?"

"We're not business partners." He leans forward. "Jenna, we are *not* partners. I'm just doing my job as I see fit."

I nod, stung by his words.

Perhaps it is because I am alone in the world, and even if the marshal is not my *friend*, perceiving him as a business associate made it seem as if I had someone, if only for a short time.

His eyes fall on mine. I cannot look away. I understand why women are drawn to him—it is not his rugged looks or the dark pools that are his eyes. It is not the gruff attitude or the fact that he exudes a sense of adventure. It is the way he looks at you. The way he sees inside you and seems to understand what you are thinking.

I stand.

"Goodnight," I mutter.

I am angry with him—I'm not entirely certain why, but I know that the woman sitting beside him is only making matters worse. It is as if my only acquaintance in the entire world has been taken away from me. It is jealousy, I suppose. Jealousy that my only acquaintance is spending time with someone else. It is selfish and shallow of me...after all, Jeremiah is not my friend. We are not even business partners, according to him.

I set the glass down. My head is spinning and, despite the cold, I am beginning to sweat.

I push my way through the men and women inside the large room and run outside, into the cold air. I take a deep breath. I feel hot, disoriented.

I stumble toward the pen, where my team is being kept. It is completely dark, aside from the small fires throwing orange light through the small settlement. The dogs are comfortable, sleeping peacefully.

"You're not much of a drinker, are you?"

I turn and face Jeremiah. His shirt is unbuttoned all the way to his chest, a jacket haphazardly thrown on.

I shake my head. My lips are numb.

He swings himself onto the pen wall and sits there, above me, looking down on me.

I am embarrassed at my spinning head and the burning sensation that has taken root inside my throat. I should have known better than to attempt to drink whiskey. Yet I keep talking, despite my better judgment.

"So this is your home," I say, tilting my chin up to look at him. "These are your people."

"They might as well be," Jeremiah agrees. "Aguta is a good man."

"You're not like other men I've known," I say. "Even Nathaniel had little to do with the native people, other than trading or selling furs or dogs."

"I grew up differently than most. When you live with these people, you understand them."

"And the woman you were sitting with inside—what's her name?"

"I don't know." He shrugs. "Just a woman."

"I imagine you know a lot of *those*."

"Jealous?"

"Certainly not."

"Ah, well, I'll take into account the fact that you're flaming drunk."

"I had ONE DRINK!" I yell, and then I cover my mouth, giggling like a child. "Sorry."

Jeremiah laughs quietly.

Such a nice laugh, I think. *He should laugh more often.*

"Cold?" Jeremiah asks.

I nod, shivering.

I put one boot on the bottom of the pen and raise myself up to Jeremiah's level.

"You have nice eyes," I say, and then I laugh.

Stop, I tell myself. *You don't know what you're saying.*

Jeremiah doesn't smile. He stares at me, searching my face.

He kisses me. Just like that.

He grabs my waist and pulls me to him, his lips pressed against my mouth. He is warm. He smells of whiskey and smoke and crisp snow. I hold his shoulders, clinging to him so I don't fall from the top of the pen. For a moment, he breaks the kiss, and there is only the feeling of his hot breath on my cool cheek, his rough fingers grasping the scratchy material of my fur jacket. He kisses me again, and this time it is harder, longer, deeper. I wrap my arms around his neck and feel his heart beating against his chest, pressed against my own.

I have never kissed anyone like this—innocent schoolyard kisses and the occasional peck on the cheek from boys in town are nothing like Jeremiah's touch. This is fierce and intense. I almost feel as if I am fighting Jeremiah, as if he is fighting *me*.

Somewhere far away, buried in the darkness of the woods, the wolves howl.

They are back. Their mournful song carries through the trees and bounces across the flat plains of fresh snow as I remain locked in Jeremiah's strong arms.

Ten

*W*hen I awake the next morning, my head is pounding. I sit up in my cot—positioned in the back of one of the communal lodging cabins for travelers journeying toward the Chilkoot Pass—and fight the urge to vomit. I don't remember how I got here. The last thing I remember is Jeremiah...

The kiss.

I swing my legs out of bed. Most people are still sleeping at this hour. I tiptoe to the stove in the center of the room and warm my hands.

Where is Jeremiah?

The memory of his kiss is still fresh on my lips. I touch my mouth, flushed.

Yes, it was a good kiss. But I was slightly drunk and he was probably *very* drunk. I'm sure he regrets it—after all, I'm not like the women he usually spends time with: dancing girls and prostitutes, women who are *experienced* and delightfully uninterested in anything serious, expecting nothing from him; no promise of love or a relationship.

I am not like that.

I am alone in the world and I long for a partner. I am aware of this desire and I do not deny it. I cannot become attached to Jeremiah. Jeremiah is a mysterious man, gruff and hardened by his experiences in this cruel world. It would be best to remain uninvolved.

Stupid, stupid, stupid, I tell myself.

I grab my coat and pull on my gloves and hat. I leave the cabin behind—filled to the bursting with men and women, eager prospectors hoping to hit it big in the Klondike. They are full of hope and anticipation, now. Little do they know the dangers that await.

Outside, I look to the sky. It is gray and freezing.

Men are gathered around fire pits, talking in hushed tones. Squaws diligently keep the flames burning inside their cabins for their husbands. I see Aguta standing on the edge of the settlement, staring at the mountains. Beside him is Jeremiah, dressed in a long black coat and black hat, his back to me.

My heart quickens.

Why did I kiss him? I wonder. *It certainly was the influence of the whiskey.*

Silly girl, my memory whispers. *Don't you remember? He kissed YOU.*

Does it matter? He kisses lots of girls.

I know that if we are going to climb the Chilkoot Pass with the dogs, we will need more supplies and a fresh sled. I have no money, but I believe Jeremiah will be able to convince Aguta to let us travel on credit. If we succeed in finding Conroy, I will have my uncle's small fortune, along with the reward money, to pay the Inuit man back for everything twice over.

A long journey...mostly uphill. Dangerous and cold.

I walk through the snow, toward the small trading outpost in the center of the settlement. Aguta's wife, the squaw with the papoose, runs the counter. Inside, it smells of sawdust and fresh soap. I see the squaw and walk to the counter. She does not smile or blink. The only acknowledgement she makes is a brief tilt of her head.

"I need Levi trousers," I tell her.

"You do not want a skirt or—"

"I *want* pants. It's not easy running a team with a dress."

She studies me for a moment. A small smile touches her lips.

"Wait here," she says.

The child on her back is silent. He stares at me with big brown eyes, like a doll. Almost too beautiful to be real. I find myself smiling at him. He looks much like my baby brother Daniel did when he was an infant. The thought fills me with a desperate ache.

I place my hand on the counter, suddenly lightheaded.

Grief is like an ocean. It comes in waves—some waves are bigger than others, and you cannot prepare for it. I cling to the counter for support, sickness and pain welling up inside of me. By the time the squaw returns, I manage to regain my composure.

"Are you all right?" she asks, quietly.

"Fine," I reply.

The squaw lays the Levi trousers out on the counter. They are small—not small enough for me, but that's okay. The material is stiff and sturdy.

"Very good," I say. "How much?"

"Free," she replies.

"Free?"

"Aguta says."

"Ah." Then, "Does Marshal Jeremiah Black come here often?"

"When he passes this way."

"How long have you known him?"

"Since I became Aguta's wife."

"How long is that?"

The squaw pauses to think. "Seven seasons ago."

She regards me with curiosity. She is beautiful and seems to be around the same age as me. Why she married Aguta, I don't know...his first wife and children perished at the hands of Cooper Mining and Conroy Parker. I suppose Aguta just wanted a family again.

"What's your name?" I ask.

"Kallik," she answers. "It means *lightning* in my language."

"Kallik," I say. "Beautiful."

"And you?"

"Jenna Renee."

"You have a gift," she says quietly. "I can see it."

Startled a bit, I say, "My mother used to say that. In those very words."

"Your mother was Inuit?"

"French."

Kallik leans forward and whispers, "We both know that's not true."

I force a nervous laugh.

"I don't know what you're talking about," I say.

"The marshal tells us that your family was killed by Conroy Parker," Kallik says, as if she didn't hear me, a knowing smile on her face. "Is that true?"

"Yes," I answer.

"I'm very sorry."

"Is there somewhere I can change?" I ask, no longer comfortable with the conversation.

Kallik nods and points to the back of the store.

"Go," she says. "I will make sure you are not disturbed."

"Thank you."

As I walk into the back room, the eyes of the silent child on her back follow me. He is adorable, but I look away. The more I look at him...the more I see Daniel.

I pull my old Levis off, torn and filthy. I leave them on a pile on the floor. There is a small mirror set up here. I look at myself— young, dark, lean face. Rosy, frost-kissed cheeks. Long black hair hanging to my waist.

I look very much like Kallik, actually.

No, I think. *I look very much like my* mother.

I pull on the pants over my woolen tights and cinch them up with a belt. They fit better than expected. I tuck the loose material into my boots, buckling my pistol holster over my hips. I braid my hair down the center of my back, tucking it under my cap. From a distance, I could easily be mistaken for a man.

I shrug my jacket back on, and then I wander back into the front of the store.

"We're going to need supplies and a sled for traveling up the Chilkoot," I say. "I can pay you for it when—"

"It has already been arranged," Kallik interrupts, holding up her hand. "Aguta says."

"Aguta says," I echo.

I wonder what deal Jeremiah has come to with Aguta—or is Aguta simply providing for a man he considers to be his son? I don't know, but I take advantage of the opportunity. I take an extra pair of woolen underwear, a fresh pair of gloves, and a box of shells for the Winchester.

I turn to leave, hovering near the door.

"What's your baby's name?" I ask, curious.

"Nukilik," she answers. And this time, she smiles. "One who is strong."

We look at each other for a long while.

"It's a good name," I whisper.

And then I leave the shop, wearing new pants, my supplies piled in my arms. I make my way to the stables and dog pen, where I see a fresh sled packed with goods. Jeremiah's doing, no doubt. The sled is finely constructed, made out of thin birch boards and oak, similar to mine. I pack my extra supplies onto the sled, but I when I walk toward the pen, my heart skips a beat.

The dogs are gone.

Cold terror shoots through me.

I stumble away from the pen, looking around. I run through the settlement, looking for Jeremiah, panicked. My mouth is dry with fear as I move, and then I see the team: they are pulling a light, unburdened sled across the open snow. They run fast and smooth and fearless. Aguta is on the back of the sled, laughing. Jeremiah is standing just outside of the woods, watching.

"What's he *doing with my dogs?*" I yell.

I am not angry.

I am *furious.*

"He's running them, obviously," Jeremiah replies, without looking at me.

"Without permission? Those are *my* dogs!"

"Careful. Don't insult the man who has just provided us with food and shelter and all the supplies we'll need to climb the Chilkoot Pass...*free of charge.*"

I swallow, a bit of the anger ebbing away.

"But he didn't ask, and that's just rude and—"

"He *did* ask," Jeremiah interrupts. "He asked *me.* I said it was fine."

I scowl.

Jeremiah turns to face me. I realize then that I haven't spoken with him since last night, when he kissed me on the walls of the dog pen. I suddenly remember how the night ended—with me pulling away, wordlessly scurrying off to my cabin, confused as to what I had just done.

Jeremiah says, "If we're going to be partners, Jenna, I think it's time you started trusting me, or we'll never make it over the Chilkoot alive, and we'll never get to Conroy, and you won't get your money and I won't get my job done."

Partners?

145

Not a word is spoken about the kiss. I can tell that he is thinking about it. I can see it in his eyes—the way he searches my face, curiously wondering if I am going to mention it.

To him, it's a game. To me, it is embarrassment.

"New Levis," Jeremiah says, nodding toward my denim trousers.

"Kallik wouldn't let me work out a line of credit."

"Aguta wouldn't allow that."

"He's very generous."

"Always has been."

Still, nothing about the kiss.

Aguta brings the dogs to a stop on the snow. He chuckles, holding his beaver cap in the air, jumping from the sled with all the enthusiasm of a child.

"Your dogs," he exclaims, breathing hard, "are marvels! Fast as the wind, wise as the wolves! I would love to breed them."

"They're not for sale," I say curtly.

Jeremiah gives me a look.

"But you are welcome to run them anytime," I go on, forcing a smile. "Thank you for your hospitality here, sir. We appreciate your kindness."

It is not in my character to be smiley, but I do my best, for Jeremiah's sake.

"You are most welcome," Aguta replies. "Anything I can do to help bring Conroy Parker and Matthias Cooper to justice. No price is too high."

I nod.

My team is fired up. They jump and vocalize their excitement to run. The fresh snow and the crisp cold awaken something in them that is primal. And there, at the front, is Lincoln. He stares into the distant woods with an intense expression, his ears shifting and twitching.

He sees something, I think.

I walk to him, Aguta and Jeremiah's conversation fading into the background. Lincoln is like a statue; the only movement he betrays is the quivering of his nose and the shift of his ears. I stand beside him, following his dark, knowing gaze.

The woods lie behind us, vast and shadowed and full of secrets.

Lincoln looks up at me, silent.

"What is it?" I whisper.

You will see, he says with his eyes. *In time, you will see.*

***

The Chilkoot Pass was once virtually unknown. Since the mad rush of outsiders traveling to this country, hoping to find fame and fortune buried somewhere in a rock or at the bottom of a river, it has become quite popular. Hundreds of people flock up the trail every day, whether it's raining, snowing, or sunny. The Chilkat Indians like Aguta's people have made a decent business out of charging travelers for supplies and equipment needed for climbing the pass, levying more fees upon them depending on the weight of their belongings.

As I wait for Jeremiah to finish loading the sled, a new dog team arrives. It is driven by a young man with a thin, wiry beard. A woman—I assume she's his wife—is seated in the sled, covered in a mound of blankets. She is as small as he is. As they pull into the settlement, the man struggles to stop the dogs, to contain them.

Jeremiah ignores their arrival. I sit on the front steps of the trading post with Lincoln; Kip, Gnat, and Moscow vie for my attention. The man dismounts his sled. He looks exhausted. He helps his wife climb out of the sled. She is quaking from the cold.

Outsiders. *Cheechakos.* They have not been here long.

Of course, it was only five years ago that I, too, was an outsider.

He puts his arm around her and they both begin walking toward me. I move out of their way, pulling my dogs back. They are harnessed together, so they are easy to lead. The man stops and looks at my dogs—at me.

"Beautiful team," he says. "Are they strong?"

"Yes," I reply. "Very strong."

"Are they for sale?"

"No."

His wife sighs. "We've been running these dogs since Skagway. A fellow in town sold the whole team to us for three hundred dollars."

"Is that all?" I ask, awed.

When it comes to sled dogs, there are few things you could buy that would be more expensive. A good dog starts at one hundred American dollars and can cost as much as four hundred—each.

Three hundred for a team of dogs is practically stealing in this country.

"We thought it was a wonderful bargain," the man goes on. "Turns out, the dogs are terribly untrained, little better than mutts."

I look toward the dogs—eight of them, not terribly impressive. I don't see any malamutes, although there are a few huskies. The rest seem to be mixed breeds, perhaps strays. Still, none of them are shabby or unhealthy, as far as appearances go.

"They look strong enough," I reply. "You just have to show them who's in charge. They'll run *you* if you let them."

"It's been an awful journey," the woman continues. "Freezing."

She is as young as me. Her skin is pale-white, her hair blond. Her eyes are bloodshot, weary.

"What brings you here?" I ask, but of course, I know the answer.

"Gold," the man replies. "Headed for the Klondike."

"Good luck. You'll need it. The Chilkoot is dangerous, especially at this time of year."

"I'm afraid we're going to die up there," the woman says, staring at the mountain pass rising up before her.

"Danielle," the man says sternly. "We'll be *fine*."

"You'd probably be better off waiting until it gets a bit warmer," I advise. "The Chilkoot isn't as difficult to climb if you—"

"We'll make it fine," the man interrupts, suddenly offended. "I can handle it."

His wife doesn't look so sure.

Jeremiah smirks. The man catches this, and he glares at Jeremiah.

"Is something funny?" he demands.

Jeremiah peers at him from beneath the brim of his black hat. A cigar is clamped between his teeth. He mutters, "No sir. Nothin's funny."

"I see *you've* got everything under control," the man continues, bristling. "You let your wife wear *pants*. I supposed you let her drive the team, too."

Jeremiah stands up. He's at least a foot taller than the husband.

"She happens to be a good musher," Jeremiah responds.

I press my lips together, resolving to stay out of this.

The thin man backs up a step, intimidated. I notice that he's wearing a white collar.

"You're a preacher?" I ask. "A man of God?"

"Y-yes," he says, bringing his gaze back to me. "I've come to minister at Sheep Camp."

"And seek your fortune while you're here. Two birds with one stone."

He flushes.

"In a way," he answers. Then, "We'd better be getting inside."

His wife never takes her eyes off Jeremiah as she's tugged inside. I suppose she's impressed with him—his dark, rugged appearance. He is a winter cowboy—a cowboy bourn from snow and ice. He's certainly much more interesting to look at than her twig of a husband.

"I think you frightened him," I remark, as the couple disappears into the trading post.

Jeremiah shrugs, teeth gritted against the cigar.

"Ready?" he asks.

"Yes."

I stand, dusting the snow off my pants. Jeremiah watches silently.

I ask him if I can drive the sled. He says no, he'll run the dogs first today.

I help him hook up the dogs, checking the harnesses and making sure nothing is knotted or tangled. I pat Lincoln's head and tell him to run fast and strong. We are about to leave when Kallik comes out of the trading post.

"Wait!" she says.

She hurries down the steps and holds her arms out to me. A hug? I hold my arms against my sides, stiff, as she places her hands on my shoulders. She holds me at arm's length, a serious expression on her lovely face.

"May luck be with you," she says.

She presses a small charm into my hand—a wolf, carved from moose bone. A leather cord is looped through a hole in the center of it.

"A gift," she goes on. "Take it."

"Thank you," I say, touched. "For everything."

She nods, retreating to the porch of the trading post, watching us. I roll the smooth charm between my fingers.

Strange, I think, *that she would give me a wolf charm. Why not an owl? Or a bird?*

It is as if she knows that the wolves follow us, always watching, always waiting.

I slip the charm around my neck. The wind is fierce today. I see Aguta, standing at the edge of camp, smoking a pipe, wrapped in a jacket and furs. He says nothing, only watches. Jeremiah tips his hat and cracks the whip. The dogs lunge forward, overjoyed to be running again. They know that we are beginning the chase once more, and this thrills them. I hurry to keep up with them, tired of running...

We leave Aguta's settlement behind. A sense of peace pervades within me. Perhaps it is just the way of the Chilkat or Inuit, but Kallik's good luck charm has brightened my spirits. In a world where I have always felt so desperately alone, even one small act of kindness is meaningful to me. I will remember it, always.

We head off at a mad pace. The dogs are wound tight, charging across the snow with a manic energy that surprises even me. They have never run in this part of the country before, and they love the newness, the freshness of it all. In the distance, I see the Chilkoot Pass rising up like a white wall, dotted with dark spots— rocks poking through the snow. I squint, straining to make out the mass of shadowy movement at the base of the pass...

I inhale.

People. There are *people* everywhere. Tents have been erected in every direction. Men and women meander about, bundled up and shivering. Fires burn. Mounds of supplies are piled across the campsite. I see Chilkat Indians perusing the boundaries of the area, making sure everyone is paying their fair share to ascend the pass.

Yet I don't see a single person on the trail. It cuts straight up the mountain, the road that leads straight up the thirty-three-mile journey.

"Do you see what I see?" I yell.

"Yes!" Jeremiah replies. "I see it."

By the time we reach the campsite, my nose is full of the scent of long-burning campfires and the sawdust used in double-tents. We come to a halt on the outskirts of the camp, and then I see it.

There has been a snowslide. An *avalanche.*

Snow has covered the far end of the campsite, near the pass. Tents and supplies are being dug out of the snow. I see several people lying on stretchers, covered in ice. They must have been caught in the slide.

That would explain the stall in the flow of stampeders.

"What happened?" Jeremiah asks a passerby.

He steps off the sled, motioning to me. I jump on the back of the sled and take the whip, yelling to the dogs to stay put. The passerby—a wiry old prospector with a long, white beard and wrinkled skin—takes a look at us.

"As you can see," he replies. His accent is heavy. Irish. "Snowslide. Happened early this morning. There was a commotion, and next thing you know, half the camp is buried. One man suffocated to death under all the ice. Many of the supplies are buried..."

I look at the trail—temporarily empty, free of stampeders.

"It was the storm," the prospector continues. "Loosened the snow, I suppose. And it looks like there's another storm on its way, brewing right over the pass. Most of the folks here are too scared to travel the trail now. They'll wait until the weather passes."

I exchange glances with Jeremiah.

I am optimistic that Conroy and his boys have been slowed by the storm, too. If they ascended the pass three or four days ago, like Aguta says, they were probably forced to hunker down and wait out the gale-force winds and falling snow. That gives us the opportunity to catch up with him.

"Thank you," Jeremiah says.

He turns to me, placing a hand on the handlebars.

"I say we chance it," he tells me.

"Me too," I agree.

"You're either fearless, Jenna, or just as crazy as I am."

"A little of both." I shrug. "But nobody's as crazy are *you are*."

I lick my lips, painfully aware of the danger of encountering a snowslide. It takes only a moment, and next thing you know...you're buried alive. It is a horrible way to die, paralyzed in darkness, ensconced in the ice.

Jeremiah goes to find one of the Chilkat Indians to pay our fare up the pass. I stay behind with the dogs, watching the stampeders frantically trying to shovel snow from their supplies. They are panicked—dying to get over the pass, desperate to reach the Klondike and begin their search for gold. Every second that keeps them from traveling keeps them from potentially making the find of their lives.

I take it all in, struck with an overwhelming sense of sadness: all of this beauty in Alaska, in the Klondike...and all people can see when they look at the mountains is the potential to dig up a yellow rock. Certainly, I need to get *my* gold back, but it is purely out of necessity and justice. These people have traveled thousands of miles to do this; they have left civilized societies to trek through a dangerous and largely empty wilderness, hoping to be one of the lucky few who will strike it rich.

Is it worth it?

I don't think so, I conclude. *Even Nathaniel didn't come here simply for gold. He came here for the adventure, before the Gold Rush even began. He just happened to be in the right place, at the right time...*

"We can climb it," Jeremiah says, returning. "But just so you know, the trail-keeper says we're insane, and that he's not going to bother to dig our dead bodies out of the snow when we're buried in a slide."

"How kind of him to say," I answer, raising an eyebrow.

Jeremiah and I stand in silence for a moment, looking up at the trail. There is something awe-inspiring about it. Something that makes me both excited and horrified, something that whispers, *Turn back if you know what's good for you!*

I look at Jeremiah. His expression is unreadable.

"Let's go," he says gruffly.

We do.

Eleven

"*T*he key is to give them a name that they can remember," *Nathanial said. He and Marilyn sat on the front porch of the cabin. It was August, and there had been torrential rainfall for two weeks. But today, all was still. The sun was shining brightly. I smelled supper on the stove. I played in the grass with a white, fluffy-tailed puppy with dark eyes.*

I stopped and gave the tiny, wriggling creature a good look. Today was my fourteenth birthday. This puppy was my present—a gift from Nathaniel and Marilyn, and a way to celebrate my first year living in Alaska.

"Lincoln," I said with confidence. "He'll remember that."

Marilyn smiled. "I like it. It's unique."

The puppy crawled onto my lap, frantically licking my fingers and crawling up my skirt, trying to reach my nose. I laughed and cradled him in my arms.

He's mine, I thought. He's all mine and nobody can take him away from me.

I would protect him. I would train him. This was my job, my task. It gave me a reason and a purpose to exist, something greater and more exciting than working the land or helping Nathaniel around the stables. We had just one horse, and only Nathaniel rode him; his name was Canoe, and he took Nathaniel back and forth from the mines every day.

But Lincoln was mine. Lincoln was my ward.

"I hope he's a good runner," I said.

"He will be," Nathaniel replied. "He is part wolf; he was born to run."

"Part wolf?" I repeated, awed.

"Yes. His mother was a malamute, Dixie was her name. His father was a timber wolf. They called him Tiger in camp." Nathaniel grinned. "He was sold to me by a fur-trapper, an Inuit man with many dogs."

"A real Inuit?" I said. "Tell me about him."

The natives of this place fascinated me. Unlike Mother—who was fortunate enough to pass as a Frenchwoman and not only obtain an education, but also avoid many of the abuses Cherokees had been subjected to—many of the Inuit here did not speak English, nor did they have anywhere to obtain an education. They were birthed from the cold tundra and raised in a type of wild freedom that I had only ever heard stories about. Even my mother, Cherokee though she was, had never experienced a life like that. Most of her younger years were spent traveling from town to town. She never truly tasted the forest and woods like her mother and father before her.

"He was old," Nathaniel replied. "And a shrewd businessman. But he was very drunk, as is usually the case with most of the savages in town."

I flinched, looking down at Lincoln, saying nothing.

If only you knew, I thought.

"You must admit," Marilyn said, "ever since the bottle was brought into Dyea and saloons were built, the Inuit and Chilkat traders have had problems."

That, at least, was true. Many of the natives in the boomtowns had never seen or tasted alcohol before—once they discovered its drug-like effects, many became addicted, as did many prospectors and disillusioned adventure-seekers taking refuge in the boomtowns along the rivers.

Still, occasionally Nathaniel would make a comment here and there about the native tribespeople in Dyea—I pretended not to hear him, pretended not be wounded when he called them "savages" or "those people." I felt a kinship with them. I, too, had once been stared at and whispered about in the streets of San Francisco, and I knew how unfair it was to be judged. I was proud of who I was and even as a young girl, I embraced it heartily, although it was something I was forced to keep secret, even from those closest to me.

I said nothing. Nathaniel was not mean spirited. In fact, he was one of the fairest, most loving people I knew. He treated the workers at the mines like family. He provided food and shelter for many stampeders who were at their wits' end—white and native alike.

Lincoln nibbled on the end of my finger. I winced. His teeth were sharp, like tiny needles.

"Silly boy," I whispered. "You will learn. I love you already."

His tail bobbed like a tiny whip. He was the most beautiful puppy I'd ever seen.

"I will make a runner out of you yet," I said. "Wait and see."

***

We begin the climb. The initial trail at the first leg of the Chilkoot Pass is a rapid slope. There are three of them, to be exact, before you reach a bit of a plateau, where both Pleasant Camp and Sheep Camp are located. I suppose, in the most technical sense, that the actual *Chilkoot Pass* is not really located here, but at the very summit of the trail, right above the *Scales*, the last treacherous height to be climbed before the top.

As we fly along the snow, the dogs' pace slows. They are pulling uphill, and the snow is deep. They blow through it, flinging ice in every direction. The cold is bitter, and I am exhausted as I run. Jeremiah and I both ride on the sled for a bit, and then we switch once more.

Up, up, up we go. When we reach the top of the first slope, we rest them. I look down the hill, toward the campsite at the base of the hill. The travelers are like tiny black specks from here. Ahead of us, all I see is a maze of rocky outcroppings poking through miles and miles of snow.

There are some mushers who do not rest their dogs often. They push them and push them until they collapse with exhaustion, until the dogs keel over and die from the strain of running at breakneck speeds for hundreds of miles.

Nathaniel taught me differently.

Dogs, he told me, *are like people. They need rest and food and love, just like us. Give all of those things to them and they will run for you like the wind.*

Perhaps I do not get to my destination as quickly as everyone else, but at least my dogs are still alive at the end of my journey. This is a sentiment Jeremiah wordlessly shares with me, because he rests the dogs as often as I would if I was running the sled. I admire him for it—although I don't voice my thoughts aloud.

"How much farther until Canyon City?" I ask Jeremiah.

Canyon City is a widening of the trail that has become a popular campsite. I've heard that as many as three thousand people have camped there at one time, resting before they attempt to climb the rest of the pass.

"Ten miles," Jeremiah responds.

"Not too far, thank God. I'm freezing."

"Lucky for you, I know my way over the pass."

"You've climbed it before, then?"

"Many times."

We continue the journey. Mostly we travel in silence. I occasionally point out something I think is interesting—like evidence of someone who has climbed the trail before us, or more importantly, evidence that there was a small snowslide on several spots along the trail. As we climb, the wind picks up speed. It is like pushing against a blade of ice.

The dogs push against it, lunging forward with frustration, fighting the invisible force that tries to drive them back. It's slow going, and it makes the journey take much longer than it should. The wind sears my exposed skin. My lips crack, my mouth dries out, my cheeks are rubbed red and raw. I bring the wool blanket up over my face as I sit in the sled while Jeremiah mushes, my eyes peering into the snow. They water and ache from the cold. I close them tight and use the wool as a barrier. I am so tired…too tired to get out and run anymore…

Yet the dogs persist. Lincoln drives them, occasionally growling, angry at the weather that threatens his leadership and his desire to run. His stubborn yowling is a challenge, a sign of defiance.

You will not win! he seems to say. *I will best you, wind.*

Hours pass, and we at last arrive at a small plateau. The dogs stumble across the top, onto level ground. The wind is still biting. It screams as it's funneled through the rocky canyon.

"Whoa!" Jeremiah yells. "Whoa, whoa!"

The dogs come to a halt, panting, tired, but excited to have made it to the top.

"I don't believe it!" I exclaim.

I climb off the sled, my boots sinking into snow—fresh, soft snow. I sink down nearly a full two feet. I grab the sled for balance. The entire sled sinks slightly, too. The dogs yip, disturbed, sniffing at the ground. They yowl and whine, looking up at us in agitation.

"Where's Canyon City?" I murmur.

The canyon is here, but I see no signs of a campsite *or* a city.

Rocks tower on each side of us. The wind carries flurries of snow. The storm is beginning to set in. And, all around us, snow. There are no tracks, no sled marks, nothing.

I sniff the air. Even through the wind and the sleet, I can make out the scent of a campfire. It is faint, but it is there.

"Jeremiah," I say. "Do you smell—"

"Yes." He steps off the sled, trudging through the snow. He knits his brow, studying the canyon. "Jenna..."

"Yes?"

"Look up."

I do. I look toward the canyon walls closing us in, at the towering rock faces dusted with snow. I study the rocks, then bring my eyes back down to the snow on the earth, covering the ground.

"*Jeremiah*," I gasp. "There's been an avalanche, hasn't there?"

He says nothing.

Cold horror grips me. Canyon City isn't empty—it is full. The camp and everyone within is buried beneath our feet...they are buried alive.

Twelve

I am horrified. I say nothing, because words are useless. I am afraid to move—to take even a single step. The canyon cliffs that tower around us now seem ominous and deadly. I no longer admire their beauty...I fear it.

"What do we do?" I whisper.

Jeremiah stares grimly at the snowy plane before us.

"You'd need a crew of a hundred men to dig through this snow," Jeremiah says. "And I'm going to wager that everyone beneath it is already long dead."

I shudder, thinking of dying like that: buried alive, slowly shutting down, becoming one with the ice.

"We've got to tell *someone*," I say. "I'll take the dogs and go back—"

"No," Jeremiah interrupts. "There's no point. These people are dead."

"But what if there's survivors? What if someone is still alive and—"

"Jenna." Here, Jeremiah looks tired—like he is trying to explain a simple concept to a child. "There's no *point.* They're *dead.*"

My lower lip trembles. The dogs try to dig through the snow, snorting puffs of air, continuing to growl and whine. They sense the bodies beneath the snow, and I shudder.

"The storm's almost hit," Jeremiah continues. "We'll have to camp here for the night."

I remain silent. I hate the thought of this—camping on snow that is burying hundreds—perhaps *thousands*—of people. Yet what choice do we have? It would be foolish to continue to travel. The temperature is still dropping, and the storm will kill us if we are exposed to it for too long.

We unload the supplies we need from the sled. We set up the double-tent. We erect the tent behind an outcropping of rock, shielded from the howling wind. Jeremiah lights the stove and piles the blankets into the tent. I bring the dogs inside—something I do only when a storm is going to be particularly brutal—and they huddle together near the stove, a furry dog pile.

"We spend more time in this tent..." Jeremiah mutters, sealing the canvas.

I settle down with the dogs, and Jeremiah settles in next to me. We share our body heat with the dogs, and they in turn share theirs.

The wind howls and the mournful solitude of the canyon settles around me like a cloak. I swallow my fear.

We are alone, and we have no one but the dead to keep us company.

***

There's not a lot I can do with my time, except try to stay to warm.

I hunker down in the blankets with the dogs and Jeremiah, thinking and thinking. I am exhausted from traveling, but I cannot erase the horrible thoughts floating through my head...thoughts of women and children being suffocated beneath the snow, a silent and terrifying death.

I lie on my side. I stare at the tent.

Lincoln suddenly sits up and growls. I watch him move toward the edge of the tent, whining, and then growling again.

"What is it, Lincoln?" I whisper.

Jeremiah stirs from his sleep, peering through bleary eyes.

"What now?" he mutters.

"Lincoln is—"

I hear a sound: a voice. It's faint, but I'm sure I'm not imagining it.

I sit up straight.

The words are muffled by wind, but I hear the voice again. It seems urgent, desperate. I scramble to my feet, throwing the blankets back, pushing into the freezing cold. I hold a lantern high. It has started snowing. The world is nothing but a swirling mass of white flakes.

"Hello!" I yell. "HELLO!?"

Again, I hear the voice. Almost a whisper. Lincoln snarls and then he lunges forward into the dizzying flurry. Jeremiah climbs out behind me.

"What the hell, Jenna?" he demands. "It's too cold to—"

"There's someone out here!" I yell above the wind. "Look!"

I follow Lincoln. He frantically digs through a spot in the snow near the canyon wall. There is a hollow cavity here, nearly hidden. The snow falls away. I see a sort of dark hole beneath the ice. I hold the lantern up. Nearly sixteen feet below us, someone is screaming. Lincoln barks.

I am awestruck.

"Good *boy*, Lincoln!" I exclaim, touching his ears. "Good *boy*!"

Then, "HELP!"

It's barely there, but it is unmistakably the voice of a child. I fall to my knees, considering the cavity. I peer into the darkness, and I see him: a little boy. I see part of his face, his right arm wrenched at an unnatural angle. He peers up at me from the snow. He is crying.

"Hang on!" I say. "Jeremiah—"

"I've got it." Jeremiah disappears for a moment, reappearing with a long rope.

"We can't dig him out," I say. "The snow could fall away and bury him—"

"Of course not. Here." He hands me one end of the rope.

"I can't...breathe!" the child gasps.

He is sobbing now that he has seen us. We must seem so far away, so free compared to the stifling confines of the snow.

"We're going to help you!" I call down to him. "But you have to stay very still. No matter what happens, *do not move!*"

"Keep the dog back," Jeremiah tells me.

I pull Lincoln away from the hole.

Help him, he says, blinking at me. *He's just a child.*

"Be very quiet," I tell the boy, lowering my voice. I do not want the snow to fall in around him. Jeremiah ties a tight, looped knot at the end of the rope. He slings the slack around his waist and lowers it into the hole. I watch as he does this, leaning over the edge. A smattering of snow slides down the hole, piling around the child's legs. He whimpers, distressed.

"Hush," I say quietly, forcing a smile. "If you're too loud, the snow will slide again. You should be quiet, like a mouse. Can you do that for me, little mouse?"

The child peers up at me. He says nothing.

The rope brushes his hand.

"Take the rope," Jeremiah tells him quietly. "Take your time."

The child inches his hand toward the rope. He can't be any older than six or seven. Dark hair, fair skin. He wraps his hand around the rope.

"Put your hand through the loop," I say.

He does. The line goes taut. Jeremiah braces his boot against the rock and pulls. Jeremiah is strong, but he is careful to move slowly to avoid causing a small cave-in. When he is close to the opening, I drop to my knees and grab the back of the child's jacket, pulling him onto level ground. The tunnel collapses, and the hole where he was curled is hidden from us.

The child shivers, staring up at me with wide eyes. His lips are blue, his fingers are blue. Frostbite.

Jeremiah kneels beside us and pulls off his jacket, wrapping it around the child's brittle form. We carry him back inside the tent. Lincoln runs after us, curiously examining the boy. I scramble to warm him. I lay him in front of the stove, wrapping him in a buffalo robe. I take his shoes off and study his feet. The toes have turned black.

I look up, meeting Jeremiah's eyes.

"He'll lose them," he whispers.

"I know."

The boy fades into an unconscious state, frozen and stiff. I rub his feet and Jeremiah rubs his uninjured hand, attempting to restore heat and blood flow. The child's left arm, I realize, appears to be broken. I work to set it, splinting it with small pieces of wood, wrapping it with strips of fur pelts, securing it firmly against his chest so that the arm can begin to heal.

Lincoln lies across the boy's chest, setting his head on his shoulder. I watch the wolf-dog warm the child, and even Jeremiah pauses to observe the sweet gesture of kindness from the dog. The rest of the team remains huddled near the stove.

The boy's eyes blink open, and he wraps his free hand around Lincoln's neck, fisting his fingers in his fur. The dog licks his face.

"Everything is going to be all right," I whisper to the child.

He looks into my eyes. He is so young—practically a baby.

"Mama...is...dead," he murmurs.

He stares at me, and then his expression turns glassy, and his chest ceases to move, and I know that he is dead, killed by the cold and the storm and the snow.

A tear slips down my cheek. I am shocked. I did not think the child would die.

Lincoln presses his nose against the boy's cheek and whines.

I'm sorry, he seems to say. *I tried to save you.*

Jeremiah covers his mouth with his hand, looking away.

I close the child's eyes, and I say a prayer for his soul. I pray that, wherever his mother is in the next life, the boy will join her.

That's what I would want.

Thirteen

The storm is fierce, but it is over in a matter of hours. As soon as the wind lessens and the snow ceases to fall, we emerge from the tent into the early morning. Jeremiah buries the boy in the snow, wordless. He angrily loads up the tent while I hitch the dogs up to the sled. We do not speak of the child's death. It feels wrong, somehow. Horrible, that we could find something so fragile and be unable to save it.

Jeremiah seems to carry the weight of the boy's death heavier than I do. His jaw is clenched, his fists are tight. He viciously ties the tent to the sled, cursing under his breath. Kip nudges Lincoln's cheek with her nose. He nuzzles her snout, as if to say,

I know, Kip. I am sorry that the child died, too. It is the circle of life.

As for myself, I move on from the death of the boy. I must. To dwell on death is to drive one's self mad with grief. I know better. So

I remain silent, my lips pressed together, concentrating on the task at hand.

We are nearly ready to depart when a traveler appears over the edge of Canyon City—an old, bearded man. I squint through the dim, early morning winter light. It is the same man we spoke to at the bottom of the pass. He is driving a small dog sled team, loaded up with a few supplies. He comes to a halt just a few yards away from our sled. My dogs bark at his dogs, and the canyon is alive with a chorus of canine discussion.

"Whoa!" the old man shouts. "Whoa, boys!"

He laughs, and then his smile melts away. He looks around the canyon.

"God almighty," he exclaims. "What in tarnation happened here?"

"Snowslide," I reply grimly.

The prospector shakes his head.

"That's a damned shame," he says. "All those people..."

"I know."

Then, "Didn't we speak at the bottom of the pass?"

"We did," I say. "I'm Jenna, and this is Marshal Jeremiah Black of the United States."

Jeremiah doesn't smile. He grabs the whip.

"We need to *leave*," he stresses, short.

"A United States Marshal?" the old man says, eyebrows raised. "What business do you have in the gold fields, Marshal? Any particular crime you're investigating?"

"No," Jeremiah responds. "Jenna...?"

Gnat lets loose a frustrated growl.

I'M READY TO RUN!

"I'm sorry to see a snowslide of this proportion," the man continues. "Poor folks."

I stuff my hands into my pockets.

"It was very nice meeting you..." I say. "We'd best be on our way, now."

The old man raises an eyebrow.

"You know," he tells us, "there was a man that came through basecamp, two days back. What was his name, now? Ah, yes. Conroy. Conroy Parker."

Jeremiah turns to face the old man.

"You saw Parker?" he asks.

"Yes. Fancy that, I know. Word had gotten around that the bastard had been shot in Anchorage." The old man rubs his chin. "Guess someone was mighty wrong."

"Did you speak with him?" Jeremiah asks, folding his arms across his chest.

"Well, not directly," the old man admits. "He had a fiery mean streak; his men were no better. We were glad to get rid of 'em and send them over the pass."

"Did he happen to mention where he was headed?" Jeremiah asks.

"Dawson, from the sound of it. His men were drunk. I overheard—couldn't help it."

Jeremiah and I share a look. This changes everything.

"Thank you for the information," Jeremiah says, tipping his hat.

The old man shrugs.

"Just thought I'd pass it along to someone who can do some good with it," he says. "You don't see much of the law in this country, so I appreciate the work of a United States Marshal like yourself."

He tips his hat, and then he heads toward the edges of Canyon City, preparing his own camp.

I look to Jeremiah and say quietly, "Aguta was right. Conroy *is* headed to Dawson City."

"We're only two days behind him. We're catching up."

I take my place on the runners, my fingers closing around the worn leather of the whip. I close my eyes. The familiarity of being the musher is freeing. Uplifting. I revel in it, and then I snap the whip through the air. It cracks. Lincoln throws a look behind him—I swear I can see him grinning—and the team lunges forward in one massive, collective heave. The sled moves through Canyon City, over the fresh snow that is a graveyard for thousands of bodies. We carry onward, because that is what you do in this place.

You fight through the storms, you bury your dead, and you pray for a fire.

Fourteen

nce we reach the top of the pass, the world turns to a pale calm. We make it past the *Scales* without killing ourselves—the steepest part of the trail—and at the very top of the Chilkoot, late into the night, we see the sunset. It is so stunning and gorgeous that I bring the dogs to a halt so we can admire it. We nestle on top of the world, suspended in the hills above noise and civilization, and watch as the sky turns to a blazing glory of red between the clouds. Snow-clad mountain peaks stand out against the fading light, turning to blue and then gray. For a single moment, there is nothing else in the world except for the sharp, gloriously clean mountain air, the steady hot breathing of the dogs, and the silence of the summit.

And then we are off again. I drive the dogs and we start to descend. The storm is behind us, and we are breaking into the clear. Darkness falls once more and I see the sky. Stars. Brilliant, glowing stars, shedding pure white light on the snow.

The air and the dogs and the running fills me with energy. When I run the dogs, I do not think about Conroy Parker or death or losing my family. I think about what it must be like to run like this forever, protected by the ancient calm of the wilderness.

When we stop to rest, we are quiet. Jeremiah says nothing and I respect the silence. We don't talk about the child. We don't talk about the kiss at Aguta's settlement. We don't talk about anything. We simply are, and that is something I can appreciate.

We are on our way again. We pass Stone Crib and Crater Lake—marvelous natural wonders that I'm sure people in San Francisco could only dream about—without stopping. We run through everything. The lake is frozen and we run across it, rather than around it. It's dangerous, of course, but we are pressed for time, and the ice is thick enough, seeing as how it is the middle of winter. On the other side of the lake, we find tracks. Only a day or two old.

Conroy Parker? Most likely.

We make it to Lindeman Lake. It is vast, bordered on all sides by stunted balsam trees and spruce dusted with white. We crash through dwarf-sized azalea bushes and skid onto the frozen lake. The dogs are excited to run across something as smooth and open as ice. We glide as if weightless. I lift one arm, pretending I'm a bird in flight.

"Jeremiah!" I say. "What are those?"

"What are *what*?" he responds, hanging lightly to the side of the sled, allowing the dogs to pull us both across the ice.

"Don't you see it?" I point. "Those strange funnels!"

White, smooth funnels of ice are sitting across the vast expanse of the lake. They are perfectly circular. We plow through a few of them. They are crushed underfoot.

"Snow licks!" Jeremiah replies. "Thin ice—the wind rolls it up across the open lake and when it gets too heavy, it just sits frozen like that!"

I've never seen anything like it. The newness excites me.

When we reach the edge of the lake, Jeremiah shouts, "Jenna, STOP!"

"Whoa, whoa!" I yell to the dogs. "Whoa, Lincoln. Slow down. Whoa!"

The dogs come to a reluctant halt. Lincoln looks at me. *Why are we stopping?!*

"What is it?" I ask Jeremiah, breathless.

"Look," he replies.

His voice is a whisper. I follow his gaze.

I am speechless.

The dark sky is ablaze with dancing light—twisting threads of blue and green and yellow. The heavens are alive. The color stretches over our heads, into the darkness of space.

"The aurora borealis," I say. "The *northern lights.*"

"It's damned spectacular," Jeremiah murmurs.

Even the dogs seem enraptured. They sit in silence. We stare, awestruck, at the theater of nature. It is stunningly beautiful. There are no words to describe it. Nothing could possibly do it justice—not a photograph or a pastel painting.

"Have you seen the lights before?" I whisper.

"Yes," Jeremiah replies. "Many times."

"Mother told me about them...when I was a child, she said her father used to tell her that there were spirit dances at the end of the world." I smile slightly. "Is that where we are? The end of the world?"

"It's Alaska." Jeremiah shrugs. "It might as well be."

"I could stay here forever."

"You'd freeze to death."

"You know full well what I meant."

We sit side by on the sled. Jeremiah's arm is pressed against mine. I know he is looking at me—watching my face, studying my eyes. I turn to him.

"Do you regret kissing me?" I ask.

The words leave my mouth before I can think twice.

He looks surprised.

"Why would you say that?" he answers.

"Because I was drunk. And so were you."

"Ah, *I* was drunk. You were *hardly* even warm, Miss Renee."

"So you admit it was a mistake. You were inebriated."

"There you go, using fancy words that poor men like me don't understand."

A playful smile tugs on the corners of his mouth. He is teasing me.

"I don't regret kissing any woman," Jeremiah says. "Except perhaps Trisha in Dyea."

"The one who was in your room when I first met you?"

"That's the one."

"Is she really so bad?"

"You have no idea. The woman drives me mad."

"And yet she was in your room." I lower my eyes. "I'm not like those women, Jeremiah."

Silence.

Then, "I know. You're better. Much better."

For a long moment, we look at each other. There is something in his eyes—curiosity? Admiration? Both? I don't know. It's strange, and very unlike the Jeremiah Black I have come to know as gruff, mysterious, and callous.

"Are you ever lonely?" I ask. "Doing the work you do…it must be difficult."

"It's my life. I handle it."

"But do you like it?"

He says, "I like the people. I like helping whoever I can."

"People like me?"

"Yes. People like you." He leans closer, and for a moment, the way he looks at me is so intense that I swear he is going to kiss me. My heart quickens and I stop breathing.

"I'll keep you safe," he says, quietly.

"I'm not worried," I reply.

I break his gaze and stare back up at the lights in the sky. We do not move for a very long time, enraptured by the wonder of the open spaces.

Dawson City, Yukon Territory

The boomtown stands before us, brimming with life, bubbling with excitement. Like Dyea, the streets are covered in snow, but unlike Dyea, it is massive and sprawling and overwhelming.

"So this is Dawson," I say.

We stand side by side with the sled, the dogs winded and exhausted from our long journey over the Chilkoot Pass. It has been several days of sledding through freezing weather, but we have arrived. At last, we gaze upon the city where Conroy Parker is hiding.

A wide main street runs down the center of two rows of log buildings with metal roofing. Lumber-hewn sidewalks front every building, piled high with snow. Signs boast every type of service and shop you could possibly think of.

Hegg Photos and Views

Pioneer Bakery and Café

Dr. Merchant: DENTIST

GLOBE SALOON

The businesses are varied and colorful, exciting, profitable enterprises waged by men who saw an opportunity to become rich with the steady influx of optimistic gold seekers. We mush slowly into the city. I cling to the side of the sled, one boot on, one boot off. Jeremiah's expression betrays nothing as we glide forward. Jeremiah brings the sled to a halt in front of a restaurant:

Jo's Juneau

Restaurant

OPEN DAY AND NIGHT – BOXES FOR LADIES

"Come on," Jeremiah says. "We need to talk to someone."

Surprised, I dismount the sled and we tie the dogs to a post outside. They happily burrow into the snow, resting. People trudge through the snow, men and women alike. Huge sled dog teams pass by us on the main street, massive sleds pulled by twenty dogs at a time. I watch everything with wide eyes. It seems especially incredible after being burrowed into the isolating heart of the wild trails for two weeks. The sounds are louder, the people are more colorful, and the excitement more palpable.

Jeremiah takes my arm and leads me through the hubbub, through the door of the restaurant. The windows are made of sheets of *real* glass. Roughly hewn wooden tables are scattered about. Two stoves are burning hot. It smells of coffee and bacon and fresh bread. My mouth waters. What I would give to eat something other than stale rations!

Women in long, thick skirts and aprons scurry around the restaurant, pouring coffee into mugs, serving steaming plates of food. Men, women, and children crowd the tables, gabbing. Some laugh, some cry. Some sit in absolute silence, their cheeks red and raw, obviously inside only to escape the arctic temperatures.

I follow Jeremiah through the crowded room, toward a counter that parallels the back wall. Every barstool is filled with travelers. Jeremiah's hand closes on the shoulder of a man dressed in a gray elk coat with a beaver cap pulled tight against his head. The man turns, stifling a yawn. He is a good deal shorter than Jeremiah, and nearly thirty years his senior. His hair is gray, and the stubble lining his fair-skinned face is the same color. He clutches a mug of coffee in a hand shaking from the cold.

"Jeremiah?" he says, blinking. "Well, I'll be..."

And then he stands up, roaring with laughter. He claps Jeremiah into a hug. Jeremiah grins and returns the gesture. I stand there, oddly out of place, watching the scene unfold.

"Well, well," the man booms. "What brings you to Dawson City, Jeremiah? And how did you know to find me here?"

"What is it—Saturday morning?" Jeremiah takes his hat off. "Not hard to predict, Amos."

The man named Amos laughs again, his gaze falling to me.

"Hey now," he says, offering his hand. "And who might you be, ma'am?"

"This is Jenna Renee," Jeremiah answers for him. "She hails from just outside of Dyea."

"I see. And she's with you?"

"For the time being, yes."

"*She* can speak for herself, thank you," I interrupt, cross.

Amos chuckles.

"Well, well," he remarks. "So she can. I'm sorry, ma'am. What brings *you* to Dawson City with the marshal?"

"We're looking for Conroy Parker," I reply, leveling my gaze. "Seen him?"

At this, Amos's jolly, crinkled smile fades away. He wipes his mouth on the sleeve of his jacket and drinks the last of his coffee

"I see," he says. "So you're back in town for Parker."

This is directed at Jeremiah.

Jeremiah nods, saying nothing.

"Well, that just makes one big—"

"Who *are* you, sir?" I ask, confused.

"Ah, he didn't tell you?" Amos asks. "Well, of course not. Ain't Jeremiah's way to be forthcoming now, is it?" He pulls his gloves back on. "I'm Amos O'Leary, United States Marshal."

Ah, of course. A fellow marshal, one of Jeremiah's friends.

"Come with me," Amos says, waving. "Quickly."

We push through the restaurant, leaving the intoxicating scent of food behind us. We emerge into the snowy street once more. We return to the sled and Amos stands beside Jeremiah, lowering his voice.

"Conroy's here," he says, eyes darting toward the crowds. "He's at the Cooper Mining Office just outside of town."

Jeremiah replies, "Good. When did he get in?"

"Not more than a day ago, I reckon. You been chasing him since Dyea?"

"We have."

"I'd say you made good time, what with the storm and all."

"We've had our share of delays."

Amos looks around, leaning closer to us.

"Why the sudden interest in Parker again?" he whispers.

"He killed her family," Jeremiah replies, nodding toward me. "I got a lead that I couldn't turn down."

"Conroy's bested you before, and he can do it again."

"Not this time, Amos."

"Just a fair warning, my friend." Amos lifts his hands up. "Anything I can do to help?"

"No. Just needed to know where Parker was."

"Well, you end up in a tight spot...you know how to find me."

"I do."

The two men exchange handshakes and Amos tips his cap to me.

"Pleasure meetin' ya, ma'am," he says. "Keep this one in line, all right?"

He disappears into the restaurant once more.

"Old friend?" I ask.

Jeremiah answers, "You could say that. He taught me a lot."

"He seems nice enough."

"Amos is as honest as they come." Jeremiah rests one boot on the sled. "We need to see what the Cooper office looks like—see how big it is. I've heard it's second only to their office in Anchorage. If

Matthias Cooper *and* Conroy Parker are both here at the same time...well, we got ourselves two birds with one stone."

"Is Matthias Cooper wanted for any crime himself?"

"Strictly speaking...no."

"Then legally, Jeremiah, you have no right to kill him. Am I right?"

"Maybe. But it wouldn't take much proof to convict him."

"You'd need a witness..."

"Conroy Parker will do just fine."

I raise an eyebrow.

"You're planning on taking Conroy Parker alive?" I ask.

"That's the idea, yes."

"But all this time, we've only talked about killing him. Dead or alive, remember?"

"Well, Jenna...I've been giving the matter some thought. And if we want to take down Cooper legally...Conroy Parker's gotta be alive."

"I suppose I don't care what you do with him, as long as he pays for what he's done."

"Trust me, Jenna," Jeremiah says. "He'll pay. He'll pay dearly."

***

We are exhausted from our journey over the mountains, so we rest in a local hotel called the Fairview. Jeremiah tells me that it is owned by a woman named Belinda Mulrooney—supposedly the richest woman in all the Klondike. This surprises me, because women in this country who manage to make something out of themselves are few and far between. She must be a force of nature to have carved a successful business in a land where mostly men have made a profit.

The hotel is impressive, comprised of three stories. The first is a bottom level with a tall ceiling, within which is a lounge and small office area. The two taller levels are nothing but hotel rooms equipped with wood stoves and beds. The entire building is fronted with snow, but men have shoveled a path to the door. We board the dogs in the back of the hotel, and Jeremiah buys us a room for the night.

The lounge is cozy and warm—certainly not fancy. It's certainly not *San Francisco*, but for this city...it's nice. I can see why the famous Belinda has made a fortune here. It is busy—men and women everywhere in the lounge, with almost every room full. The vibrant excitement of the city seems to soak into the walls of the hotel, lightening my mood a bit.

Jeremiah and I climb the stairs to the third story. Our room sits on the far corner of the building, a window overlooking the streets below. Jeremiah unlocks the door and I step inside. The floor is bare wood, and a single, wide cot is pressed against the wall. I bite my lip, wondering if Jeremiah knew that the room had only one bed. Most likely he did...he probably told the clerk that I am his wife while I was outside, tending to the dogs.

I walk to the window and look across the street. The city is dark, yet glowing with lamps, fire, and candlelight. I smile despite myself: under better circumstances, this town might be a fun adventure. I would love to explore the small shops that have sprung up on the main street. So many people...from all over the world!

"You can take the bed," Jeremiah says, gruffly.

He tends to the woodstove, and soon tendrils of warmth fill the room. I light a lamp sitting on the nightstand. The room glows with orange, calming light. I watch as Jeremiah takes off his hat, sheds his heavy outer-coat, pulls off his gloves. He warms his fingers in front of the woodstove, never looking at me. He stares at the flames, impassive, avoiding my gaze.

"Is something bothering you?" I ask.

He doesn't answer.

"Jeremiah..." I say again, cautiously. "Is everything all right? Has something upset you?"

He turns around, meeting my eyes.

"Everything," he replies, "is *fine*."

"If it's the bed," I say, "I don't mind sleeping on the floor. Really, you can take it—"

"Jenna, no. You take the bed."

"But if it's bothering you—"

"It's not *bothering* me." He steps toward me, inches from my face. I can see the tiny, hardened crystals of ice on his unshaven cheeks. "What's bothering me, Jenna, is that we're pretty damn close to closing in on Conroy Parker and Matthias Cooper—"

"And you think we're going to fail?"

"No. I don't want you to get hurt. I want you to stay here, in town."

"Absolutely not, Jeremiah. This is my fight."

"This is my *job*."

"I can take care of myself."

"I'm well aware. But this is going to be a lot different, Jenna. You may be killed."

I pause, and then I take a step closer.

"You're worried about me?" I whisper.

"I don't want you to get hurt," he repeats.

We stand there for a moment, staring at each other. I remember the kiss at Aguta's settlement. I remember the way he looked at me while we watched the Northern Lights. My heart flutters inside my chest, warmth spreading through my face.

"You're very kind," I tell him. "Kinder than most give you credit for."

"I hide it well."

"I know."

Still, we don't move.

"I suppose," I say, "that we should get some rest. If we're going to Cooper Mining's camp tomorrow to find Conroy...we should keep our strength up."

The words fall out of my mouth, forced and sudden.

I don't know what else to say.

Jeremiah reaches his hand out, tracing the edges of my face with his thumb. He wraps a strand of my loose black hair around his index finger, thoughtfully studying my face.

I feel as if the breath has been taken out of my lungs. I don't dare move—breaking the quiet peacefulness of this moment would seem nearly criminal.

"Am I pretty enough for your taste, Marshal Black?" I say, half-joking.

"You," Jeremiah replies, slipping his hand behind my head, "are not pretty at all, Jenna."

Embarrassed and hurt, I open my mouth to sling a stinging retort in his face, but he interrupts.

He pulls my head forward, fingers tangled in my hair, his free hand gripping my waist.

"You're hardly pretty," he says, pressing his lips against my cheek. "You're *beautiful*."

He kisses me, and, like the kiss at Aguta's, this kiss is full of power. He kisses me like a man drowning, like a man clinging to the banks of a river, dying for air. My hands are pinned against his broad chest. His hand on my waist tightens, pressing me against his body. I feel his heartbeat pounding against mine. His tongue brushes my lips. I shudder, and Jeremiah moves his right hand from my hair to my back. He swings me around and pushes me against the wall. My head rattles against the wood, but I hardly notice. Jeremiah is everywhere—his hands, his kiss, his touch is fire. How many times did I watch his strong, capable hands wield a gun or run the dogs? How many times did I see flashes of a predatory undercurrent of strength—a darkness and a danger that seeped from his pores? And now that power is turned on me, in an entirely different way.

I do not think. I only feel. I wrap my arms around his neck and taste his lips, hungry for more. Jeremiah tears away my thick buffalo robe. It lands in a heap on the floor, and his hands brush the bare skin of my collarbone. He tips my chin up and touches my cheeks with his fingers, a careful, rough smile tugging at the corners of his mouth.

"What is it?" I ask, breathless.

"Jenna," he whispers, over and over again, kissing the soft places of my neck, pulling my jacket and shirt down to the shoulder, pressing his mouth against the hot flesh there. I inhale sharply, and I turn his face back to mine.

"Jeremiah," I say.

He pauses, breathing hard, every part of his strong, muscled body fitted against mine.

"Don't sleep on the floor," I whisper.

He smiles.

"I don't intend to," he replies.

***

The next morning, I slip out of bed to find that the room is empty. Jeremiah is nowhere to be found. Frowning, I dress and gather our belongings, sweeping my hair back with my scarf, pulling on my gloves.

Flashes of what happened between Jeremiah and me flit through my head...

"Jenna Renee," he whispers, holding my wrists above my head, "are you afraid?"

"It takes more than you to scare me."

He laughed with amusement, then. Kissing me, caressing me, exuding a powerful sense of confidence and strength, holding me against his bare chest. For the first time in ages, I felt excitement. For the first time in ages...I no longer felt alone.

My cheeks flush red, thinking of the way he touched me, the way he kissed me. Was I out of my right mind? I pull my hat on, unconsciously smiling. I catch myself in the mirror and sigh. I am not smiley—I'm not! I force my lips into a thin line and I leave the hotel room. Downstairs, Jeremiah is sitting in the lounge, reading a newspaper from the States. It looks to be about three months old.

His boot is propped up on a footstool, and he is drinking a steaming mug of coffee. When I approach him, he slowly raises his eyes from the paper. He does not smile. He gestures to the seat beside him instead. Strangely nervous, I feel a thrill in the pit of my stomach as he looks at me, and I find myself staring at his hands...hands that caressed my cheeks...

"Ready to go?" he asks simply.

I nod.

He folds the paper and leaves it on the couch, standing.

"Let's get on with it," he says.

Hurt, I stand and follow him, my expression sliding into one that is familiar to me: cold...stony. We go to the back of the hotel to harness the dogs. They are comfortable in their pen, and happy to see us after a good night's sleep.

Jeremiah is about to open the pen door when I place my hand on his.

Furious, I say, "Jeremiah. I am *not* like the other women I'm sure you've spent most of your life sleeping with. I do not intend to be used and then thrown away like a piece of trash! I want that to be *perfectly* clear!"

My face is calm, but I am confused. Wounded. Why would he act so coldly after last night?

To my surprise, his rugged, handsome face softens with a slight smile.

"Jenna," he says, touching my chin with his finger. "I was just keepin' it professional."

He kisses my lips, and the tip of my nose.

"I'd never hurt you," he promises.

I stare at him, dumbfounded. Am I really so bad at reading people? No, I decide. It is simply Jeremiah. *He* is hard to read, but his reassurance is enough to quell my nerves for now. We get the team together and leave Fairview Hotel behind, heading for the place where—if we're lucky—we will find Conroy Parker and put an end to the pain he has caused both of us.

***

Cooper Mining's office is about three miles outside of Dawson City. It's hardly an office: it looks much more like a fortress.

Walls have been erected on all sides of a cluster of buildings, including a stable, a dining hall, and several other cabins that look as if they are being used to house Cooper's employees. It is a massive operation, bigger than anything I could have ever imagined.

"It's huge," I whisper, shaken. "Jeremiah, how—"

"We'll have to check it out first, of course," he interrupts. "You look a little pale, Jenna."

There is a touch of sarcasm in his voice.

"I'm just wondering if you should round up a posse," I suggest. "Do you have other friends in Dawson? Marshal Amos O'Leary seemed willing to help."

Jeremiah sighs. "Let's take a look around. Just trust me."

"It's a fortress, Jeremiah. If Conroy's down there, he could be *anywhere*!"

"Again, *trust* me."

I sigh. Jeremiah ties the dogs in the trees. I rub Lincoln's head and I check the chamber of my hammerless Smith and Wesson. I drop a few extra bullets into my pocket for good measure, and then I'm off, following Jeremiah down the snowy hill, toward the fortress stretched across the clearing below.

We come around the back of the camp. Twenty or thirty dog sled teams are coming and going, hauling supplies in and out of town. A sign is erected above one of the gates leading into camp: COOPER MINING CAMP AND OFFICE.

Jeremiah pulls my hat lower over my face. I pull my scarf tighter, and I follow him as he walks through the front gate, as if we belong there. I follow him, shoulders hunched, heart beating wildly in my chest. I can smell the food being cooked in the dining hall. Everywhere, there are gruff men and tired-looking prospectors. Men who are exhausted from fighting the bitter cold, day after day.

We walk in front of the stables. A tall, sinewy man with a hooked nose waves to Jeremiah as we pass. "Hey!" he calls. "Who are ye?"

Jeremiah pretends as if he can't hear him.

"I asked ye a question!" the man yells. He trudges after us in the snow. "What in tarnation! Is that a *woman* you got with you? There ain't no women allowed in camp!"

Several passerby have stopped to observe the commotion. I feel like a naked tree, stripped and laid bare in the winter air. Jeremiah turns to face the strange-looking man.

"We're here to see Matthias," Jeremiah says. "He's expecting us."

The sinewy man raises his brow, and then he bursts out laughing.

"Like hell you are!" he shouts. "I say we find out what you and your lady friend are doing here, ay?" He waves to a few men on the other side of the camp, yelling, "Aye, we got a bit of a trespassing situation, if you catch my drift, why don't you—"

"Get back to the dogs," Jeremiah hisses. "I'll deal with these men."

He shoves me forward. I stumble in the snow, and the motion excites the curiosity of the strange man and the prospectors headed our way. I look toward the gate—it is crowded with people. I glance at Jeremiah as his hand rests against his jacket. There is a pistol hidden there, and I do not doubt that he will use it if he has to…

I slip into the stables. A commotion breaks out in camp. A gunshot shatters the air. My blood runs cold. Two more gunshots. Yelling. Men, running by outside. Someone yells, "SHE WENT INTO THE STABLES!"

I hurry through the rows and rows of horses and dogs, searching frantically for a rear entrance, all the while praying under my breath that Jeremiah has not been shot. I round the corner of the stable. There is an empty pen here, filled with hay. It is being used for dogs, currently. I can tell by the smell and droppings on the floor, as well as the—

"Gotcha!"

A terrified scream sticks in my throat. Hands close around my arms. Someone drags me backward, flinging me to the ground. I hit the muddy, hay-strewn ground. The air goes out of my lungs. I roll onto my back. A man kicks me. His boot connects with my ribs and my chest explodes with pain. I gasp for breath and raise my arms to block him. I reach for my pistol, pulling it from the folds of my jacket, blindly pulling the trigger. The shot goes wild, and the man looming over me—a brute of a man, shoulders as wide as a bull, hair bald as a china plate—wrenches it out of my hand, driving the muzzle into my cheek. The metal is cold, and I shrink away, shuddering for breath.

"Now, now, is that any way to treat a lady?"

Conroy Parker.

His voice. I clearly recognize it.

I slowly lower my arms, pressed up against the stable wall, blood dribbling from my mouth, hair plastered against my face. Conroy stands at the door, his shotgun casually laid flat across his shoulders.

"Little Jenna Renee," he says. "What brings *you* all the way to Dawson? I figured by now you'd be dead or back in the States."

I take a deep breath, wiping the blood from my chin.

"You figured wrong," I say at last.

He looks at the bull-like man.

"I'll take it from here, Ed," Conroy tells him.

Ed doesn't argue.

Conroy takes a few steps toward me. I lean away from him.

"I was looking for you back in Dyea," Conroy says, grinning like a madman. "Who woulda thought you'd come crawling right to me? Makes my job easier, that's for damn sure."

"I've come to see you arrested," I grit out, holding my chin up. "For what you did to my family. For what you did to my *home*."

"All by your lonesome?" Conroy clicks his tongue. "Tell you what, little spitfire. I don't believe that. I think you're traveling with somebody. Am I right?"

I glare at him.

He kneels in front of me and grabs my chin with his fingers. I jerk away and spit in his face. For a moment, his skin purples with rage. His hands turn to fists. He grabs my throat and holds me against the stable wall. The edges of my vision begin to turn black right before he drops me. I cough and stutter for breath, holding my burning throat with my hands.

Conroy throws his head back and laughs, standing up.

"Damn," he says. "I *like your attitude.* It's downright inspiring. Right, Ed?"

"Inspiring as hell," Ed deadpans.

"How about this," Conroy goes on. "Why don't we take a little walk down to the office and see what Matthias has to say about all a' this?"

Still, I say nothing.

Conroy rests his arm on the barrel of his shotgun. He's still wearing a malicious smile. Charming, I suppose....like a snake.

Ed hauls me to my feet. My chest and my ribs ache. I grit my teeth and he ties my wrists together. I refuse to look at Conroy.

Jeremiah must have gotten away, I tell myself. *He must have!*

Ed tightens his grip as he shoves me forward, out of the stables. Conroy walks beside us. He whistles and tips his hat to the men in camp. They glance at me, then continue about their business. I see no signs of Jeremiah, but there is still a commotion on the far side of camp. I force myself to stare straight ahead.

The big building at the far end of the camp is ominous. It's two stories. The wood is tarred; almost black. The windows are made of real glass. Smoke billows from the chimney. A huge, round window overlooks the camp, and I see the dark shadow of a man standing behind it.

Conroy and Ed drag me up the front steps of the building, and we go inside.

The first thing I notice is the smell: spice and leather. The inside of the house is luxurious. It's more lavish than anything I have ever seen. The walls are peppered with pieces of artwork and the heads of hunted animals—moose, bear, and...wolf. I stare at the wolf head mounted in front of me, feeling ill.

A staircase leads to a shadowy second level. Conroy takes me to the dining room. A table sits in the center of the room, draped with a red cloth. We pass the table and enter a drawing room— couches and another table sit here. A marble chess set sits on the second table.

Ed shoves me onto the couch. I sit there, covered in dirt and mud, a stark contrast against the beauty of the room.

"Get out," Conroy tells Ed.

Ed frowns, but he does not argue. He leaves us, and then I am alone with Conroy. He grins and sits across from me. He helps himself to a cigar. He lights it, filling the room with smoke.

"So," Conroy says. "Don't tell me you followed little ol' me all the way to big ol' Dawson just so you could get your uncle's money back? Because that would be the damned most pathetic thing I've ever heard."

I press my lips together.

"You seem a mite bit angry," Conroy says.

He touches my cheek. I flinch.

He laughs again.

"You got spunk, and I like that in a woman," he says. "I think you'll suit me just fine."

I keep my eyes focused on my hands.

"Why were you looking for me?" I ask him. "*Why* did you kill my family, Parker?"

Conroy shakes his head, leaning his head against the couch cushion.

"I got my reasons," he replies. "And it's none of your business, pigeon."

My hands are sweaty inside my gloves. The warmth of the house is almost too much.

"Is this her?"

Conroy looks up. He jumps to his feet, satisfaction lighting his features.

"Yes sir, Mr. Cooper," he says. "This is her."

Matthias Cooper. He is tall, skin pale and flawless. He has a thick, black beard. Colorless gray eyes study me from beneath bushy eyebrows. He wears a suit, a gold pocket watch tucked into his vest. He is younger than I thought he'd be—perhaps thirty years old. There is something vaguely familiar about him, as if I have seen him before. Impossible, of course, but still...

"Jenna Renee," Matthias says. "A pleasure to meet you."

He crosses the room and bows slightly.

"I apologize for the restraints," he continues, gesturing toward my bound wrists, "but you must understand...it's nothing personal."

I stare at him.

Matthias sits on the couch directly across from me. He pours himself a drink from the chess table and takes a long swallow.

"Are you thirsty?" he asks.

His voice is smooth, calm. I say nothing.

"This one here," Conroy says, looking at me, "was sneaking around in the stables."

"Ah, curiosity killed the cat, so they say," Matthias replies. "Tell me, Jenna...did you come all the way to Dawson City on your own?"

I smile slightly, defiant.

"It will go better for you if you talk," Matthias says, taking another drink.

Still, I remain silent.

"Mr. Parker..." Matthias sighs.

Conroy pulls my hammerless from his jacket and holds it against my knee.

"Start talkin'," he says. "Otherwise, I'll have to blow your kneecap off, and I'm a mite sure that'd be the end of your life in Alaska. Am I right, darlin'?"

I hide the fear racing through my veins, arranging my expression into a mask of stone. I say, "I came alone."

"Is that so?" Matthias asks.

"It is."

Matthias laughs. It is a tinny, girlish sound.

"Tell me the truth, Jenna," he says.

"*Why*?" I demand, flushed. "You killed my family. You took *everything* from me!"

"How quickly you change the subject," Matthias says, raising a finger. "But that is an inaccurate statement indeed. *I* did not kill your family—Mr. Parker did."

"On *your* orders! Why? What was the *purpose*? You're not allowed to play God, you can't simply choose who lives or—"

Matthias stands, crosses the distance between us, and slaps me. His palm connects with my cheek. My teeth rattle in my head. I taste blood. My forehead smacks against the armrest. I look up at Matthias, dizzy. He stands still, like a marble statue. He stares at me, a fascinated expression on his face.

"That was very rude," he whispers. "Don't do that again."

The way he says it, the way he stares at me, it's like looking into the empty eyes of a pale doll, flat and detached.

I look at the floor, at the patterns in the ornate carpet beneath the couch.

"My family stood in the way of your company's expansion," I say. "Nathaniel's mines...you wanted them, didn't you? That's why you had him killed. I know you bought his mines after his death."

"Miss Renee," Matthias says, crossing his legs, picking up his scotch. "You must understand that I am a man of business, and there is never a move I make that is not logical or meaningful. I did not build my empire by mere luck. I used my *mind*. I colluded with the *best*."

"You're a murderer," I say.

"Everyone is," Matthias responds. So cold. So unfeeling. "Everyone kills someone or something to get what they want—be it will, love, or body. There is no escaping that fact."

Conroy stands up, nervously pacing to the window.

"I'll see you dead yet," I promise. "Both of you."

"Very bold promises for a woman with no weapons and no friends," Matthias replies coolly.

Conroy snorts, making a comment under his breath.

"You had no right to—" I begin, but Matthias interrupts.

"I never kill without reason," he goes on. "I told you before: I am a man of logic. I am a man of reason and thought. Your uncle brought his fate upon himself."

I lift my eyes from the carpet and look at Matthias. His face is intense—he seems desperate to communicate with me, as if impressing me is important to him in some way.

"Then *what* was your *logic* in murdering my family?" I demand.

"You seem to be functioning under the false assumption," Matthias says, "that I had Nathaniel Renee killed because I wanted control of the gold he was mining. Nothing could be further from the truth."

"Then *tell me* the truth," I answer.

"I didn't need your uncle's mines. I already *had* them."

I blink, puzzled.

"Oh, you didn't know," Matthias says. He shares a secretive glance with Conroy. "How silly of me—of course Nathaniel wouldn't have told you. You were his pet, weren't you? The little child he saved, the little girl he always wanted. He wouldn't want to burden you with unglamorous truths."

Angry tears spring to my eyes.

"Matthias," I grit out. "I swear to God, if you just brought me here to torture me, *do not mock my pain*. Just kill me and be done with it."

"I'm enlightening you!" Matthias counters, offering a smile. "I'm not a cruel man. Nathaniel Renee was little more than a naive optimist when he came to Alaska, searching for gold. It was long before the rush. He was ahead of his time. I funded his operation, loaned him money. I took a chance on him. I said to myself, *Now here is a man who knows how to work.* I was right. His prospecting was quite profitable. He was a good businessman."

"Nathaniel worked for you?" I whisper, dumbfounded. "Impossible."

"Quite possible, actually." Matthias stands and begins pacing. "We were business partners, on equal footing. I funded him, and he, in turn, split his profits with me, as I have done with men before him and after. It was quite simple, really. It was a lucrative agreement. But you see...I found out some things about your beloved uncle. The gold turned him greedy, as it does all men."

"Nathaniel was an honorable man."

"As am I. But we all have our dark sides, don't we?"

Conroy breathes a cloud of cigar smoke into the air. Matthias takes another drink.

"He was withholding profits," Matthias tells me. His voice is cold. "Embezzling. He wasn't paying his dues, as we had previously agreed. On and on this went. Thousands of dollars, missing. He'd broken my trust, you see."

Shock and disbelief course through me—Nathaniel, an embezzler? Surely not.

"I did what I had to do." Matthias shrugs. "When he died, the full ownership of the mines reverted to me, as it always should have."

"If that's true," I spit, "then *why* have Marilyn killed, as well? She did nothing to you!"

"Nothing?" Matthias snorts. "Hardly. She knew about the money—of course she did. She knew why Nathaniel had been killed. Tell me, Jenna, the money that Conroy took from your family...was it not Marilyn Renee who hid it away after Nathaniel's death?"

Yes. God, yes. I remember watching her hide it. After Nathaniel was dead, after the small funeral we'd had. She'd taken the money, everything...hidden it in the floor and told me never to speak of it. It was our way out, she said. It was what we would use if we ever needed to leave Alaska.

"Ah, I'm right, aren't I?" He smiles.

The horrific revelation of Matthias' words settles on my chest. I feel stifled, suffocated. If this is true, then Nathaniel brought his death—and Marilyn's—down on all of us.

He brought *all* of us judgment.

This is what Matthias wants you to believe, I tell myself. *He's lying.*

"You see," Matthias continues, "I'm not a murderer. Merely a harbinger of accountability and justice in a country where there is neither. Someone has to do it."

His voice cuts like a knife; sickly sweet, dripping with poison.

"I understand," I say, leveling my voice, forcing a semblance of calm into the lie. "But I'd still like the money that Parker took from my cabin. I think we can both agree that you have more than enough to go around, and I would prefer to leave Alaska behind and return to California."

"I am sorry, Miss Renee," Matthias replies. "That money is rightfully mine."

"Mr. *Cooper*," I say, attempting to sound innocent—childish. "I swear, if you let me have the money, I'll let this go. I'll never tell anyone what you did. I'll drop it. Honest to God I will."

"It doesn't matter if you drop it or not," Matthias replies. "The fact remains that Nathaniel Renee stole a great deal of money from me."

"Then just let me go!"

"It's not that simple!" Matthias throws his head back and laughs. "The gold and dollars Conroy brought to me from your cabin are nothing. A drop in a large bucket. Nathaniel stole thousands and thousands. Fettered it away on gambling and the bottle."

"Nathaniel neither gambled nor drank," I say.

"You, little girl, are living a fantasy." Matthias drinks the last of the scotch. "Nathaniel was a good businessman who lied to his family to hide his faults, and who betrayed his business partner because greed drove him mad."

White-hot anger fills my veins.

This can't be true. It can't be. It's NOT!

But the memory of Nathaniel's long and frequent business trips to Dawson City flashes through my mind. Was it possible that he came to town to pay up to Matthias on his business trips, and then spent the remainder of the trip drinking and gambling? Marilyn would have been horrified if she knew.

Or did she know? Did she condone it? Did she try to stop it?

"I want you to leave Alaska," Marilyn told me, so many times.

Trying to push me away, to convince me to return the city. Perhaps she knew that Conroy Parker would come back for her from the beginning, but she didn't have the heart to tell me.

The pain of that possible betrayal cuts deep.

"It's shocking, isn't it?" Matthias asks, watching me closely. "When you find out that the people you thought you knew, weren't at all who they pretended to be."

"I don't believe you," I say.

But I am shaken. Hurt. Wounded.

"Unfortunately for you," Matthias continues, "the remainder of Nathaniel's debt falls on your shoulders."

"The remainder of—"

"Thirty thousand American dollars, to be precise."

"Good God, you can't be serious."

"I'm afraid I am."

"I don't have that kind of money. Obviously. Otherwise I wouldn't be here, trying to get Nathaniel's *back*."

"I'm quite aware."

A heavy silence falls over the room. Conroy leans against the windowsill and takes a long drag on the cigar. He never moves his eyes from my face. I feel violated, somehow, and wait for Matthias to go on.

"I'll make certain you pay the debt in full, don't worry," Matthias says.

"But how—"

"Mr. Parker, she's all yours."

"Wait, what are you—"

Conroy looms over me and grabs my wrists. He yanks me to my feet, pulling me close to his face. "Welcome to the business," he says.

There is amusement in his voice. I look to Matthias. He never moves from the couch. He watches in silence as Conroy drags me out of the drawing room, through the halls and out the front door. I jerk against him but he holds tight.

Outside, a few of the men from Conroy's posse are waiting with their horses. I clamp my mouth shut, refusing to make eye contact with anyone. A few of the horses whinny and stamp the ground.

"Logan House," Conroy says, matter-of-fact. "I'll need two extra hands."

Ed volunteers, and so does another man, the same strange-looking fellow who approached Jeremiah: a tall, sinewy robber with a hooked nose and a clean-shaven face. He and Ed swing on the back of one of the horses, forcing me onto the back of a brown mare. Conroy swings up behind me, sliding his arm around my waist. His breath is hot on my cheek.

"Uncomfortable?" he asks, roughly.

I close my eyes.

They're going to kill me, I realize. *They're taking me outside the camp to kill me.*

I open my eyes and search the edges of the camp for any sign of Jeremiah.

Where is he? Did he escape? Was he captured? Dear God—what about my dogs? What about *Lincoln?* I think I'd rather die than see Lincoln fall into the hands of someone like Matthias Cooper.

That is precisely what is going to happen, Jenna. You are going to die.

Conroy takes the reins and the horse trots forward, Ed and the skinny man beside us. We ride through camp and I cling to the saddle.

If what Matthias Cooper said is true...this is Nathaniel's fault.

A tear slips down my cheek. How could he bring this judgment down on us—especially on Marilyn, the woman he loved?

There is quite a lot you don't know about Nathaniel, my conscience whispers, *so it stands to reason that there was a lot you didn't really know about Marilyn, either.*

Was I really so blind? How I could miss this?

I don't notice anything as we ride. I clutch the saddle so hard that blood seeps from my fingernails. I don't notice that the snow from the roads has been cleared away by the Cooper Mining Company, making it possible for horses to ride along the company trail. I don't notice the hundreds of miners crossing the roads as we ride, worn and dirty, aching and covered in grime. I don't even notice how long we ride, or how long the horse breathes and moves beneath my sore body.

We stop. That is all I know.

Conroy dismounts and yanks me down after him. I stumble and right myself. Conroy never lets go of my wrists. I take in our surroundings—the Yukon River. It lies before me, massive and mighty and frozen.

A dock extends into the river. Behind it, there is a building marked *Logan House*. Three dog teams are being loaded up with supplies—each team consisting of fifteen to twenty dogs.

Conroy says, "It'll be a good few years before you see this country again."

"Where are you taking me?" I demand.

"You'll see."

Our boots thump against the dock.

I don't see any signs of Jeremiah or the dogs. That, at least, is a blessing. It would seem that neither Conroy nor Matthias are aware that Jeremiah has been my companion these last few weeks, and it is better that way. Perhaps Jeremiah escaped...that is the only explanation.

Perhaps he'll come for me. Perhaps...

Conroy forces me onto the first sled, wedged between barrels and blankets. He stands with me at the rail, overlooking the frozen shore. Dawson City hovers in the distance, full of smoke and noise. The men finish loading the supplies onto the heavy sleds. They exchange a few words, and then Conroy is standing behind me, cracking the whip, driving the massive team.

Where are we going? I wonder. *Why all this trouble to take me, too?*

The hills rise around us. The trees are thick and white.

Something flashes through the woods, then. It is a white-gray blur.

The wolves, I think. *The pack. They've followed me, even here.*

But I am wrong. It is not the wolf pack that has haunted our steps ever since we left Dyea. It is a slightly smaller dog—a wolf, a malamute...

Lincoln.

My eyes widen, and I clutch the railing of the sled. Lincoln breaks through the trees, running toward us. He barks wildly, frantically.

"LINCOLN!" I cry.

Where is the rest of the team? Why is Lincoln alone?

He barks again. I call to him.

"Lincoln!" I yell. "Lincoln, no! Go back, go back!"

Lincoln's eyes are brimming with fear.

Why are you leaving me? Jenna, come back! I need you—we all do!

Conroy brings the sled to a halt and says, "Shut up, girl!"

"Lincoln, NO!" I scream. "Go back, don't! Go back to the team!"

No, I will not leave you!

Conroy swings his shotgun into his arms and pulls the trigger. The shot rips through the silence of the woods. He misses Lincoln. I jump from the sled and scream, "RUN, LINCOLN! RUN!"

Terror and confusion flash in his face.

Conroy grabs my arm and flings me against the ground. Lincoln runs toward us. I scream at him to stop. I clutch Conroy's legs, attempting to bring him to the ground. He kicks me. His boot strikes my face. I taste blood in my mouth. My head spins. Conroy takes two more shots. I know nothing except that I can't stop screaming. I don't see if Lincoln escapes. I don't see if he is dead. I don't see anything—I simply see red, feel pain, and taste the salt of the tears on my face, turning to ice in the cold. Conroy cusses and yells and I am thrown back into the sled. He slaps me across the face. My teeth rattle in my skull. I press my face against the blankets and cry as if my heart is broken—because I believe it finally is—until Conroy growls at me to shut up.

I cry in silence until the cold numbs me so much that I no longer feel anything.

I am broken. I am alone.

I am ice.

***

Lincoln's devastated barks and whines loop through my head, over and over again.

Why are you leaving me? Jenna, how could you? Where are you going?

He must think I have betrayed him.

I blink back tears.

No, I tell myself. *Don't cry. You have to stay strong.*

What if Lincoln is dead? What if Jeremiah is dead?

I cannot allow myself to think thoughts like that.

Instead, I peer at the horizon, toward the early sunrise. I see a dark square in the distance...a cabin? I squint against the sunrise. It *is* a cabin. It's massive—crudely constructed, fitted together with imperfect logs, as if sprung out of the very forest itself. It has two levels. Smoke pours from the chimney. Two small dog teams are tied up outside.

The closer we get, the larger the building becomes. It blends into the trees that surround it, nestled in shadows. Conroy brings the sled to a stop just outside the front door. I hear laughter.

"Out," Conroy growls.

He jumps off the sled and yanks me after him. I am struck now with the urge to kick him between the legs—to run for all I'm worth into the forest and hide in the darkest place I can find until he gives up the search.

"We'll only be a minute," Conroy tells the men on the other sleds. "Keep an eye on the goods."

Conroy and Ed each take an arm, and I am led to the front door. I press my lips together, remaining silent. Conroy shoves the door open without knocking. Inside, I am hit with the overpowering stench of booze and sweat. A fireplace blazes in the back of a large, open room dotted with worn couches and rugs. A door to the right leads to a kitchen that smells of fetid onions.

And there are women—everywhere. They are dressed in ill-fitting dresses with too-tight corsets. Blazes of red and yellow and green cotton, tangled piles of hair and ghostly white-powdered faces with dark lipstick. They sit with equally dirty and harrowing-looking men on the couch, some kissing near the fireplace. A few of the women stumble through the room, talking loud and dancing with men.

"Welcome to Darling's," Conroy says. "This is gonna be your new home. This is how you're to pay off your uncle's debt."

I stare at the scene unfolding in this room, and the truth becomes clear to me:

Neither Matthias nor Conroy ever had any intention of killing me.

"I'll make sure you pay the debt in full, don't worry," Matthias says.

They intend to work me to death.

This is no lodge...this is a whorehouse.

I am speechless. Full-fledged terror takes root within me, and I break free from Conroy's grasp. I kick him between the legs, just as I had imagined, and make a mad dash for the door. Hopeless, futile...yet I still try. Conroy curses. Ed grabs me before I reach the door. He throws me against the wall. Conroy grits, "I'm about to lose my temper, girl," pulling me close to his face, squeezing my jaw between his fingers.

The other women in the room watch me with sad, knowing eyes.

They say nothing. They avert their gazes and return their attentions to the male companions they are being paid to entertain— or forced to entertain. I scream at Conroy and Ed as they drag me up a staircase. I wrench away again. Conroy grabs my hair. Tears of pain slip down my cheeks. I claw at his hands, bite his fingers.

He flings me into the upstairs hallway.

I hit the floor. My teeth rattle in my skull. I reach out to grab the wall, to right myself. I barely register the darkness of the hall or the mazes of doorways that seem to extend forever. I am dragged to the last room in the hall. There is an empty, threadbare cot. No window. A nightstand, a mirror, a chamber pot, a small stove, and a spittoon. Nothing else.

Conroy slams me against the floor once again. I feel my wrist pop: sprained or broken. I kick up at him. I'm blinded by maddening fear and panic. Conroy looks down on me, tilting his head, examining me like I'm a wounded animal.

"I'll warn you," he says. "The ones who start off like this end up being a liability to the company. If you start losin' us money, next time I visit I won't be so charmin' and hospitable. We'll make a quick visit into the woods with the shotgun. That will be the end. Am I makin' myself damned clear, little girl?"

I nod, trembling.

"Good."

He reaches forward, grabs my head, and slams the back of my skull against the wall.

Everything is black.

***

When I dream, I see the wolves again. I see the alpha, with his fierce, all-seeing gaze. He watches me through the window as I lie silently in my prison, waiting for death.

Lost?

"Yes," I say.

He seems to move through the window, sitting beside the bed.

Do not abandon hope.

"I'm not, but I'm trapped." I begin to cry. "There is no coming back from this. I've heard stories of women who were forced to live this way. They are broken and used."

You are not those women.

"I don't see—"

You do not see because you have not opened your eyes.

The wolf leans forward and touches his nose against my hand. His teeth glint in the moonlight.

Open your eyes. There is a way out. Find it.

"How?"

He is gone. All that is left is the darkness, and the memory of his muzzle pressed against the palm of my hand.

***

I sit up.

The room is glowing with a barely there light. A lantern burns in the corner. I try to swing my legs off the bed, but I am clumsy. My foot slips and I fall to the floor, weak. I lift my head. I see the room through a fog of confusion and amplified sound.

I struggle to stand, but fall back to the bed. I'm wearing a long white shift. My hair has been braided, and I'm barefoot.

Somewhere in the recesses of my mind, I know this is wrong...but I am fuzzy. The world is blurry, and it dimly occurs to me that I have been drugged. My heart does not race and I am not filled with worry, like I know I should be.

I simply *am.*

I tell myself to muster the energy to stand again.

Sorry, much too tired. Better to just lie here for a bit...it's much more comfortable, anyhow. The floor is so cold.

My instinct to run is buried beneath a hundred pounds of lead weight. I know that staying here is bad—lethal, even—but I cannot think clearly enough to make my body move.

I am my own prisoner.

The door opens, and I blink as if peering through fog. Is it a man?

It's not.

It's a woman—slight of build and fair-haired, younger than I. She locks the door behind her and carries a glass of water to the nightstand. She touches the back of my head. I grit my teeth.

"God almighty," the girls says. "They knocked you a good un'."

I stare at her. What do I say? I haven't forgotten how to speak, too, have I?

"What's yer name?" she goes on.

Her accent is unusually thick. She looks to be about fifteen or sixteen.

"Jenna," I tell her. "Jenna Renee."

"I saw you come in with Conroy an' Eddie," she replies. "Couple a' rough sons-a-guns, they is. I don't like 'em much. They was the ones what brought me here last year."

I don't know what to say.

"Here," she says. "Drink this."

She holds the water to my lips. I take a few gulps. I cough.

"Who...are... you?" I ask, squinting.

"Baby," she answers. "That's what they call me here."

"Baby," I repeat.

"How old are you?" She rubs my hair between her fingers.

I don't answer.

"Listen, ya don't have to tell me. Didn't mean it how it sounded... How'd you end up with Conroy an' Eddie?"

"Long...story," I answer. "I don't...feel so good."

"I reckon you wouldn't." She shrugs, picking at her blue dress. "They keep you like this, the first few weeks. It helps."

"Helps what?"

"You'll see."

I force myself to sit up. The girl is watching me with large, round eyes like I'm some sort of specimen to be closely examined. This makes me uneasy enough to bring clarity into my mind...for a moment, at least.

"Baby," I say, my words heavy and slow. "Where are we?"

"Just outside of Eagle," she replies. "This place is called Darling's. Biggest whorehouse on this side of the Yukon River."

"Owned by Matthias Cooper, no doubt."

"Yes. I reckon you met him, then?"

"Have you?"

"All the girls do, sometime. He's 'spected to visit about once a month."

"How long have I been here?"

"Two days. They rung yer' bell good."

"And drugged me. Baby, I have to get off these drugs. I can't move."

"That's the idea, girl," Baby says, seriously. "They'll keep you like this until ya learn to work. It's for yer own good..." Then, sheepishly, she adds, "Trust me. It's better this way."

I lick my lips. I taste dried, crusted blood.

"I cleaned ya up, mostly," Baby continues. "You gotta be clean in this business. Men don't like women what smell like dogs and sweat."

I say nothing.

She stands up, shaking out my pants and shirt.

"What kind of girl are ya, anyhow?" she asks. "When they brought you in, you was dressed like a man."

"I wanted to kill Conroy," I say, matter-of-fact. "He murdered my family."

Baby stares at me.

"Damn," she exclaims. "Is that right?"

She folds the pants and belt.

"Then whatcha doin' working fer Cooper?" Baby probes. "If Conroy killed your family and—"

"I'm not here because I want to be, Baby," I say. "Are you?"

"Sure I am. A woman's gotta make a living somehow, ain't she?"

I look away.

Baby sighs. "Sorry, girl. I didn't know. There's two kinds a' ladies here, Miss Jenna: ones like me, what choose this cuz we need the money. Or ones like you; the ones Conroy and Matthias bring in."

"They can't keep me here."

"They will."

"I need to get out."

"You *crazy?* They'll kill ya."

"Conroy and Eddie are gone by now, I'd suppose."

"Sure they are. But we've got men guarding the house at all hours a' the day."

Well, that's most unfortunate...

"'Sides," Baby remarks, "you ain't going nowhere like this. You can't hardly even sit up. They ain't ever gonna stop shooting you up, neither, until you learn to comply. They got you scheduled to work tomorrow."

I shudder.

And then I remember Jeremiah and Lincoln and everything hits me like a wave. Even under the influence of whatever drugs I have been given, I am struck with an overwhelming sense of loss.

If Jeremiah was going to find me...he would have been here by now.

It would seem that I'm out of luck, at last.

"I can see yer havin' a hard time with this," Baby says, sitting on the end of my bed. "Let me tell ya: when I first come here a year ago, I thought I couldn't do it either. But a woman's gotta do what she's gotta do. The pay is good and—"

"No!" I exclaim. "I won't live like this! I'm getting *out.*"

"Ain't possible. Like I said before, there's guards outside and—"

"How many?"

"About four."

"Anybody else?"

"There's thirty women what live here. They've all got eyes an' ears."

"When do you eat?"

"About six. Why?"

"When do you work?"

"All hours. Whenever we get customers. Usually at night but—"

"Good. Thank you, Baby."

She raises an eyebrow. She may be young, but she's not stupid.

"Don't get no ideas," she warns. "You can get real hurt if ya try to cross the guards."

"I'll be fine."

"The women don't like traitors, neither."

I settle back onto my pillow.

If they've scheduled me to start *working* tomorrow, I've got one day left to get out of here before it's too late.

And then where will you go, Jenna? You have no dogs...no money. You don't even have Jeremiah anymore. You might as well stay here and earn some cash.

The thought shocks me—that I would even consider such a thing.

But desperation makes a person crazy. I have nothing left in the world. Would I be better off living here, anyway? What else can a woman do in Alaska aside from marrying a prospector or working in a whorehouse?

"Where did Conroy go?" I ask. "Back to Dawson?"

"Nah," Baby replies. "From here he always goes and checks up on the Dorsey Mines."

"What's that?"

"Mines what belong to Cooper. He spends a few days there. Always stops here on the way back to Dawson."

I consider this.

"Where is Dorsey's?"

"Up the road about ten miles." She blinks. "Why do you care, anyhow?"

"I'm just curious, honest."

"I can see that." Baby stands up. "I'll be back with some food. You need ta' eat."

"Thank you."

She nods and whisks out of the room. She locks the door from outside. I wait until her footsteps disappear, and then I crawl out of bed. I am dizzy and weak, but I press my ear against the wall. I hear the faint echo of women's voices, mingled with men's. I hear fiddle music downstairs, and I smell the scent of burning wood and scalded coffee.

I close my eyes.

Baby is kind enough, but she is not going to help me escape. The door is locked. There is no window. The effects of the drugs have not worn off yet.

The only chance I have of escaping, I realize, is if I avoid more drugging.

I'll have to fool them.

I crawl back to the bed. My head feels heavy, and I have only just begun to realize that my wrist is sore, too. I feel the coldness of this place creep inside my bones, and I imagine Jeremiah's warm hands around my waist, picture his gruff, handsome face leaning close.

I pull my knees to my chest.

Promises mean nothing. In the end, only I can protect myself.

***

The drugs give me nightmares. I dream of Nathaniel and Marilyn's deaths over and over again. I dream of blood and murder and Conroy's leering face. I dream of Jeremiah turning his back on me and disappearing into shadows. I dream of being devoured by the wolves, eaten alive, screaming for help.

When I wake up, I am alone in the room, and I have a pounding headache.

But I feel lighter in my head; clearer.

I sit up. I hear the fiddle downstairs again.

I stand. The floor is cold against my bare feet. I shiver, standing in front of the mirror. Baby has braided my hair to one side, a long trail of black against the white shift. She has even tied a ribbon there. I bite my lip, not sure if I am what might be considered *pretty*.

Footsteps.

I scramble to the bed and lie down, closing my eyes.

The door creaks as it is unlocked and opened. Baby slips inside. She touches my shoulder, shaking me. I slowly open my eyes, feigning grogginess.

"It's time," she says. "You get yer first customer. Annamarie is sick with a fever, so's it's gonna be you what's taking her place. Your man's name is Patrick, an' he's a regular." She looks hard at me. "So don't screw it up. Conroy'll have yer head if he finds out you're not working."

I stare at her, pretending I'm speechless. Pretending that the drugs are still wreaking havoc on my mind—but the wheels in my head are spinning so fast I can hardly keep up with my own thoughts. Clarity revives my senses. I feel a rush of relief to be myself again. My fingers and toes tingle.

"The drugs are hittin' you harder than most," Baby remarks as she leaves. "I'll be sure to dose you after Patrick, though, just in case." Then, "Have fun."

She winks.

I stare after her. As soon as the door clicks, I jump out of bed. My pants and jacket have been taken. My boots sit in the corner, but that is all that remains of my belongings.

I look around the room, under the mirror.

The spittoon. I slide it under the bed. I roll up the sleeves of the white shift. More footsteps—heavy, down the hall.

My first customer.

I take a deep breath. I feel as if I'm going to throw up, but I tell myself to hold my wits together. I'm going to need them.

I perch on the end of the bed like a bird, allowing a slight smile to touch my lips.

Be charming, Jenna. Surely you can do that for just a few moments.

I straighten my hair. The footsteps get closer.

My heart thunders against my ribs.

The door opens, and in steps a man who looks to be about forty years old. He has a thin beard. His eyes are a dull brown, his skin worn and burnt like leather. He wears the hat of a prospector. A long black jacket is unbuttoned over pants and suspenders. I swallow a lump in my throat as he walks in, shutting the door behind him.

"Howdy," he says.

His voice is scratchy, low.

He's been drinking.

I size him up. He's about my height, fairly thin. But he looks strong, as most prospectors do.

"Howdy," I echo.

Do I sound as scared as I feel? I don't think so.

"Usually I see Annamarie," he says. "I reckon you're her understudy or something of that sort."

"Somethin' like that," I reply. "I'm Jenna."

"You still look fresh as a daisy." He grins. "I like that."

He moves closer, sitting beside me on the bed.

"I'm a gentleman, miss," he goes on. "I can see plain as daylight that you ain't ever done this before. Am I right?"

"Right as rain," I reply.

I can feel his breath on my cheek. My hands fist around the sheets.

"Well, I suppose the best way to get started..." he says, trailing off.

He leans forward, grasps my cheeks between his dirty fingers. He kisses me. I taste the booze on his lips. I put my hands on his shoulders and playfully shove him backward, against the pillow. He laughs and throws his hat off.

I crouch over him, studying the lines in his face.

What is his story? I wonder. Does he have a family? A wife? Has he found gold? Most likely not. If he had found gold, he wouldn't be here...he would be taking it home and rejoicing in his newfound wealth.

I lean down to kiss him again. It is not a kiss I enjoy—I think of Jeremiah when I do it, and I am struck with the feeling of betrayal. I flatten myself against the prospector, feeling the rise and fall of his chest. He takes this as a sign of affection, but I slowly slip my arm off the side of the bed. My fingers close around the rim of the spittoon.

I sit up for a moment and pull the ribbon from my braid. I keep smiling for the prospector, shaking my long hair around my face. He chuckles low in his throat, and I say, "Do you like long hair, sir?"

"I daresay I love it," he replies. "Nothin' like a woman with long, beautiful hair."

I smile again.

I tell him to close his eyes. He does.

I slam the spittoon against the side of his head. It rings loudly. The prospector—Patrick—slumps against the bed. His eyes flutter shut. A bruise begins to blossom on the side of his temple.

I stay there, frozen, staring at his face.

I am shaking from head to toe.

I slowly climb off the bed and creep to the door. I pray that the sound of the spittoon colliding with his head was drowned out by the downstairs' laughter and fiddle music. I set the spittoon on the floor and pull off the man's jacket and pants, his long-johns and his wool tights. I take his shirt and his belt.

I exhale.

I yank the shift over my head and stuff it under the bed. I pull on the pants and shirt, fastening the suspenders over my chest. It's too big, but close enough. I am lucky that this man is of similar height and build as me. I layer on all of his warm, thick clothing, knowing that this will be the only thing that keeps me from freezing outside, dying in a matter of minutes.

I take his socks and pull them on. I slip on my boots. I take the bandana from around his neck and tie it around my forehead, using it to sweep my hair away from my face. I stuff the rest of my hair beneath his hat. I button his jacket over the ensemble. I look in the mirror. I pull the hat low across my face, wrap his long, thick, fur-lined scarf around my mouth and cheeks. I rifle through the pockets of the pants.

I find a small knife.

I take a deep breath. I hold the knife flat against the palm of my hand, hiding it beneath the long sleeve of the jacket. I cover the prospector—now stripped naked—with a blanket.

"Sorry," I whisper. "I'm sure that you were a nice, honest man once."

Perhaps he still is. I'll never know.

I pause at the threshold of the door.

Four guards outside the cabin. Thirty women inside. Customers coming and going.

I'll have to be quick.

I open the door and step into the dark hallway. I click the lock behind me, moving swiftly across the floor, throwing my shoulders back as I walk, holding myself like a man would. I descend the staircase. The wood creaks under my weight.

I am sweating.

I reach the first floor. The large, open room is filled with women and men once again. It's a busy night. A man plays a fiddle in the corner, grinning despite his missing teeth. I spot Baby out of the corner of my eye. She is sprawled across the lap of a young man, tracing her finger along the curve of his face.

I keep moving. A dark shadow sifting through the faces in the room. The front door opens, throwing cold air into my face. Two men walk in, fresh from the mountains. I brush past them, keeping my head down, and step outside.

I may have hours—or mere minutes—before the prospector awakens.

When he does…

The moon is shining bright against the crusted snow. The temperature is unbearably cold—the kind of cold that punctures your lungs and makes your bones ache. I pull the jacket tighter and I run. I run into the woods, into the forest.

I am headed to Dorsey's Mines. Only ten miles, according to Baby.

I'm still coming for you, Conroy. Nothing has changed.

I am coming for Conroy and I will get what I came for:

Justice.

Sixteen

I don't know where I am or where I'm going. I follow the road, like Baby said, hoping to God that it will lead me to Dorsey's Mines. I've come so far! I can't simply return to Dyea empty-handed. If I can find a way to bring Conroy to justice and collect the reward money, then I'll at least have three thousand American dollars...enough to start a new life, at the very least.

I must find Jeremiah first. I can't bring Conroy in alive without the marshal...as tough as I like to make myself out to be, I am not stupid. I will need help, and that is why I am hoping that my hunch is right...that Jeremiah will be where Conroy Parker is. Besides that, I don't want to continue without him. I'm worried sick about the man. When I think of him, I think of his dark eyes, his hot kiss, and the night we shared in Dawson City before we were separated...

I exhale, flushed. Even thinking about that night makes my heart race.

Time to think of something else.

Lincoln, where are you?

The thought of my beloved dogs—especially Lincoln—running loose and alone is, to me, the most piercing of all the tragedies that have befallen me so far. I have cared for each one of my dogs since the moment they came into this world. I feel as if my children have been wrenched from me. The pain cuts into my heart, making it hard to breathe.

You can mourn later, I tell myself, willing strength into my soul. *You have to finish this, even if it kills you. Conroy Parker cannot be allowed to get away with this.*

My thoughts are interrupted.

Nearby, a wolf howls. I stop, shivering and breathing hard.

Impossible.

The wolf howls again. I see flickers of shadowy movement between the trees, eyes and ears flashing in the moonlight.

I gasp.

I am being hunted.

Have I escaped one death only to die here, eaten alive?

Up ahead, a wolf bounds out of the trees, blocking the path. He is lean and gray, his eyes glowing yellow. I stumble backward, falling into the snow. It seems to happen in slow motion. I look up, and I see the lean wolf. He has not moved. He stares at me. His lips pull away from his teeth; sharp white razors, made for tearing and killing. I do not move.

The distant wolf howls again, and the lean one disappears into the woods. I remain frozen for a moment, terror-stricken. And then I am on my feet. I run through the forest, light on my feet. I barely make a sound. I move as if carried by the wind, and I imagine that perhaps my grandmother and the rest of my ancestors once ran as free and fast as I am now, before the Trail of Tears disrupted their lives.

How would my life today be different?

Another feral growl disrupts my thoughts. A wolf is running beside me. I trip again, taken by surprise. I roll to my feet, dashing forward once more.

The wolf on my right can smell my fear. Another wolf is running on my left.

I don't stop.

I am a deer. I am the prey, and they are the hunters, and I have fallen into their trap.

I keep moving, running through branches and dancing over fallen trees, crunching through snow. I am running with the wolves as they form a moving ring around me. How many are there? Impossible to tell. I only see two. There are more—I can hear them. I can *feel* them.

I burst into a clearing in the trees. The crusted snow is untouched. I halt in the center of the clearing, knowing that I could run for days and never escape. I drop to one knee, gloved hands closing around the knife in my pocket. It is the only weapon I have.

The forest is silent. I walk in a circle.

Where are they? Why are they waiting?

They're circling.

One wolf moves out of the trees.

I know him. He is the alpha, and I am sure he is the same one I saw back in Dyea, before Marilyn died. Am I mad to think so? I don't know. I suppose it doesn't really matter anymore.

I recognize his eyes. I recognize the way he holds himself.

I recognize him from my dreams.

I stare at him, frozen. My small knife is pointed at his face. My hand is shaking badly. My face is crusted with ice and frost.

He does not move. We simply stand there, facing each other.

I sense the presence of the pack around us, closing in. There are five—no, six. Six, including the pack leader.

Put the knife down.

I shake my head, muttering, "No."

I am imagining this. This is not real.

I don't move. I don't know what to do. I am trapped. I will be torn limb from limb.

"I've seen you in my dreams," I whisper, hardly able to control my quaking now. "Why have you been following me? I know you have been. I *know*."

The alpha steps forward. His movements are slow and purposeful.

Do not be afraid.

I blink, now completely certain that I am losing my mind. Animals don't *really* speak to us. My *gift* of communicating with creatures was a parlor game that my mother simply encouraged. It does not really exist. It is part of my imagination, a careless projection of my own emotion...

"I'm ready to die," I say, "if that is my fate."

I exhale. I lower the knife. I drop it into the snow. My hands are free, and I stand again. I look around me. The wolf pack is standing around me, stoic and silent. I have never seen or heard of anything like this. It's as if they are waiting for the alpha to give permission to destroy me.

"I have nothing left," I whisper. "Everyone I love is dead. Just *kill me.*"

In this moment, I am defeated. The weight of my losses is too heavy, and I am at the end of the road. It's over for me, and I know it.

I hang my head.

The wolf takes another step forward.

Not everyone is dead, Jenna.

I bring my eyes back to his, awestruck.

"You know my name," I murmur.

I have known you for a long time.

One more step forward. I do not move. He lowers his head. His nose quivers as he tests the air.

Trust me.

I don't know why I do it: I lift my hand and stretch my fingers out. The alpha slowly touches his nose to my fingers, and all at once I remember my dream at Darling's: the wolf touching my hand, willing me to escape.

I feel the coolness of his nose and the soft fur around his muzzle. I slip my hand into the coat around his ears. He is silky, like what I imagine a cloud to be.

Follow me.

I stare at him, mesmerized by his eyes.

"I can't," I say, shivering. "It's too *cold.*"

Again, ***Follow me, Jenna.***

I pick up the knife and tuck it into the pocket of my jacket. I stand. The wolves don't move. The alpha shakes his head, and he stalks into the forest. I don't know why or how I do it: but I follow him. I trail his path like a lost puppy, pushing through snowy branches. I am painfully aware of the rest of the pack ghosting through the forest as we move—but they never touch me. They keep their distance, always.

This is a dream.

This is real.

I do not know what the truth is.

I follow the alpha as if hypnotized. I don't pay attention to the time or the sky. I trek onward, through the woods, walking until my feet ache and I am dizzy with hunger.

We climb uphill for what seems like an eternity. When we reach the crest of the slope, I am panting for breath. The alpha waits for me, unblinking. I step beside him and look across the vast expanse before me.

Mines.

A series of small mountains bubble across the valley below us. They are peppered with mining sites. A camp has sprung up near the banks of a frozen creek.

"Dorsey's Mines," I whisper.

The sun rises over the mines, deep red through the twilight. Below, prospectors are just beginning their early day, slaves to the strange daylight hours of this winter arctic wilderness.

Go and find him.

I look to the wolf. In the light of the sunrise, he seems more real than ever before. His eyes and the full strength of his size are clearly defined. He seems too beautiful to be real.

"I can't take Parker by myself," I say.

No. Find him.

I chew on my lower lip, confused. The alpha walks forward and again touches his nose to my hand.

Never look back.

I say nothing. He cocks his head, and then he bounds into the woods. I take a step backward, startled. He disappears into the shadows, and the pack vanishes with him. It happens so fast that I have no time to react. I can only watch as they go, and I am alone at the top of the hill, looking down on the mining camp that will most likely bring my final doom.

***

I sit for a moment, surveying the mining camp. I shake myself, slap my cheeks. Did I imagine the wolves? Am I delirious from hunger? Traumatized from my near-enslavement into prostitution?

I don't know.

I watch as the prospectors in camp rouse from their tents and get to work. The mines from here look like small pinpricks of black pressed into the hills. The camp itself is a sea of canvas double-tents. The air smells of campfire smoke. Hundreds of crude wooden platforms connect the different mines. The men swarm the platforms like ants.

The sheer size of Dorsey's Mines is staggering.

How can I possibly find Conroy here?

I lean against a tree. At the very least, I need to move. It is too cold to stay rooted to one spot. I will turn to ice.

I watch for a bit longer. I watch the men moving and I look for signs of Conroy, and I think about the wolves who led me here. Dream or not, I have ended up where I need to.

Find him, the wolf said.

I will. I have to.

I take the next few moments to study the zig-zagging structure of the camp—the paths that wind between tents.

I can do this. I know I can.

I look behind my shoulder, expecting the wolves to appear again, but they do not.

I move downhill, staying in the shade of the trees. By the time I reach the bottom, camp routine is in full swing. Men are talking, laughing and cursing. I hear the constant rhythm of pickaxes striking rock. Smoke rolls out of the caves—an effort to keep the walls from freezing solid.

I pull my hat low across my face and make sure my hair is tucked in. My cheeks are smeared with dirt and grime. I'm confident that I can pass for a man at a distance. I hunch my shoulders and slip into camp. A pickaxe is leaning against a small outhouse building. I grab it, slinging it over my shoulder. I stick my free hand in my pocket and amble into camp, feigning calm...but I am searching. I look at every face, and I peek into every tent. Inside camp, there is constant noise and bustle. It is a stark contrast from the isolation of the woods I have traveled for the past few weeks.

I notice something strange: a fence is erected around the camp, just beyond the creek. It is crudely constructed, made of timber that has been hacked into sharp points. Several men patrol the fence. I stop and duck behind an empty tent as a large group of young prospectors walks by.

I press my face against the canvas, holding my breath.

They walk close together, silent and stony.

They are chained.

I stifle a gasp. There are eight men. Their hands are chained to a long piece of wood, binding them together. One armed man walks on each side of them. The young prisoners appear to be exhausted. The one on the front left is taller than the rest. He seems strong, but his face is bruised and bloody. There are burn marks on his neck. He's limping.

Jeremiah.

Recognition strikes me like a lightning bolt. It's *him*. I recognize the broad shoulders, the thick, dark hair. He keeps his head down, glaring at the ground, jaw clenched. He does not see me. My heart buoys in my chest, and suddenly everything makes sense:

Find him, the alpha told me.

I understand at last.

Seventeen

I follow them. I ghost behind the tents and slip through the camp, watching the chained men walk. A thousand questions tumble through my head:

Why is Jeremiah here? He must have been captured in Dawson, when I was talking to Matthias Cooper in the drawing room.

Matthias brought him here...to enslave him?

Why didn't Conroy kill him?

Why bother to bring him here?

The thought that Matthias Cooper is not only killing innocent people, but enslaving them in isolated mining camps, is the icing on an already very bitter cake. I clench my fists and run to keep up with the men. They are cursed at, spit on and occasionally hit from behind with the stock of the guards' shotguns.

Jeremiah is at the front, and he bears it all with a level of icy calm.

If Jeremiah is here…and Lincoln and the dogs are loose…

Did he let the dogs loose, or did they escape their harnesses after we did not return for them?

I follow the men to a mine on the edge of camp. It's a large, black opening supported with wooden beams. Sealed, icy flumes sit outside. During the spring and summer months, they flow with water, where prospectors can pan for gold dust and nuggets in dirt and mud.

The shackled men are unbound, handed tools, and sent one at a time inside the mouth of the mine. Guards are stationed outside the mine, around the fences. They patrol the streets of the camp.

This is far from a mining camp: this is a prison.

While I'm sure some of these men are working, it's obvious that many of them have been brought here by force. Who are they? Men who owe Matthias Cooper money or a favor, perhaps. He seems to be the master of cashing in on debts in the most ruthless way imaginable.

I wait in the shadows.

One of the guards shoves a pickaxe into Jeremiah's arms. They push him forward, and he disappears into the bowels of the mine. I swallow, nervous. The remaining men are escorted inside. I wait until the last ones are gone, and then I rest my own pickaxe over my shoulder and look at the ground, ambling casually toward the mine entrance.

I concentrate on putting one foot in front of the other, not daring to look up and make eye contact with someone on accident.

I walk into the mine. It's dark and grimy. The air is thin and cold. Torches and lanterns light the tunnels. Mining carts are pushed along makeshift tracks. Men hack at the walls. Some whistle, some talk, and some cuss. The mine spirals into four different passageways, diving into the heart of the mountain, interconnecting with the rest of the mine entrances around the camp.

Where is Jeremiah?

I hesitate, knowing that if I *look* lost, someone will notice.

I take a chance. I veer to the far right, following the sounds of voices. A group of laughing men round the corner. I slip behind them, falling into step. I shadow their movements. The guards from outside are standing here, leaning against the rock walls, smoking cigars. I stay just behind the men and make it past them without a second glance.

Men are spaced out along the walls. One man for every twenty feet of rock, I notice. I walk until I see familiar faces—some of the men who were chained up with Jeremiah. I feel lightheaded and sick. This is crazy—how am I going to get out of here alive?

I push the fear away and keep moving.

There he is. At the end of the mine, beside a curve in the tunnel. It's eerie. The lanterns cast strange shadows across the walls. Jeremiah swings at the rock with ferocious strength. I see the shimmer of gold dust in a few places.

Jeremiah is wearing a coat and pants, thick boots and gloves. I can see the fury in the way he moves, and I wonder how long he has been here.

I move behind him.

"Jeremiah," I whisper.

He stops mid-swing. He looks left, looks right. He turns around. I pull my hat up a bit, breathless.

He stares at me.

"It's me," I say. "*Jenna.*"

He exhales. He drops the pickaxe and grabs my shoulders, pulling me around the corner of the tunnel. He crushes me against his chest. He kisses me. I taste sweat and dirt on his lips.

"Thank God, Jenna," he whispers.

He holds my face in his hands. I see the worry in his eyes, weighing him down.

"What are *you doing here*?" he demands.

"I came for Conroy," I reply, looking up at him. "I found you instead."

His face is cut and bruised.

"What happened to you?" I ask.

"What happened to *you*?"

"Jeremiah, we don't have time for this!" I poke my head around the bend. "We need to leave!"

Jeremiah slips his fingers under my chin and turns my face to him.

"You've never looked more beautiful, Jenna," he says.

There is a slight smile on his lips.

"Marshal," I whisper. "I do believe you missed me."

"You have no idea."

"Come on," I reply. "Let's go."

"Whoa, hang on," he says. "We can't just walk out of here. I'm a prisoner."

"I walked *in* here just fine."

"Getting in is a lot easier than getting out."

"Then what do you suggest?"

"I've been here for three days…" Jeremiah pauses. "Long enough that I was working out my own escape since I got here."

"But you hadn't bolted yet. Why?"

"I was hoping they'd bring you into camp, and we could get out together. I had no idea where they had taken you, so I figured staying in one place was my best chance of finding you…"

"Is Conroy even *here*?" I ask.

"No." Jeremiah shakes his head. "But I know where he'll be."

"Well then, let's go!"

Jeremiah jerks his thumb over his shoulder.

"The mining carts," he says. "That'd be the only way to get out of here without being seen. And trust me, they'd notice if *I* tried to walk out. They're watching me closer than the rest of the men."

"Sounds about right."

A mine cart sits near us on one of the tracks.

"You'll have to push it," Jeremiah says. "They don't know you—they'll assume you're with the employees, not the prisoners."

"And if they assume otherwise?"

"We're dead."

"I can live with that," I remark.

"That's my girl." Jeremiah grins.

I take a deep breath, checking the corner again. So far, no one has taken notice of Jeremiah's lack of mining.

"Now," I tell him.

He nods, and then he's gone, walking toward the cart. He checks to make sure nobody's watching, and then he slips into the mine cart, hunkering down. I grab my pickaxe and bring it with me. I set it aside as I shove dirt over Jeremiah.

"Not so much," he whispers.

"Shut up!" I hiss.

I keep shoveling. I pile enough dirt over him to hide the shape of his body, and then I set a roll of canvas and two pickaxes parallel across the rims of the cart. I steady my nerves, and I begin to push the cart. It groans and creaks as I move it, but nobody so much as blinks. There is plenty of noise in the mine—lots of talking, singing, and clattering. I move at a steady pace, keeping my hat pulled down, acting as if I belong—as if I know what I'm doing.

The guards are talking amongst themselves. They don't notice me as I pass.

"Hey, you!"

I shut my eyes.

A burly, bearded man with a black jacket stops in front of my cart. We're only halfway through the tunnel. My face is still hidden in shadow.

"What'ya think you're doing with this cart?" he demands.

He's got a gun in his hand.

"Takin' it outside," I reply, lowering my voice. "Checkin' it for gold dust."

I know as soon as I say it that I have said something stupid. There is no gold dust in this dirt, and I'm sure everyone here knows that.

The burly man leans forward, squinting at my face.

"I ain't ever seen you in here before," he goes on. "Who are you?"

My mind races.

"Silas," I reply. "Silas Rigby."

"You staying down in the free camp?"

I have no idea how to respond, so I say, "Yes, sir."

He nods.

"I hear the food's better down there."

I exhale.

"I suppose," I say. "It depends on your definition of what better food *is*."

He roars with laughter.

"True, true," he agrees. "Listen, mind if I join you tonight for dinner, then? I've been gettin' the short end of the stick with food lately. Conroy said I had free rein, now that I've been promoted to the upper mines."

"It'd be my pleasure."

"Good, good." He claps me on the shoulder—almost knocking me over. "And by the way..."

He grabs my hat and tosses it to the ground.

"No women allowed in camp," he growls.

Jeremiah rises from the mining cart. He slams into the burly man, knocking him to the ground, driving his shoulder into his chest. The burly man yelps with pain. Jeremiah crushes his fist against his face. I hear his nose crack. The man screams. Jeremiah grabs his gun.

"Jeremiah, what are you—"

Jeremiah clutches my hand, and we're running. The burly man is cursing us to hell and back again and the mine erupts with activity. Guards crawl out of the tunnels. Someone rings a bell. An escape warning?

"Run fast, Jenna!" Jeremiah shouts. "Don't stop, no matter what happens!"

"I plan on it!"

We burst out of the mines, into the light. I see people and movement everywhere. Are they after *us*? I don't know, and I cannot stop to find out. We run. I push myself harder than I've ever pushed before. We barrel through camp, toward the woods. We slip over the frozen creek. Jeremiah never lets go of my hand. I keep pace with him. My legs burn with fatigue as we climb the hill.

Gunshots pepper the woods. Bullets whiz by our heads. I lose my balance and almost twist my ankle. Jeremiah's steady hand keeps me upright. We never stop. We keep going, even when we reach the top of the hill. My hair is flying behind me and the wind is cold and the entire mining camp is up in arms. I can hear their footsteps crashing through the underbrush. More gunshots and yelling.

How many men are chasing us?

If they catch us…

I don't think about it. I'm sure it wouldn't be pleasant.

We run until we are dripping with sweat, until we are one with the pain firing through our muscles. At last, Jeremiah drops to the ground and pulls me down with him. I stumble into his arms and he rolls me beneath the hollow shell of a fallen tree. He pushes me farther into the darkness and crawls in after me. My cheek is flat against his chest. I hear the rapid beat of his heart.

"Don't move," he whispers.

I close my eyes, praying.

"It's all right," I say, suddenly, as if everything is clear. "They'll protect us."

"*Who*, Jenna?"

Footsteps, voices, boots crunching against snow and twigs. Men move past us. At one point, someone steps on the fallen tree. The hollow stump rattles and snow falls into our faces.

"I don't see them," someone says.

"No, I don't—"

His voice is drowned out by a horrible scream.

"WOLVES!" somebody shouts. "Wolves! Get out, get out!"

Cursing, more footsteps. Gunshots. Growling. I lift my head and stare through the small opening in the tree. I can't see much— just flashes of men, sprinting, panicked. The howl of a lone wolf echoes through the trees.

I look at Jeremiah.

"They're leading them away from us," I whisper.

"Doubtful."

I bring my eye back to the slit in the fallen log, and I gasp, face to face with a single, yellow eye. It's the lean younger wolf, part of the same pack that I have come to know.

Thank you, I think.

I don't breathe.

He stands up.

And then he's gone, bounding after the men in the forest, pushing them away from us, saving us.

Watching over us.

***

"Conroy's heading back to the Yukon River," Jeremiah says. "There's a warehouse there, and he's loading it up with gold and supplies. They'll be shipped out on a steamer as soon as spring sets in and the Yukon thaws."

We are walking through the woods, keeping a steady pace. We've been moving for several hours through the twilight daytime hours, and so far, I've seen no signs of pursuers. Perhaps the presence of a wolf pack scared the men from the forest.

Again, I think the words: *Thank you.*

"At Dawson, when we were separated," Jeremiah tells me, "Conroy kept me locked up in a holding cell. I was brought to Dorsey's the next day. I thought Conroy would show, but he never did. Heard from some of the boys around camp that he was headed to someplace called *Logan House.*"

"I know where that is!" I exclaim.

"Good. Then we've got somethin' to work with, at least."

"I'm sorry you ended up here," I say. "I was hoping you'd escaped, back at Dawson. I heard gunshots, and I just kept going. I thought if I could get out, I could come back and help you, but I got cornered in the stables..."

"One of the men fired a wild shot," Jeremiah admits. "It started a brawl. There were just too many men. I underestimated Matthias Cooper's organization and numbers." He grimaces.

"Jeremiah," I say. "What about Lincoln? What about the *team?*"

"I got out of camp, and I cut them loose," Jeremiah replies, confirming my suspicions. "Cooper's men were closing in on me—I knew they'd take the dogs, sell them off, breed them...that's what they do with confiscated goods, so to speak. I told them to run. I figured they'd be happier out in the woods than with Cooper's company, anyway."

"Lincoln found me," I say. "I think Conroy may have shot him. I'm not sure."

Jeremiah frowns, then reaches over to squeeze my hand.

"How did you find Dorsey's Mines?" he asks. "It's pretty well hidden."

I explain to Jeremiah how I was taken to Darling's, and how I escaped. I tell him how the wolves surrounded me and how the pack guided me to the mines—dream or not, I ended up in the right place, somehow, and I am learning to accept these slights of fate with gratitude.

I tell him that the wolves have been following us since the beginning; that it all started with me, running the dogs from a supply trip to Dyea. The same wolves, the same pack. I tell him that I believe they are watching over us, that they are acting as our guardians. There is no other explanation.

Jeremiah considers my words in silence.

"You think I'm crazy," I say. "You think it's a wild story."

"No," he replies.

"Then what *are* you thinking?"

He shakes his head.

He stops me, then, right there in the middle of the forest. He brushes my hair away from my face and kisses me, gentle and soft.

"I trust you, Jenna Renee," he whispers.

I search his eyes—dark pools, eyes that have seen much more than I have.

"I know," he goes on, slowly.

I raise my eyebrows.

"You know *what*?" I ask. "About Nathaniel?"

"No," he answers. "Although that sounds interesting. I meant, Jenna...I know. About you."

"What about me, Jeremiah?"

Jeremiah halts again.

"I know part of you is not French," he states. "I know there's some native in you. On your mother's side, judging by the way you've talked about her."

I go still, and the small part of me—the part that is not made of ice—freezes over again. I lift my chin and regard him coolly. "You don't know what you're talking about," I say.

"I hate to tell you this, Jenna," Jeremiah says. "But I'm a bit older than you are, and I ain't stupid. I'm not holding it against you. Hell, I don't care if you're Inuit or German. I'm just telling you: I *know*, and I intend to keep your secret."

I nervously scratch my cheek, replying, "Do you now?"

"I do."

"I told you I'm French, *why* don't you believe me?"

Jeremiah tucks a strand of long black hair behind my ear.

"Because my own mother," Jeremiah says, "was Cherokee, and she looked a lot like you."

I blink at him, awed.

"Impossible!" I exclaim. "You said that your mother was married to a Union soldier, and that she drank herself to death."

"My mother," Jeremiah replies, "was a young woman working on my father's plantation. The woman who drank herself to death was my stepmother. My father, Jenna, cast my mother out of his life once she gave birth to me. I never saw her past the age of six. My father protected me. He knew that my life would be different if he did not claim me as his own, completely. Lucky for him, I take after him in appearance...it wasn't hard to pass me off as Delilah's son."

"Delilah?"

"My stepmother."

"So you're..."

"Illegitimate, yes. My mother...I never knew what happened to her."

"I'm so sorry, Jeremiah."

"Don't be."

"So you..." I say, staring up into his face, dark eyes, tanned skin, black hair. "You're part *Cherokee*?"

Jeremiah nods.

"I hide it well," he says.

"Yes, you do."

"Almost as well as you do."

"Better, I'd suppose."

Jeremiah kisses me again.

"Two halves make a whole, so they say," he whispers.

For the first time in my life, I press my face against the chest of someone who is like me, and this revelation is as thrilling as it is terrifying. How could it be that Marshal Jeremiah Black shares the same ancestry as me? Fate, indeed, works in mysterious ways.

"I don't believe it," I tell him. "How can it be?"

"I don't ask questions like that," he says. "I just accept the things that happen to us."

I'm shocked at this knowledge, and terrified that someone knows my secret...for the first time in my life, someone *knows*. I try to control the smile creeping across my lips.

"Jeremiah," I say. "There's something I need to tell you about Nathaniel."

"Yes?"

"He was working for Matthias Cooper."

"There you go, Jenna. Breaking a damn romantic moment with a sentence like that."

"I'm sorry, but facts are facts! Matthias says he was embezzling money. That's why he killed him."

"And Marilyn's murder? What purpose was behind that?"

"Tying up loose ends, so he said. Conroy was looking for me only because Matthias had requested I be sent to Darling's to make up the rest of Nathaniel's debt—thirty thousand American dollars! I never would have been set free. I would have worked until I died, surely." I close my eyes. "Nathaniel co-owned his mines with Cooper from the beginning. I've been a fool, Jeremiah. I never knew. How could I have been so blind?"

"Whether your uncle was embezzling or not," Jeremiah says, sharply, "is still no reason to murder a man and his wife. Cooper is still corrupt, and Conroy is still a killer. They deserve justice and punishment."

I nod.

"Jeremiah," I say. "I heard what Amos O'Leary said to you in Dawson: about Conroy having bested you before. What did he mean by that?"

"After Conroy destroyed Aguta's settlement, years ago," Jeremiah replies slowly, "I had a personal score to settle with Parker. I wasn't always a lawman, Jenna. I ran with men who robbed and killed. I fell in with the wrong sort of folks. I was working for a man named Yul Mallard, stealing a vault of money from a bank just outside of Skagway. Turns out, Yul was workin' for somebody, too."

"Conroy Parker," I say, understanding.

"The very same."

"What happened?"

"I felt like the stupid boy I was," Jeremiah answers, shaking his head. "Realizing I was working for the same man who destroyed my second family...I was ashamed. I found out where he was. Sitka, in a hotel. I tried to kill him, Jenna. I was roaring drunk, raging. I didn't stand a chance. Conroy would have killed me if my friends at the time hadn't intervened. I felt like a child again..."

I say nothing.

"I had nothing left," Jeremiah continues, "except Aguta. I found my way back to his settlement, and we had a talk. I changed my ways, you could say. I knew there was a shortage of lawmen in Alaska...hell, it was one of the reasons I was a robber in the first place. But I knew all the tricks, all the men out there. The United States was looking for some young men to be new marshals in the rough country, especially with whispers of gold springing up all over the States. I signed up, got a badge. And here I am, I guess."

I look away, struck with the sadness in Jeremiah's voice.

"I wanted to kill Conroy Parker for so long," Jeremiah says, "that I admit I didn't care if you were telling the truth or not when you first came to me in Dyea. I *wanted* to believe you. What he did to

249

you was what he did to me, and I want to bring that son of a bitch to justice, Jenna."

"Well," I say, taking his hand as we walk. "I suppose we'll just have to do it together."

Jeremiah searches my face. His eyes are red—painful memories resurfacing, dancing across his steely gaze. It is a devastation I understand far too well.

"We can't stop him if it's just the two of us," Jeremiah says, choosing his words with care.

"What other choice do we have?"

At this, Jeremiah finally smiles.

"Trust me," he says. "I have a plan."

Eighteen

This is crazy. I stick my hands in my pockets and look across the white, frozen Yukon River and that's all I can think: *This plan is crazy. We're both off our rockers.*

But I don't leave. What else can we do?

If nothing else, bringing Conroy Parker to the authorities will at least get us enough reward money to split between the two of us, and then we can go our separate ways...

I clutch my chest, as if choking.

Will we really go our separate ways?

What will I do without Jeremiah? I have no dog team. I have no family...

He has no real obligation to me, I suppose.

But there is something more between us, now. Something fateful. Something that has brought us together throughout this long journey of ours across the snow and up the Chilkoot, into Dawson, despite our separation and abuse at the hands of the Cooper Mining Company.

We are both Cherokee. He understands what it is like to live with a secret.

I remind myself that Jeremiah Black is an infamous womanizer. I'm sure he has made many women feel special and loved. Yet, for some reason or another, I am able to look past that. I glance at him, crouched on my right, surveying the sweep of trees and the expanse of the Yukon before us. He is hardened and serious, handsome in a rugged, wilderness-worn sort of way. How did I not see the Cherokee in his dark eyes before? How could I have missed something so obvious?

Because it was never obvious. Jeremiah is right: he looks like a white man who has spent years in the sun, darkening his skin. One would not know he had Cherokee blood unless they looked very hard...and I imagine that is something he avoids...just as I always have.

The Yukon stretches before us, mighty and still and completely oblivious to the human drama that is unfolding on its shores. The warehouse that is Logan House sits next to the dock. There is a second, larger storage building where the supplies are being stored, fronted by a small office. Men scurry to and from over a dozen dog sleds, loading crates and barrels into the building.

It is six o'clock in the morning, dark as night. In nearly an hour, the sun will crest a bit in the strange half-daylight, half-nighttime way that it does during the winter.

On the edges of the dock, a dog team of ten canines are brought to a halt. The musher is no one I am familiar with, but the dogs are.

"Jeremiah!" I exclaim, gasping. "Those are *my* dogs!"

I recognize them from here—every single dog, every slash of color in their fur, every movement of their body. At the very front is Lincoln, who stands dutifully in his spot, sniffing the air. One of the men approaches Lincoln, his hand outstretched. Lincoln shakes his head and growls, sinking his teeth into the man's arm. The man screams and starts beating Lincoln with his whip.

I stand up, fury flashing through me. Jeremiah grabs my arm and pulls me back to the ground.

"No, Jenna!" he hisses. "Keep your head. We'll get them back. We have to wait!"

I feel the tears building, and I fight them back.

Lincoln is beaten into submission. He snarls and whines, and then he is tossed into the snow while the man stalks away, cursing the dog to hell and back again. Lincoln lies there for a moment. For one horrifying moment, I am afraid that he is dead. But he stirs a moment later, and I can see the weariness in the way he holds himself.

I take a deep breath and attempt to harness my fury.

"We can do this together," Jeremiah whispers. He leans close to my face, his breath hot on my lips. "I promise you, I won't let Conroy get away this time. For both our sakes."

I nod.

I see Conroy at the door of the warehouse. He walks back and forth from the inside of the building to the sleds. He carefully oversees the unloading of the goods.

Over the past few hours, Jeremiah and I have been doing nothing but watching the men unload, working out how to get to Conroy as more men arrive with more supplies. It comes down to the fact that we are only two people, and Conroy has at least forty of Cooper's men with him at the moment. We can't storm the docks— we'll be overpowered and killed on sight. After losing both of us— twice—I doubt Conroy will bother with imprisoning us again. A bullet in the head would be a much easier fix.

"Maybe we should wait until most of the men are gone—" I begin, but Jeremiah cuts me off.

"No," he says. "Conroy will leave once everything is unloaded. We have to get to him before that."

"We need a distraction, then," I conclude. "I can do that. I'll distract them, and you can get to Conroy."

"I'm not letting forty men chase you through the forest, Jenna."

"Don't be ridiculous. Only *half* of them will chase me."

"So that's twenty men, then. Still, too many."

"Worried about me?"

He says nothing, but he gives me a wistful look.

"I do declare, Mr. Black. You almost looked sentimental for a moment there."

He is about to reply when I spot movement on the horizon. A wagon is rolling up the road, pulled by a team of the biggest, darkest dogs I have ever seen. There is a small detachment of armed men riding alongside it, pulled by smaller teams. The wagon is being driven by a burly man with a mustache. The passenger is wearing an expensive fur-lined coat and scarf.

I flush cold, recognizing him.

"Matthias Cooper," I whisper. "He's *here*."

I remember Baby's words back at the whorehouse, when we were discussing Matthias Cooper and his connection to Darling's:

"Where am I?"

"Just outside of Eagle," she replies. *"This place is called Darling's. Biggest whorehouse on this side of the Yukon River."*

"Owned by Matthias Cooper, no doubt."

"Yes. I reckon you met him, then?"

"Have you?"

"All the girls do, sometime. He's 'spected to visit about once a month."

"He's coming to visit Darling's," I whisper. "I was told to expect him once a month."

Jeremiah frowns, tightening his grip on the rock we're hiding behind.

"Two birds with one stone," he mutters.

"He's probably here to meet with Conroy before he goes on to Darling's."

"Most likely." Jeremiah squints against the glare. "He's only brought five men with him. That brings our count up to forty-five."

"Which means an extra five men will be chasing me through the woods," I reply wryly.

"Very amusing, Jenna."

"I thought so."

I am joking because I'm afraid—because I am terrified of failure. If we fail today, we fail forever, and I am back to the doom of working in saloons to earn a wage, so that I can at least feed myself.

"We need a *big* diversion, then," I say. "Bigger than just me. It needs to be enough to draw most of the men away from the warehouse. Away from Conroy."

"I can take them all if they're scattered," Jeremiah tells me. "We have to break them up." He points at the river. "See there, near the shore?"

Barrels of gunpowder are waiting to be loaded.

"We blow it," I state, guessing at his idea. "Send it up in flames. And then what?"

"We don't just blow that," Jeremiah goes on. "We blow the office and the storage building behind it. We blow up everything, send it up in flames. Destroy it all."

"I like it," I agree. "But how do we get the gunpowder into the other buildings?"

"We'll split. I'll sneak behind the buildings and plant the gunpowder..." He nods toward the gunpowder stash. "There's dynamite down there, too, for blasting at the mines. I'll use that. You just worry about the one area by the shore. Can you do that?"

"Of course I can."

"Good."

Matthias Cooper's sled stops in front of the office. He climbs out, shaking the frost from his coat. He walks into the office. Conroy sees this and barks something at his men. He makes a beeline for the office, too, and disappears inside.

"Perfect," Jeremiah says. "Are you ready?"

"Yes," I say. "*But,* what if something goes wrong? What's our plan?"

"We'll have to make it up as we go along, I reckon."

"Jeremiah! If something goes *wrong*, where should we meet?"

I don't want to get separated again. I can't go back to Darling's.

"Here," he says. "Wait for me *here.*"

I agree.

He presses three cold objects into my hands. I look at them—bullets.

"Not much," he says. "For the gun."

He tries to hand me the gun he took from the guard at Dorsey's.

"You should take it," I say.

"No. You keep it; use it if you have to."

"I will."

We stay there for a few tense moments longer, and then Jeremiah is moving. He slips down the hill and I follow him, staying close behind him in the trees and the shadows until we are so close to the small river port that I can hear the voices of the men.

"Go," Jeremiah whispers.

I head toward the shore. Jeremiah follows. We stay low in the bushes until we reach the barrels. The Yukon is only a few feet away. I smell the frozen river water and the dirt that turned to mud and then to solid ice. The boxes of dynamite are stacked up behind the barrels. Jeremiah inches his way toward the crates, pausing as someone walks by with a box in his arms, headed toward the warehouse.

I hold my breath as he pries the crate open. It's not sealed very well—it's beaten and crushed in one place. Probably the victim of a long journey from the States...although why anyone would be careless enough to roughly transport a crate of *dynamite* is beyond me.

Jeremiah pops the crate open and very, very carefully pulls several sticks of dynamite from within. He stuffs them in his pockets and nods at me.

"Do you have something to light it with?" I hiss, embarrassed that I hadn't thought of that one important detail.

"I've had matches in my pocket since we left Dyea," Jeremiah replies. "They didn't notice I had them at Dorsey's."

At least *one* of us is thinking.

He hands me a few of his matches, and then he is gone. He crosses a small open stretch of dirt. He ducks behind the office building, hovering there, waiting for a clear shot toward the storage building. I hold my breath. A group of men pass, toting a huge crate between the four of them. They walk by without noticing Jeremiah. I exhale, and Jeremiah disappears behind the storage building.

Work fast, Jenna. Hurry!

I close my fingers around the rock-hard plug on top of a barrel of gunpowder. My fingers are so stiff from the cold that I can hardly get a grip on it. After several minutes of working at it, I manage to pull it open. The powder inside is black and filled to the brim. I duck and press my back against the barrel as yet another group of men moves by. They are chatting about how much they're looking forward to going to Anchorage—about drinking and gambling and women.

After they pass, I jump up and grab a handful of the black powder. I pile it in a thick line across the top of the barrel, creating a trail that leads straight into the barrel itself. If I light the trail at the very edge of the barrel, I'll have only a few moments to run for cover before it explodes.

Never play with fire, Jenna, Nathaniel always warned me. *Fire in this country can destroy hundreds of acres and dozens of people's homes. It's not something to be trifled with.*

Here I am, playing with fire.

Nathaniel would not be happy.

Well, we can't always have what we want, can we? I think, glumly. *If Nathaniel hadn't double-crossed a man like Matthias Cooper, he and Marilyn would still be alive. I wouldn't be in this mess in the first place.*

I shake the thoughts from my head and finish my job.

I stay low and watch for Jeremiah's signal. I am supposed to blow the gunpowder first, before he blows the storage building. He'll have more time to run than I will, and while everyone is looking in my direction, he'll be able to plant more explosives in the office.

We'll be able to get to Conroy...if the blast doesn't kill him.

Frankly, I wouldn't be devastated if it did.

The reward money guidelines for Conroy Parker are clear: dead or alive.

Although Jeremiah has made it clear that Conroy Parker is one of the few men on this earth who can implicate Matthias Cooper, and for that...perhaps he *should* be kept alive.

I watch for Jeremiah, the matches clutched in my fingers, the chilling breeze of the Yukon River blowing my loose pieces of hair in wild circles. Jeremiah is barely visible from the other side of the building. He nods in my direction.

It's time.

I shake a little as I strike the first match. The tiny flame hisses as it burns. I hold it to the line of black powder. It catches fire, moving in a slow march toward the contents of the barrel.

I run.

I run as fast I can, heart pounding against my chest, diving for the cover of the rocks and the trees. I peek behind me just as the small flame disappears into the barrel.

Nothing.

I stare, breathless.

No, it has to work! It has to!

I begin to stand, and then it detonates. The blast is thunderous. The force of the explosion knocks me off my feet, slamming me flat on my back. My ears ring. Pieces of wood and metal shower through the sky. Smoke and dust and heat cloak the river port.

I lie there for a moment, dazed.

Why did I stand up? Stupid girl...

I stagger upright. Several men lay dead and bloody on the ground. I peer through the haze and see men running toward the gunpowder, yelling and screaming. Guns are loaded, dogs are set loose. I shrink back into the trees, circling around the far side of the port.

And then the dynamite explodes. The storage building detonates in a shower of splintered wood. Flames erupt from within, licking at the roof. More damage, more destruction. I see Conroy

Parker and Matthias Cooper stumble out of the office. Matthias is screaming bloody murder. Conroy's face is twisted with rage.

He knows.

He knows it's *us*. I can see it in his eyes.

He shouts something to the men—I don't know what it is, because my ears are still ringing—and he grabs his shotgun. He runs toward the woods, and just as he does, the office explodes, too. The blast throws him forward. His shotgun falls from his arms. He hits the ground. Blood gushes from a cut on his forehead.

My fingers tighten around the gun in my hand.

Now's my chance!

Someone grabs me from behind. I didn't hear them coming— my ringing ears have temporarily rendered me deaf. I'm thrown into the snow. I roll onto my back, bringing my boot up into a kick. My heel collides with a bearded man's jaw. He's wearing overalls. One of Cooper's employees. I scramble backward. He grabs my leg and drags me toward him.

I twist sideways.

He twists back, flipping me flat on my back, driving his knee into the center of my chest. The air bursts out of my lungs. I see stars.

The gun is still in my hand. I raise it up and pull the trigger. The bullet explodes from the barrel. My aim is terrible—I can hardly breathe. But the shot is good enough. It hits the bearded man in the chest, entering just below his ribcage and ripping upward, through his shoulder. His face goes still and white. His body slows. He stares at me, terror flashing in his eyes.

He falls forward, on top of me.

Dead.

I struggle to crawl out from under him. I stand and survey the chaos around me. Smoke and flames everywhere. The heat from the fires is incredible, an unreal contrast with the freezing temperature. There is nothing Cooper's men can do except watch the buildings burn—the Yukon is frozen. There is no water. Just snow.

I plunge into the smoke and search for Jeremiah. I don't see him anywhere. I see more of Cooper's men, dead on the ground, killed by the blasts.

Did Jeremiah make it away from the blast in time?

I don't have time to worry—to think—and so I run toward the warehouse.

The dogs. Get to the dogs.

I hear Lincoln's worried bark echoing from the inside of the burning building, despite my pulsing eardrums. I see him through the door, chained to the wall.

"Lincoln!" I scream. "I'm coming for you!"

I think, *Jeremiah, please be safe!*

I still don't see him...but he is not dead. I know it. I feel it.

I run into the building. There is hardly a soul left inside. It is dark, filled with cloying smoke. Lincoln sees me. He snorts and shakes his head, howling desperately. All around us are piles and piles of crates and barrels.

All of it, gold and money.

I run to Lincoln and throw my arms around his neck.

Tears stream down my face.

"I thought I'd lost you forever," I whisper. "I love you, Lincoln."

He licks my face, knocking me over.

Jenna! Jenna! You're safe, you're safe! What happened?

"Long story," I say.

I unfasten the chain from the ring on the wall. Kip, Dasha, Moscow, Gnat, and the rest of the team paw at the ground, barking and terrified of the flames closing in around us. I free them, and they converge on me as a pack, covering me in slobbery kisses, a moving mass of warmth and fur. I laugh with joy, but common sense prevails.

I shout, "Run! Get out, go!"

I lead them through the maze of supplies, and the dogs follow me. I take them outside, and I tell them to wait.

Someone fires a shotgun in our direction. The bullet misses me and lodges itself into the wooden support beams of the warehouse.

"GO!" I scream.

Lincoln pauses.

I will not leave you again.

"Trust me!" I tell him. "Please, Lincoln."

I kneel down and touch his nose.

"Trust me," I say again. "Lead the team. *Go.*"

He bumps his nose against my forehead.

I will be watching.

He darts into the trees, away from the gunfire and the flames. I know they will wait for me—I know they will be here when this is all over, if we are still alive at the end of it—

Another gunshot.

This one is dangerously close, and I see the source of it: Conroy.

The smoke swirls aside and he is standing there, glaring at me. There is nowhere to go, nowhere to run. I whirl around and disappear into the warehouse, narrowly avoiding his next shot. There is a second level inside the warehouse—a wooden platform that parallels the walls, looking over the goods.

If I can get up fast enough, I may be able to shoot Conroy from above.

I tear up the stairs, putting all of my strength into it. The roof has begun to catch fire, and the smoke is growing thicker, making it difficult to breathe. I see Jeremiah flash by near the office outside, and then he's gone again.

I come to a halt at the railing of the platform, kneeling in the smoke. I raise the gun, waiting for Conroy to emerge through the smoke.

"Drop the gun, girl."

I feel the cold barrel of a shotgun on the back of my neck. A stone drops to the pit of my stomach.

Impossible!

I don't move.

"Drop the *gun*, Jenna."

The gun presses harder against my skin. I drop the gun onto the platform. It clatters against the wood.

"Stand up."

I stand.

"Keep your hands above your head, girl. Face me."

I turn, slowly.

It's not Conroy. It's Matthias. He's covered with grease and dirt. His perfect fur jacket is burned, and he's bleeding. He glares at me.

"I knew I should have killed you," he seethes.

Gone is the calm and cold demeanor he portrayed in Dawson.

He's enraged, his face flushed red.

"Is this your idea *of a game*?!" he screams, spit flying from his mouth.

He shoves the barrel of the shotgun into my ribs, driving me against the rail of the platform. There's nothing but open air behind me. I stare at him, breathing hard.

"How many times have I *allowed* you to live?" Matthias growls. "I could have had you killed in Dawson, but instead I sent you to Darling's. And how do you repay me? By *running* away? By helping one of my prisoners to *escape* Dorsey's Mines?" He lifts the shotgun and presses the barrel into my cheek. "You are *far* more trouble than you're worth, Jenna. I should have had Conroy kill you a long time ago and avoided all of this."

I cough, smoke filling my lungs. Conroy appears on the platform, holding a shotgun in his hands, too. Blood streams down his face, pouring across his nose. He looks fit to kill.

My heart pounds so hard, I can feel it in my skull.

"Drop the gun, Matthias."

Jeremiah.

I feel a rush of relief—but it is momentary. This is not over yet.

Jeremiah stands at the top of the stairway, a pistol in each hand. One is pointed at Matthias, and the other is pointed at Conroy.

His jacket is torn apart. He is covered with streams of blood and smudges of ash...but he stands there, unflinching, his badge pinned to the collar of his jacket.

"You're under arrest," Jeremiah says. "The both of you, for murder, grand larceny, kidnapping, and forced imprisonment of over one hundred men and women."

"Well look here," Conroy says, grinning wickedly. "We got ourselves Marshal Jeremiah Black...again. I'd heard you escaped from Dorsey's. Guess it's true. You needed your lady friend to make it out, eh? Couldn't do it by yourself?"

"I had no reason to," Jeremiah replies, cold. "Drop the gun, Conroy. Or I shoot."

"Go ahead. Matthias'll still kill the girl."

"I'll kill you both."

"You'll fail, boy."

Conroy is sure of himself. He does not falter. He just looks at Jeremiah like he's a child—like we're playing some kind of game. Matthias trembles with rage.

"Do you have *any* idea how much gold you just blew up?" he demands. "How much *money*?"

Matthias strikes my jaw with the stock of the shotgun.

"DROP IT!" Jeremiah commands.

I hit the floor. My jaw throbs with pain. My vision goes fuzzy. Matthias drops the gun. He looks to Conroy.

Conroy doesn't move.

"You shoot me, Jeremiah," Conroy says, "and I guarantee you, I'll get a shot off at the girl before I'm dead. You know I ain't lying."

Jeremiah holds his pistols steady.

He is calling Conroy's bluff, and my life is hanging in the balance.

I hold a hand to my cheek.

"Come now," Matthias says, sneering. "This is nothing but business gone bad. I should have had the whole lot of Renees killed *years* ago and saved myself the inconvenience of dramas like this."

"You'll pay for what you did!" I say, spitting blood from my mouth.

"Why?" Matthias says, raising his hands. "This pain is far from *my doing*."

"The fact that Nathaniel double-crossed you is no excuse for murder or—"

"Nathaniel never double-crossed me!" Matthias scoffs, laughing sourly. "Did you think I was telling you the truth, Jenna? Did you *truly* believe me?"

I blink, confused. I exchange a glance with Jeremiah, and I can see that he, too, isn't grasping what Matthias is trying to get at. A ploy to distract us—to buy more time?

No.

Footsteps on the platform. Cooper's men surround us, armed. Pointing their guns at us, forming a human blockade. My heart sinks. We are done—finished.

A tall man steps out from behind the crewmen. He's dressed in a suit, a hat pulled snug against his graying hair. The air goes out of me. I recognize the kind eyes, the wrinkles around the mouth, the long, worn fingers.

"Nathaniel?" I whisper.

Shock, utter shock.

He stares at me, a sad smile on his face.

"I'm sorry, Jenna," he says. "I'm truly sorry."

Nineteen

cannot believe my eyes. I blink several times, sure that I am hallucinating.

Yet he's here, in the flesh. The Nathaniel Renee who adopted me, who raised me like his own daughter, who taught me to run dogs and love them, who taught me how to survive the cold and to be as strong as any man and easily as self-sufficient.

"I don't understand," I whisper, numb.

My head swirls with shock.

This can't be true. How could Nathaniel be alive? I was there when he was killed last year—they dragged him away. He was screaming. I'd heard the gunshot...listened to Conroy's laughter and Marilyn's devastated sobbing...

"I don't understand," I say again.

I relive his murder, and I realize something integral that never before occurred to me:

I never saw his body. We never buried him…

"You…faked your death," I murmur, eyes widening.

Nathaniel licks his lips. He looks toward the ceiling—a familiar gesture of his, one he used to make when he was thinking long and hard about answering one of my complicated questions—and then meets my gaze.

"It was for the best," he says. His voice is flat. "I did what I had to."

"What are you *talking* about?" I slowly stand. "I saw you and Conroy—Marilyn mourned for a year. She dug a grave for the body she never found behind the cabin. She was heartbroken. How could you leave her like that? How could you leave *us*?"

"Oh, this is delicious," Matthias remarks, rubbing his hands together. "A family drama, unfolding. I was hoping for a brilliant display of theatrics. It would seem that I have gotten it, at last."

"Matthias, shut up," Nathaniel thunders.

I grasp the platform handrail. Nathaniel—giving Matthias Cooper orders? How is that possible?

"You seem *confused*, the both of ya," Conroy guffaws, a snarl on his lips.

"Why did you do this to me?" I ask Nathaniel, rage coursing through me, exploding like a stick of dynamite. "EXPLAIN YOURSELF!"

My voice is a scream—a cry for him to make sense of this.

He's been dead for a year…why would he pretend? Why?

"Jenna," Nathaniel says. "I own Cooper Mining Company. Matthias…is my son."

"Impossible," I snap. "You have no children. You had *me*."

"Matthias is my son," Nathaniel repeats. Is there sympathy in his voice? "Born long ago, before I met Marilyn."

"So he's illegitimate?"

"And richer than God, so watch your mouth," Matthias growls.

I glare at him. I see no resemblance to Nathaniel in his face. None. There is nothing there but cold greed and unrestrained animosity.

"I don't understand," I whisper.

Nathaniel sighs.

"I first came to Alaska to find wealth," he says, his voice cracking. "I brought Marilyn with me. We were both younger then, and full of optimism. Matthias was in a fine school in San Francisco, and I sent for him when he was old enough to join us."

"Marilyn knew about this?" I demand.

"She knew about most of it...certainly not all of it. She wouldn't approve of all of my...methods..."

"Impossible!" I yell, horrified.

"Marilyn wanted a normal life." Nathaniel shrugs. "I gave her the cabin, I let her have *you*. She was always reminding me of my romantic dalliances in San Francisco. She said that *I* had a child, so she wanted one, too. That's why we sent for you, Jenna. Because Marilyn needed a *hobby*."

The words are brittle and asinine.

They are alien words—words from an enemy, not from the uncle who lovingly taught me the ways of the woods, who rescued me from a poorhouse in the city, who swept me away from the tragedy of my parents' deaths.

"Your business trips," I whisper. "You were managing Cooper Mining all along, weren't you, in Dawson City?"

"Indeed I was," Nathaniel admits.

"Why fake your death? Why do this to your family? You were such a good man!"

Everything is coming together, like fragmented pieces of glass, finally forming a whole window. I see the deception and I question myself. I wonder how I never put this together. How I could have missed this.

Was I so blind? Or was Nathaniel simply *that* clever?

Or maybe, you saw what you wanted to see, I think, sadly. *Maybe you told yourself you had a family, and you made yourself believe it was wonderful because you had nothing else.*

"I needed to spend all of my time in Dawson, to put it simply," Nathaniel. "The company...Cooper Mining. It started so small. I killed a man, once, to secure my hold on his mines. I was terrified I'd be arrested for murder. But I did it again...and again...." He shrugs. "I knew I had to protect myself. I separated myself from the company as much as I could, as soon as the damned lawmen from Canada and the United States started sniffing around, investigating everything. But there came a point, you see, where I had so much wealth...so much *power*...that I no longer wanted to live a double life. Not even Marilyn was aware of the extent of Cooper Mining's powers."

"So you faked your death so that you could leave us...so you could live your extravagant lifestyle without any strings attached," I say flatly. "How noble of you. Matthias was right about one thing...the gold turned you greedy."

"It became more convenient." Nathaniel looks straight at me. "I always meant to return for Marilyn. I was going to tell her the truth...she didn't know about the murders. I protected her from that, at least."

"And what about me?" I say. "What were you planning to do with me?"

"I wanted to send you away. Out of the mess, out of the wilderness. Honest to God I did, Jenna."

"But *why*?" I ask. "Was I not like a daughter to you, Nathaniel?"

"You were."

"Then why send Conroy to the cabin to kill me?"

Nathaniel replies, "He was never meant to kill you, Jenna. He was meant to send you home."

"Yeah, but you pissed me off, girl," Conroy interrupts. "And look what happened."

"But why pretend to die?" I press, unsatisfied.

"What I do, Jenna, is guarded with the utmost secrecy," Nathaniel explains slowly. "Matthias is the face—"

"And *you* are the puppet master," Matthias interjects, grinning.

"I told you to *shut up*."

Matthias shuts his mouth, irritated.

"I couldn't risk jeopardizing everything I had ever worked for by bringing you into the fold," Nathaniel goes on. "The things I've had to do to establish my empire...not all of it has been pretty, or legal, I'm afraid. I needed to disappear, and I needed a valid reason to do so. You were meant to be sent on a steamer back to San Francisco when spring came and resume your life there."

"All this deception and pain," I say, trembling. "And for *what*, Uncle?"

"To keep my name clear."

"It would seem that you have failed in that respect."

"She's really unforgiving," Matthias comments. "And to think, we're actually *cousins*."

"Again...shut *up*," Nathaniel says. "I named the company after Matthias. Most men know who I am, Jenna...but you never did. I kept you isolated. And perhaps, I *could* have brought you into the fold...but the fact that you were the daughter of a *redskin* was...well, less than attractive to me."

He says the words, but there is no life in them. It is as if he is forcing himself to say them, forcing himself to hurt me so that I will stop asking him questions he does not want to answer.

I blink back angry, hurt tears.

"You know," I say, hoarsely.

He nods, regarding me with a cold expression. I have never felt so betrayed...I have never felt so utterly destroyed.

I gather myself, despite everything.

"Why kill your own wife, then?" I demand, trembling. "*Why,* Nathaniel?"

"I didn't kill Marilyn!" Nathanial growls. "I am many things, Jenna—but I always took care of Marilyn. I sent Conroy to the cabin to *collect you*. I was coming back for Marilyn after you'd been dealt with." Here, he throws an irritated glance at Conroy. "I didn't know

Marilyn had been sick. I didn't know she had already died. I would have been there for her. Of course I would have."

I stare at him.

"She didn't simply die," I hiss. "She was MURDERED!" I point to Conroy. "He shot her in the head. I saw her body!"

Nathaniel cocks his head. He gives Conroy a shaky smile.

"She's lying," he says. "...*Isn't* she?"

"Of course she is," Conroy spits. "I did what you said, boss. She was dead when I got there."

"LIAR!" I shout. "You killed her!"

Nathaniel stares at me, and I can see him turning this over in his head: the wife that he sent for...murdered by his own hit man.

"You didn't send Conroy to take me to San Francisco," I say, finishing the rest of the story. Suddenly, I understand. "I was meant to be taken to Darling's all along. I would be out of your hair, there. Out of your life—because that's all a *savage* like me is good for, in your line of thinking. I don't believe that Marilyn would have condoned this. She was like a mother to me."

"Marilyn knew nothing of Darling's," Nathaniel answers, matter-of-fact. "She didn't need to."

"So I'm right."

"You wound me, Jenna," Nathaniel says, holding a hand to his chest. "Did I not care for you—clothe you, feed you? Give you a dog team of your own? Teach you to mush, teach you to survive? I was a good father."

"You were. Until your lust for wealth turned you into a monster, Uncle."

Nathaniel shrugs, but I can see that he is shaken: he is still thinking about what I said, about Conroy murdering Marilyn.

"She's dead," I say quietly, looking into his eyes. "She's dead because of *you*."

A pause.

Nathaniel looks at Conroy.

"You told me Jenna wasn't at the cabin when you got to it," Nathaniel tells him, his tone accusatory. "You said she was long gone. And yet here she stands...and my wife is dead. How can this be, Parker?"

Something glints in Matthias's eyes: amusement.

He is enjoying the show.

"She was dead," Conroy grits. "She *was*, boss. Swear to God, she was."

"She was alive," I say, never breaking my gaze from Nathaniel's face. "He shot her, and then took the gold. Why do you think I'm *here*, Nathaniel? For *fun*? I'm here for *revenge*! I came for justice. I wanted to bring your killer and Marilyn's to justice...and it looks like it's *you* who needs to be hung from the noose."

As I watch Nathaniel, his expression falters.

I can see it in his eyes: the realization that he has made a mistake.

That he has ruined everything. That his life as he knew it...is over.

And my heart is broken.

"Are you telling me that you were behind the Chilkoot killings all those years ago?" Jeremiah interjects. I had almost forgotten he was there, I was so engrossed in Nathaniel's seeming resurrection from the dead. "You killed a lot of good people."

"Again, I wasn't directly involved," Nathaniel replies quickly. "That was Conroy's—"

"Is that the name of the damn game now, shit-face?" Conroy bursts, turning purple. "You gonna blame me for every kill you've ever ordered—every execution you've ever planned? We're equal partners in this. If you're going to lie like a dog, lie to someone else!"

His gun swings left—pointed straight at Nathaniel's head.

"Someone has to take the fall," Nathaniel whispers. "It would be bad business for that person to be me."

The tension is thick; I could cut through it with a blade. The crewmen on deck hold their weapons tighter, ready for the burning to erupt in a bloodbath. Jeremiah never lowers his pistols. The stalemate continues. He looks at me, and I look at him.

Conroy's gun is no longer trained on me, and Matthias is not paying attention.

This is our chance.

"Do it," I mouth.

Jeremiah nods. He pulls the trigger. The bullet bursts from the gun—a piercing shot that echoes through the building. Conroy's head snaps forward. Blood explodes across the deck. Some of it hits my face. I run toward Jeremiah. Conroy falls to the floor.

Dead.

At *last,* dead.

God, he killed him. He really killed him. WE did.

Apparently, Conroy Parker will not be taken alive, after all.

Bam, bam, bam!

Three more shots. Jeremiah covers me while we dive down the staircase, onto the ground below. Matthias screams profanities at us. I fall on the stairs, struggling to my feet. Jeremiah pulls me upright. Shotgun shells rain through the air.

"They're shooting through the platform!" I yell, horrified.

"Jenna, get out of the building and—"

Nathaniel is blocking our path. He has swung down from the upper platform, and he's standing at the front door of the warehouse...the only escape from the flames that will surely consume us if we can't get out. He has Conroy's shotgun in his hands. His arms are slicked with his dead hit man's blood.

"I'm sorry, Jenna," he says. "I really am. But this is the way it has to be."

"You killed your wife," I reply, cold. "And you lost me forever."

Nathaniel doesn't flinch.

I can hear the rest of the men coming. Everything is happening in seconds, but it feels like hours, as I look into the face of the man I once loved and called father—the man I once thought was my rescuer.

And perhaps he was, once.

Just not anymore.

He is going to kill us—there is little remorse on his face. He is angry. I can see that. Angry that his own greed and maniacal need for power caused him to trust the wrong people—caused him to be the death of his own wife.

I know what I must do.

"I'm sorry, too," I whisper.

I pull my gun from my pocket.

I lift it up. Nathaniel goes pale.

"You wouldn't—" he starts to say.

But I would. And I do.

I pull the trigger and the gun goes off and Nathaniel's head snaps backward. He falls back in a heap. I see it all in slow motion—the blood, the shocked expression on his face, the realization that he has been beaten at his own game.

I killed Nathaniel. I killed him. I killed him...

"Jenna, go!" Jeremiah says.

He is sliding sticks of lit dynamite across the floors of the warehouse, into the maze of crates and barrels.

Jeremiah, always thinking ahead...

He jumps up, grabbing my arms, dragging me toward the door. We stumble past Nathaniel's lifeless body. I force myself to look away.

You killed him because you had to. He left you no choice! He was going to shoot you.

"Oh, God," I gasp, suddenly horrified with what I have done. "Jeremiah—"

"I'm here for a reason! TO KILL CONROY AND PROTECT YOU!" he says. "NOW RUN!"

I sprint forward, the spell broken. Jeremiah slips his hand into mine and we clear the doorway together. We dash away from the warehouse. Lincoln and the dogs are standing at the edge of the trees. Jeremiah and I never look back. Not once. Not until we reach the trees do we glance behind us. I see Matthias Cooper stumble out the door of the warehouse, covered in black, hacking his lungs up. He collapses to the ground in a heap, his eyes settling on us. I see terror in his face.

Justice, I think. *At last.*

The warehouse explodes. It is the biggest detonation I have ever seen. The initial burst of flames consumes Matthias immediately. He dissolves into ashes, and the warehouse seems to crumble within itself, the already burning structure destroyed by the dynamite.

I stare at it, not realizing I am crying until Jeremiah puts his arm around my shoulders.

"Come here," he says.

He pulls me to his chest, and I cling to him.

"It's over," Jeremiah whispers. "Jenna, it's over."

I look up at him. He strokes my sooty cheek. Both of us are shaking with cold.

"Lincoln," I state, hoarsely.

My beloved wolf-dog moves out of the woods, silent. He walks to us, and the rest of the team gathers around him. They are stoic. I have never seen them like this. Lincoln presses his head against my leg, whining softly. Kip presses her nose into my shoulder. Moscow nuzzles Jeremiah. They are full of warmth, ensconcing us like a blanket, shielding us from the cold.

I hang my head, and I know.

It *is* over.

Finally.

Twenty

The warehouse smolders, a dying fire in the dark civil twilight of the arctic winter.

"We have to get out of here," I say. "I don't want to be here anymore."

Jeremiah says nothing. He only hugs me tighter.

Lincoln licks my hand.

"We have no sled," Jeremiah murmurs. "No horses. We'll have to walk back to Dawson."

"I'm not going back to Dawson," I say. "Cooper's men are still there."

"Cooper and everybody connected with them is dead." Jeremiah leans forward, holding my face in his hands. "Do you understand, Jenna? It's over. The leadership no longer exists. Cooper Mining will crumble without your uncle at the helm—not only that, but I've got names and locations to report to the United States now.

It won't be long until a posse is sent up here to smoke out Dorsey's Mines and anyplace like it."

A sad, animal sob escapes my chest.

"Nathaniel," I whisper. "How could he do this to me?"

Jeremiah shakes his head.

"I don't know," he says.

"He wasn't always like this. He was kind, once."

"I believe you."

"He raised me like a father."

"I know, Jenna."

A flush of embarrassed humiliation burns through me: all this time I have been chasing Nathaniel. All this time I have been thirsting for vengeance for a man whom I thought loved me.

He did love you, a voice whispers. *His love turned corrupt.*

Would a hateful man bring Lincoln to me? Would a hateful man clothe me and feed me? Teach me the ways of the woods? Talk to me about hunting and tracking and running the dogs?

No. There was love in him, once.

It simply got lost somewhere along the way.

"I'm sorry, Jenna," Jeremiah murmurs. "But he's dead now. As he should be."

I accept this, somehow.

"Come on, let's get out of this mud. It's too damn cold." He forces a smile. He slings his strong arm around my shoulder, and the dogs trot around us, following us.

"No body," I say.

"What?" replies Jeremiah.

"Conroy's body. No body, no reward money."

Jeremiah shrugs. "Ah, that's okay."

"How is that *okay*!?" I push away from Jeremiah, furious. "I promised you we would at least split the reward money! I have *nothing,* Jeremiah! I ended up with nothing, even after all this!"

Jeremiah stops.

"Jenna," he says, calmly. "You came to me because you needed someone who would bring justice to these men. We did that, together. When you were taken by Conroy to Darling's, I *failed* my job. But I think I have something that will make it up to you." He smiles. "Come on."

He takes my hand and leads me through the burning wreckage of the port.

"Where are we going?" I ask.

He replies, "Curious, Jenna?"

"Of course I am."

The dogs sense his excitement and jog along with us. We move until we have circled around what used to be the office building. Pieces of charred wood are scattered everywhere. Jeremiah walks straight through the ruins, toward the place where the office used to be.

"Feast your eyes, madam," Jeremiah says, mock bowing.

In the center of the rubble, there's a square lump.

I gasp.

"Is that what I think it is?" I say.

"It sure is," he replies, grinning.

I've never seen him so happy.

It's a vault. I walk slowly, making footprints in the ashes. The vault is very small, but it's fully intact. I study it.

"There's no way we're going to open it," I say.

"Oh, is that so, Miss Renee?" Jeremiah answers, raising an eyebrow. He twists me around and pulls me into his arms. His hands grasp my waist and he presses a hot, long kiss to my lips. I feel the power of the kiss all the way to my toes.

"What was that for?" I ask, breathless.

"For luck," he says.

"You can't possibly hope to open it up," I reply. "Or is there something you're not telling me?"

"I'm good at everything I do, Jenna." He winks at me.

"So optimistic."

"Am I now?"

He's back to his usual, obstinate self, and this cheers me a bit, despite the shock of everything that just happened. He approaches the safe and kneels down, touching the door. It creaks open, ever so slowly.

"Impossible!" I exclaim.

"Quite possible, actually." Jeremiah smiles. "It would seem that Conroy Parker and Matthias Cooper and your uncle Nathaniel Renee were in the middle of a business transaction when I blew the dynamite. Unfortunately for them, they left the safe unlocked."

My eyes widen.

I kneel down and push the door open a bit further.

I inhale.

"I don't believe it," I breathe.

Jeremiah laughs.

There are piles and piles of American paper money— thousands upon thousands of dollars. A small box is pressed against the back of the safe. It's filled with gold dust. Another velvet bag is filled with solid gold nuggets; small, but worth hundreds.

Jeremiah stands up and whoops.

"I'll be damned!" he hollers. "Jenna Renee, how does it feel to be rich?"

The money in the safe alone could set me up for life. It's far more than any reward for Conroy, and far more than the savings he took from the cabin when he murdered Marilyn.

I cover my mouth with my hands and start to cry.

Tears of relief, tears of sadness, tears of disbelief.

Jeremiah searches the rubble for something we can use to carry the money off. He finds an old burlap sack on the edges of the port, and we start piling bills into the bag.

Recompense for all the pain you've caused me, Uncle, I think. *Payment for everything you took from me, and everything you took from dear Marilyn. I suppose that since I'm you're adopted daughter, I should inherit your money anyway.*

Lincoln trots in circles around us, and we leave camp with the dogs surrounding us like a ring. We are moving through woods, headed toward the sled trail, when there is movement on the horizon.

I stop and hold my breath.

I don't think I can take another fight.

Not one more.

Silly girl. You have just toppled an empire today.

I had help.

You've come far, Jenna.

285

I straighten my shoulders and slip my fingers through Jeremiah's. He looks at me, and I see love in his eyes. I don't see a drunken, womanizing, hurting man who takes his anger out on the world and in a bottle. I see someone who has risked his life to help me, who stuck by me even when there was no promise of success. I see a man who is the only thing I have left in the world, aside from my dogs.

"It will be okay," Jeremiah says, quietly.

I nod.

I believe him.

A dog team prances over the crest of the hill, and two more follow it. Chilkat—I'm sure of it. My dogs yip and run to meet them, excited and frenzied. Lincoln cocks his head, taking the scene in.

"Aguta!" Jeremiah yells. He is laughing. "Aguta, *you son of a gun*! What are you doing here?"

Sure enough, I recognize the man on the first sled. He comes to a dramatic halt, pulling his cap off.

"My friends!" he exclaims. "You look well! This is good news!"

His wife Kallik is riding in the sled. Her baby is not with her today.

"What are you doing here?" Jeremiah asks.

Aguta claps him into a hug. Kallik climbs out of the sled. The other two mushers come to a stop. They are smiling—chipper and cheerful.

Aguta holds Jeremiah at arm's length.

"I thought you might need some help," he says, his eyes crinkling. "It would seem that we have come too late. What happened?"

He surveys the port—the ashes, the smoke, the crackling licks of fire...the empty vault.

"How did you know we were here?" Jeremiah presses. "You came all the way over the pass and—"

"Jeremiah," Kallik says, holding a hand up. "Do not question. Just accept."

Jeremiah doesn't look convinced, but he is beaming.

This is his family, and they are here. He is happy.

Kallik walks to me and takes my hands.

"My friend," she says. "It is good to see you."

I am still confused. Kip and Dasha and the dogs crowd around the other teams. The air is filled with a chorus of yipping and barking.

"Cooper and Parker," Aguta says, low. "They're dead, aren't they?"

"They are."

He nods, satisfied.

"At last," he says. "Cooper Mining is finished."

"How *did* you find us?" I whisper to Kallik.

She tilts her head, a mischievous smile touching her lips. She presses her smooth fingers against my collarbone and touches the wolf charm hanging around my neck. She caresses the curve of the wolf and looks at me, still smiling.

"You know," she replies, simply.

She stares at the woods behind us, and I turn to follow her gaze. Something shifts in her eyes, and I understand.

He is there. The wolf, the alpha, the one from my dreams; the one that led me to Dorsey's and kept me alive. The one who has been with me since the beginning. He is standing between the trees, almost one with the shadows. His eyes seem to glow like the embers of a fire. He looks right at me, and I feel tears of gratitude welling up within me.

"He watches over you," Kallik says quietly. "All of the wolves do. I could feel it. I knew you were in trouble. They told me. I said to Aguta, *We must go. They need us. Your son is in danger.* I dreamed of a wolf leading through the forest, to the river." She squeezes my hand. "The wolves do not lie, Jenna."

"I know."

I look back toward the hill, but the wolf is gone.

He is gone, but he is emblazoned in my memory forever.

The wolf who saved me. The wolf who protected me.

The wolf who was my friend.

After

When it was all over, we went back with Aguta's people and stayed with them for a while. We counted the money. Fifty-seven thousand American dollars, not counting the gold. We bought a new sled. Lincoln and the dogs ran day and night. Jeremiah and I ate heartily and dreamed of what we would do with the money. *Buy a thousand bottles of wine! Build a mansion in Paris! Buy a steamer and open our very own shipping company! Purchase a velvet couch and lounge on it all day, eating nothing but cake and fruit.*

Our dreams were ridiculous...but exciting.

The world was open to us. We could do anything, now. *Be* anything.

Jeremiah informed the Canadian constabulary about Dorsey's Mines and Darling's illegal activities. He also informed the United States government and assisted in many of the arrests that were made at Cooper Mining camps around the country. He told them that

Conroy Parker and Matthias Cooper were dead. It was big news: Cooper was dead, and so was his right-hand man.

Needless to say, most were happy to hear it.

Some of the constabulary was angry. They had been on Cooper's payroll, after all, and their bribes had vanished. Like the sheriff in Dyea, they were unwilling to do much, except pass along the message. Most people were relieved to hear the news. At last, Cooper was dead. His mining offices had begun to fall apart without Parker to keep them in line. The smaller mines were bought up by private, more enterprising prospectors, breaking Cooper Mining's monopoly on the mines in the country.

Jeremiah and I returned to Dyea in the spring. We took the money with us—every last penny of it—and made the journey home. It was a pleasant one. The weather was warm. The dogs were happy. We rode horseback and walked the dogs, since we were well into the summer months and the snow had melted away, turning to long hours of daylight, heavy humidity, and swarms of monstrous mosquitos.

When we returned to the remains of my cabin, I found everything untouched. I had money now. Split between the two of us, both Jeremiah and I had more than thirty thousand American dollars.

A fortune. I used those funds to rebuild the cabin, to make it stronger and better.

"I should go back to San Francisco, like Marilyn wanted," I told Jeremiah. "I could start a new life there. Away from all of this."

Away from the memories.

Yet the memories were what I loved. Despite everything— despite Nathaniel's utter betrayal, every piece of Alaska sang to me. I remembered every curve in the trails, every tree in the forest. It was familiar to me, comfortable. The more I thought about leaving it, the less I liked the idea.

This was my home.

Besides, where would I keep a team of dogs in San Francisco? I certainly wasn't going to leave them behind. They were my family.

Jeremiah, for his part, lingered at the newly resurrected cabin. He slept in the cot beside me at night, listening to the wind and howling of the wolves. I no longer feared them. To hear the wolves was to know that I was being watched over, guarded. I believed in my heart that it was my mother who had sent the wolves to me. My mother who, despite her untimely death, was still watching over me, even from the next life.

"I'm going to California," Jeremiah told me every day. "It's time."

"And what will you do there?" I'd ask.

"They have work for men like me. Men willing to build. San Francisco is growing." He smiled. "Sooner or later they're going to want to build a bridge across the bay, and I've got some ideas. I can't be a United States Marshal forever, Jenna."

Every day he talked of leaving, and every day, my heart grew a bit heavier.

I knew it was inevitable. I had come to him to help me find Conroy. He had done his job, and we had emerged from the journey richer than we could have imagined. I couldn't expect him to stay forever, no matter how much love I carried in my heart for him.

One day, in the hours of the early morning, when I rose to make a pot of coffee, he was gone. His belongings, his supplies.

Everything. There was a note. It read, *I'll always love you the most, Jenna. – Yours, Jeremiah Black*

I sat on the floor for hours after that, staring at the wall, too sad to cry.

I kept the letter pinned to the wall over my bed, along with the wolf charm Kallik had given to me. Days passed, and I knew: I was never going to San Francisco. I belonged here. Jeremiah was gone, and I was here, and it was over. All of it.

I kept to myself. I worked the land and used the money to buy up a few mines around Dyea. I bought Timothy Healy's general store. I hired men to rebuild my cabin, to add more rooms than we had previously, and to build a full stable for more dogs and more storage. Days turned into months. The seasons changed. I grew older. The Gold Rush and all of the frenzied glory that it brought to Alaska melted away, as all rushes do. Peace and still settled over the countryside. My businesses in town flourished. The people here began to call me Madame Renee, the mysterious, wealthy young woman who lived in a cabin in the woods with no one but her dogs. I met many young, eligible bachelors, but none of them could match the dark beauty and intense power of the Jeremiah Black from my memory.

I carried him with me wherever I went, just as I carried my family with me.

Two years went by, and I began to accept that I would live a solitary life. Lincoln spent all of his days with me now. He was getting too old to run, so instead he slept in the cabin, at the foot of my cot, his wise, knowing eyes sparkling with affection. The fur around his nose was beginning to gray. Every day I sat with him and stroked his soft head. I wrote books...story after story of my journey with Jeremiah to find Conroy Parker. Some of them were published in magazines in California. I was even paid a visit by a writer who was traveling through the country. His name was Mr. London, and as I understood it, he went on to become quite famous for his books about Alaska.

I lived. I ran the dogs, I took care of Lincoln, I wrote my stories, and I managed my businesses. In 1901, when I was twenty-one years old, I was sitting on the edge of the fence around my property. Winter was rolling in. I could smell the snow and the storm in the air. I could taste it on my tongue. Lincoln lay in the grass beneath me, enjoying himself. I was writing a note to my friend, Mr. London, who was celebrating his first anniversary with his wife, Bess. Lincoln suddenly stood up, ears erect. He barked once—a loud, definitive bark that I had not heard in years.

"What's the matter, love?" I asked, frowning. "What do you hear?"

I climbed off the fence, my long hair curling in the wind. Someone was coming up the road.

"Never you mind," I told Lincoln, rubbing his ears. "It's only Mr. Healy. He's here to deliver my mail."

Mr. Healy had moved down the road from me in his retirement, and he prided himself in delivering my mail to me whenever it arrived. I dusted off my skirt and snapped my notebook shut, intending to finish the letter in a moment.

I walked to the road that curved through the trees. I squinted through the half-light of twilight. It was indeed a man...but it was not Mr. Healy. I knew who it was—I knew the broad shoulders, the black hat pulled low, at an angle. The pack slung over his back, the way he walked, quiet yet strong.

"Jeremiah," I whispered.

Lincoln ran to him, wagging his tail. He had known long before I had. Jeremiah knelt to the ground and embraced the dog. His shoulders heaved, and I could see that he was crying. I wanted to run to him—but I could not. It had been too long. I was frozen with disbelief. My heart was beating so hard, I was afraid it would tear through my chest.

And then he stood. He looked the same. The clothes he wore were nicer, the hat was new. But the dark eyes were unchanged, the hungry way he met my gaze was the same.

I ran to him. I ran and I threw my arms around his neck and he embraced me. I smelled the scent of him—so fresh and familiar. I felt the strength of his hands on my waist and the taste of him on my lips and I knew: I was home. Truly home.

"You came back," I whispered.

"Of course I did," he replied. His voice was thick with emotion. Tears streamed down his cheeks. "Jenna...I couldn't do it without you. San Francisco held no shine for me without you there." He took my cheeks in his hands. "I love you, Jenna Renee. I want to marry you."

I searched his face.

I had no idea what he had been doing since 1898. How many women had he loved? How many times had he gotten drunk? How had his life changed in the city, while I was here, living quietly in the wilderness?

I kissed him.

I didn't care, because I loved him and that was the end of every argument and the beginning of every promise.

"Come home," I told him. "Come home and stay home."

He smiled, pressing his lips against my fingers.

"Always, Jenna," he said. "Always."

The End

About Running with Wolves

This book is dedicated to the memory of a great writer, Jack London. Anyone who knows me well, knows that I should probably just go ahead and build a shrine to Jack London in my office, because the man is quite seriously my favorite author of all time. Hands down, London's writing speaks to the deepest parts of my soul. I identify with his work, and I love the stories that he crafts. At the heart of his novels is a respect for the wilderness and a deep understanding of the way of the wild, especially wolves and dogs.

London – an adventurer who spent much of his life drifting from one rugged trade to another (among them, pirating as the infamous Oyster Pirate of San Francisco Bay and exploring Alaska as a gold prospector in the Canadian Klondike) – was a fighter. Born poor and illegitimate, he clawed his way out of the slums of San Francisco and was considered, at the time of the publication of *The Call of the Wild* in 1903, the wealthiest and most successful author in the world. Jack London lived firsthand many of the adventures that he wrote about in his fiction, transferring his own human emotion into timeless characters such as *White Fang* and *Buck*. London has inspired me for years, and the mystery and utter breadth of the land in Alaska begged a question: what sort of story could I tell about this world? So entranced by Alaska itself, a tale sprung into being about a year or two ago in my mind. An adventurous tale that showcased the brutality and challenges of living in Alaska during the 19th century. A story that showed the unforgiving nature of both the wilderness and the lawlessness of the land. Something that put a new spin on a gold rush that was, quite frankly, short-lived but epic and exciting nonetheless.

Thus Jenna Renee was born. The character of Jenna occurred to me organically. Being a woman in 1898 came with its restrictions – and being a woman in the wilderness only made things more complicated. Add to that a Native American heritage, and you've got an entirely different level of problems!

In the days of Jenna Renee, to be woman and native was simply a disadvantage. In Alaska, you were granted a sort of small reprieve – because it was in the middle of nowhere, and many people did what they had to in order to survive...even accepting a woman doing a man's work. But the issues that Jenna complains about are quite true: women in Alaska during the 1890s came to the wild arctic world to find a husband, find gold *with* their current husbands, or work in a saloon or whorehouse. There were few options available to women.

Belinda Mulrooney was actually a real businesswoman in Dawson City during the gold rush, and she *really* did own a hotel called the Fairview. She was also considered the richest woman in the Klondike. You see, Alaska offered something that the rest of the world did not: room to grow, and expand. Women were, perhaps, granted a bit more freedom because of the isolation and complete struggle to survive, day after day. This struggle brought everyone to the same level, therefore offering many of the same freedoms to both sexes.

Jenna's Cherokee heritage is something that was inspired, partly, by a black and white photograph I came across during my extensive research for *Running with Wolves*. The photo was taken in the 1880s. It depicted a lovely young woman with long, black hair, gazing off-camera. Her name was Marica Paschal, and she was the half-Cherokee daughter of Lieutenant Colonel George W. Paschal (information provided by the *Bureau of American Ethnology*). She had an incredibly "modern" look, and I immediately thought, "That's Jenna Renee." The Cherokee heritage was, I thought, very important to the story: to realize how not just Native Americans were treated in those days, but how women were treated, too.

As an author, I'm just so grateful for the opportunity to write. There was a time when a woman had to use a male pseudonym just to sell a book! Yes, the world has changed. For the better in some ways, and I'm sure some would argue that it's changed for the worse, as well.

Running with Wolves was also inspired by my love for sled-dog racing. I first was entranced with the idea of dogs running in the snow as a child, watching the animated film *Balto* over and over and over again (every week, for years). The Iditarod (a modern sled-dog race through the freezing, icy expanse of Alaska, clocking in at over 1,000 miles in length) is an incredible tribute to the heritage of sled dogs and how they provided strength and transportation for explorers and gold-seekers during the 19th century and beyond. I read *The Incredible Journey*, by Sheila Burnford as a child, as well as *Born Free,* by Joy Adamson. I loved books like that, which spoke about animals and our connection to them, as well as the unavoidable fact that, when it comes down to it, so many times Man himself ends up being the villain...it is not the terrifying wolf that causes the most damage to the world. It's Man, in his greed for wealth or power, that brings the wilderness to the brink of extinction.

I consider myself a conservationist, someone who loves the wild places – the woods, the trees, the animals, the open sky. I believe that it is our job as stewards of this planet to take good care of the beautiful things God has made, and perhaps that is why writing by authors like Jack London or John Muir resonates so deeply with me.

In my opinion, modern society is so far removed from the wilderness and the outdoors, that the romanticism of the "old west" and the "great frontier" days has become somewhat mythic. It's sad, really, because those things are the heritage of man himself. The façade of modern society is fragile...which of course, is the thought process that inspired the entire *Collapse Series*. But that, my friends, is another story entirely.

Jack London, for all of his success and wealth, was an intensely unhappy man in the end, troubled by the treatment of the poor in the 20th century, and even more troubled by the fact that men acted more like animals than the animals did. He committed suicide at the age of 40. A sad end to a story of a man who did great things, and had high ideals. While the closing of his story was tragic, it perhaps makes his writing all the more important. If anything, I hope *Running with Wolves* is a tribute, in some small way, to the intelligence of the animals in the wild and the deep emotional capacity of dogs. I hope it inspires some of you to read *The Call of the Wild* or *To Build a Fire*. I hope it reminds you that the days of steamers and gold mining and Winchester pump-action shotguns really wasn't very long ago, and that the modern world would benefit from a little of yesterday's courageous, adventurous spirit.

Sincerely,

The Author

Enjoyed this novel?
Check out the complete works of prolific,
#1 bestselling author Summer Lane!

THE COLLAPSE SERIES

The #1 bestselling, smash-hit phenomenon! Over 100,000 copies sold!

Join Commander Cassidy Hart as she fights for survival amidst the ashes of society, striking back at a shadow enemy, protecting her friends, and finding love.

IT'S A FIGHT YOU WON'T FORGET.

The complete series is available on Amazon & Barnes and Noble.

THE ZERO TRILOGY

The #1 Bestselling Companion Novella Story to the Collapse Universe!

One girl. One sword. One dog.

Survival is a game. Are you ready to play?

Available on Amazon and Barnes & Noble today!

THE BRAVO SAGA

Civilization, fallen. Society, destroyed.

But there was a dog. And his name was Bravo.

The #1 bestselling 2-part saga from Summer Lane!

The 2-part set is available on Amazon and Barnes & Noble today!

UNBREAKABLE SEAL

A #1 bestselling military adventure story of love, loyalty, and vengeance, starring Chris Young from the Collapse Series.

Available on Amazon and Barnes & Noble today!

SUMMER LANE IS GIVING THE WORD 'PROLIFIC' A RUN FOR ITS MONEY

PROLIFIC YOUNG WRITER KEEPS THE HITS COMING

PROLIFIC

WRITING A HIT

NOVEL

[LANE] IS A PROLIFIC WRITER

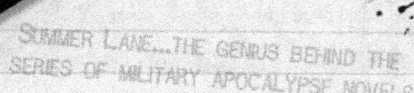

SUMMER LANE...THE GENIUS BEHIND THE SERIES OF MILITARY APOCALYPSE NOVELS

FROM #1 BESTSELLING AUTHOR

SUMMER LANE

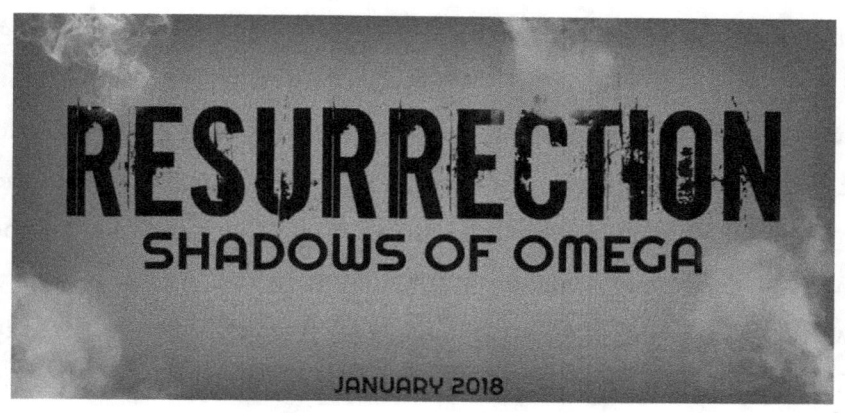

Cassidy Hart is back, and this time...

She's in charge.

Tweet #PresidentHart and #Resurrection on Twitter.

Catch the official release date at SummerLaneAuthor.com.

Acknowledgements

Many hands make work light...or at least, *lighter*. I would like to specifically thank Marcie Zorn Smith and Stephanie Parent for their editorial work and insight. To Don Lane, for your proofreading. To Andrew Dubravushkin, for your stunning cover art collaboration with Writing Belle Publishing. To my advanced readers. To my friend Ellen, for being my best writing buddy. To my dog, for making me take breaks during the writing and editing process to take her for walks. To my husband, for putting up with the craziness that a writing life brings, and for fixing everything that breaks. To my friends, who bring me laughter and blessings. To my readers...thanks for sticking with me, always. This is my first historical fiction novel, and I'm very proud of the work that went into it. While I am still submerged in a post-apocalyptic landscape (I am currently working on the *Resurrection Series* as this novel is being released), the story of Jenna Renee was an uplifting and refreshing challenge for me to tackle.

Thanks for reading. You make my world go round.

About the Author

Summer Lane is the #1 bestselling author of 18 books and counting, including the smash-hit books of the *Collapse Series.* She is the owner and founder of *Writing Belle Publishing*. She also owns *Writing Belle*, an online magazine where

she has interviewed hundreds of authors from around the globe. Summer is an experienced journalist and creative writing teacher. At heart, she is a dreamer and an entrepreneur. Summer lives in the Central Valley of California with her husband, Scott, and their German Shepherd, Kona. Look for Summer's upcoming releases by visiting her official website, following her on social media, or signing up for her email newsletter.

Connect:

Website: summerlaneauthor.com

Magazine: www.writingbelle.com

Twitter: @SummerEllenLane

Instagram: @writingbelle

Facebook: @SummerLaneAuthor

Publisher: writingbellepublishing.com

Email the author here: summerlane101@gmail.com

Write to the author:

Writing Belle Publishing/Summer Lane

P.O. Box 994

Reedley, CA 93654

Professional Photography Provided by:

Jen Eileen Photography

Cassidy Hart Promotional Art:

Lindsey Goudreau